Speak of the Devil

Speak of the Devil

Lachá M. Scott

www.urbanchristianonline.com

Urban Books, LLC
97 N18th Street
Wyandanch, NY 11798

ISBN 13: 978-1-60162-689-9
ISBN 10: 1-60162-689-4

First Trade Paperback Printing January 2015
Printed in the United States of America

10 9 8 7 6 5 4 3 2 1

Distributed by Kensington Corp.
Submit Wholesale Orders to:
Kensington Publishing Corp.
C/O Penguin Group (USA) Inc.
Attention: Order Processing
405 Murray Hill Parkway
East Rutherford, NJ 07073-2316
Phone: 1-800-526-0275
Fax: 1-800-227-9604

Acknowledgments

Thanks to God first and foremost for birthing the gift of writing in me.

Ronnie, thank you, love, for allowing me to do what I do and sharing me with my readers, within the ministry among the various engagements I partake in to share what God has placed inside of me. Thanks to my girls, Jasmin, RhonShay, Maliya, and ShayLa for loving me in spite of my imperfections and for always telling me that my stories sound good and are believable. Most of all, thanks for lending me your ears time and time again and for answering my many questions and giving me your literary input.

Thanks to my mother, Evangelist Carolyn Riddick, my sisters Melina Mitchell and Marina Santos for your support. Elissa Gabrielle, thank you for the encouragement and support on putting me out there with the interviews you have blessed me with and the road map on how to be a successful authorpreneur.

Brenda Foster Love, for providing me with encouragement and literary nuggets in pushing me through the process of staying focused and completing the work.

JoyLynn Ross, thank you for being the best editor ever. I'm extremely grateful to be a part of Urban Christian books.

Big thanks go out to Michelle Chavis, who is working hard at getting me the publicity I need to take my dreams to the next level.

Acknowledgments

Bestselling author Renee Flagler, thank you for just being you. I'm grateful to you for taking the time out to share with me the tools that helped get you to where you are now.

Thank you to everyone who purchases *Speak of the Devil*. I appreciate you more than you know. A writer has no need to write if no one is reading. I hope each person who reads this book will be blessed and encouraged. Please tell all of your friends about it.

Thanks to all of my favorite authors, seasoned and new, who encourage me to keep my passion for writing alive.

Thanks to Jahzara Bradley, Carla Nix, Kisha Green, Dedrea Day & Chyna Blue and Ella Curry of *Black Pearls* magazine, *Women's Essence* magazine, Vanessa Richardson of *The Certain Ones* magazine, *21 Black Street*, and many others providing me the platform by hosting me as a guest on your radio shows or for featuring me and or allowing me to write in your magazine as a platform to share my testimony and showcase my work. I'd like to thank De'Marte Bullock for designing my photo for the cover.

Love and Blessings,
Lachá M. Scott

Chapter 1

Applause erupted from the congregation throughout the Atlanta Georgia Dome as Serena Sampson worked her way in and out of the throngs of screaming women. It was evident that the ladies were seeking something from God. Serena knew that her ministry was to preach and minister to those who were broken and wounded. She encouraged women to remain steadfast instead of throwing in the towel by walking away from God. Then there were those who were there looking for the weakest link because they weren't there on God's assignment, but the devil's.

"Women of purpose, God sent me here to give you a personal message. God said don't faint in the process because He ain't through with you yet. I know you are going through a lot and have endured long days and weary nights. God has seen your tears because of wayward children, a no-good, low-down man, folks talkin' 'boutcha on your job, and mockers laughing behind your backs." Serena drew in a deep breath and exhaled before continuing.

"Truth be told, you thought you could trust your best friend, but she turned out to have switched teams. Well, glory be to God that you made it over the threshold to your breakthrough, to your deliverance, to your freedom, to restored minds, and one mo' thing: you're about to get your happy back." Serena's eyes swept the crowd in awe of God as the anointing from heaven fell heavily on the women's backs. It was evident by the bent knees and the war cries that came from many as Serena's prophecy dripped like honey, a salve, or even as some would say, a healing balm.

Serena lowered the microphone from her mouth and stood in the midst of the unrestrained worship taking place, while her armor bearers were strategically aligned at arm's length of her. Their stance let the crowd know that they were in warfare mode, ready to be of assistance. Careful not to quench the spirit, they remained quietly and watchful in position. The Holy Spirit was free to have His way as it was clearly His service that they were just invited to attend.

Serena was grateful and humbled that God had moved on hearts all over the world. The conference was even being televised and millions were seeking healing, deliverance, and empowerment from their struggles. Each year, the conference goers increased by leaps and bounds.

Sounds of praise caressed Serena's ears, but she wasn't fooled for one moment. In spite of all of the running, jumping, dancing, and crying women, many were slain in the Spirit. There was no doubt that God was ministering to the women, but there were also plenty of women there playing Russian roulette with God. They deceived themselves, trying to make everyone else believe that they were true worshippers. Serena was on guard and knew a fake when she saw one. God wouldn't leave her blind about the snakes trying to suck the life out of those who wanted to be free.

The Atlanta Georgia Dome was so huge that when the praises went up, they transcended the ceilings and continued to go straight to heaven. Serena wanted to believe that God was pleased with the praises. She felt in her spirit that all was not well and knew it was her responsibility to call out anything unlike God. This was the only way true deliverance would be attainable. The Word had gone forth and yokes were being broken, but Serena knew that she had to bind the devils cloaked in sheep's clothing. God revealed that their agenda was different than the one set for the house during this hour.

Serena drew the microphone back up to her mouth. "My question to you today is, who's willing to take the mask off in order to receive your breakthrough?" Serena waited for a response and when only a few called out that they would be the one, she continued. "You are seeking something supernatural from God; however, you refuse to fully come clean with Him. God knows you and is aware of your weaknesses. You may believe that you have deceived many here with your hollow praise and your fake worship. I caution you that God cannot be mocked."

Loud cries diminished to small whimpers as amens rang out from the crowd. Those who weren't laid out fell to their knees in prayer or stretched out wherever they could find space. The hard chairs were in disarray as they were knocked out of the way by those slain in the Spirit. Ladies dressed in white were assigned to be catchers to break the ladies' fall if they went out as a result of Serena laying hands on them.

An ungodly sound caught Serena's inner ear and her head followed the sound. If one weren't sensitive to the Spirit, they would have mistaken the sound for spiritual tongues. It was a counterfeit, demonic force masquerading like a pure praise unto God. That spirit had to be stopped before it undermined the reason the conference was being held. Serena didn't think twice as she moved toward the woman who was loud and out of order. As if on cue two armor bearers flanked Serena's side, two were right behind them and two walked in front of her sideways.

Microphone in hand, Serena spoke to the atmosphere and began to speak. "Satan, you may as well take your bag of tricks someplace else because your potions, witchcraft, and uttering won't work here. I see you slithering and winding your way into the lives of these women. God's chosen, you have used all in your arsenal to destroy them. I bind up every work and put every demon, imp, and witch on notice right now. You have no power here." She continued her trek through the throngs of women. Many were moving out of the way as she approached them.

Under the power of the anointing, women fell like flies as Serena walked by with authority, and the power of God in her humbled them. Serena didn't stop until she reached the back corner of the dome. The musicians played softly due to the fact that many were still in worship mode. The woman continued to screech in a high-pitched voice. The armor bearers and intercessors surrounded their woman of God as she handed the microphone to her head armor bearer and niece, Amina Sampson. Amina used her free hand to pour some praying oil into Serena's hands.

"Bring her to me," Serena commanded, which caused the armor bearers and intercessors to be on guard. She knew that there would be a battle in order to get the young woman set free from her inner demons.

The woman's countenance was very pale and she had a wild look in her eyes. The evil spirit had caused her to thrash about and even cursed when it was found out. "What do you want with me?" the demon-possessed woman questioned Serena. The demonic spirit spoke through the woman and began to hiss like a serpent.

The dome grew quiet. Those close enough to see what was happening jumped to action. Hands went up in the air and some pointed toward the direction Serena was standing. Prayers filled the air as the prophet began to cast the demon out of the woman. Although the monitors were supposed to stay on Serena, they were fixed on the musicians. Worship music played throughout the dome and many were on one accord. The atmosphere that started out being replete with heaviness had now been broken and the fallow ground remained. Amina knew her role well and she held the microphone up to Serena's lips as she began to minister. Serena felt that it was important to make a show of this demon so that others would be able to witness the power of God in their midst. "Satan, I bind you up in the matchless name of Jesus. I command that you release this woman under the authority of Christ Jesus. You have no power over her," Serena declared.

The woman began to buck like a bull. However, Serena knew that the evil spirit was trying to destroy the lady. Serena remained focused and continued to bind every spirit contrary to the spirit of God.

"Argh, help me," the lady cried out. The throaty voice that rose up in her took a back seat to her desperate cries.

"Woman of God, you need to repent. God has revealed to me that you have been operating in a spirit of witchcraft," said Serena.

The lights dimmed to the others, but Serena acknowledged the very existence of God and let Him use her mouth to spring forth rivers of living water. A haze draped over the altar section of the platform and Serena took it as an indication of His pleasure. Instead of speaking to the crowd, Serena bowed her head and closed her eyes as the Lord ministered to her.

The musicians played "Song of Strength" and as if on cue, anointed praise and mime dancers began to minister. The music was slow and the keyboardist played with grace. Serena moved back to give room for the worshippers, and her armor bearers covered her as she bowed in submission to God in prayer. Seven warriors stood alongside Serena watching, while some prayed in the Spirit. The intercessors closed their eyes and prayed for their leader as she poured out, and the men kept their eyes open for spiritual and physical protection.

Amina handed Serena a glass of colored drink. Serena's drink of choice after preaching was Gatorade. She turned the goblet up to her mouth and let the cool liquid hit the back of her throat, gliding down her throat and quenching her thirst.

Once the dance ministry exited, Serena felt refreshed and she reached out for her handkerchief. The pure satin piece matched her black and gold three-piece suit. She wiped the perspiration from her face and kicked off her four-inch heels that had become cumbersome. Serena didn't need to be tied down for the next transition God would move them into. She was more than ready to expose the enemy in attempt to get the women set free. Serena passed the microphone to Amina as her eyes swept over the crowd. She didn't move forward until she had made eye contact with a lady who had been weeping loudly. Taking slow steps, Serena hurried over to the lady who seemed to be drowning in despair. She didn't see Serena and her team approach her. "Get her!" Serena yelled over the worshippers.

The intercessors sprang into action and grabbed the lady gently by her forearms. The woman began crying loudly with a deep voice. Serena was prepared to deal with the demonic influence over this woman's life.

Serena addressed the lady. "I see witches and Ouija boards."

"Argh sssss." The woman bucked and began chanting in worship to Satan. Two more intercessors moved into position to encompass the wild woman who was now cursing at the prophet.

"What do you want with us?" the raspy voice inquired.

"I bind you in Jesus' name. Satan, you have no power over her. You must pack up your potions and go. I cast you out under the authority of the power in me in Christ Jesus according to my faith." Serena reached for the oil that Amina was holding and nearly poured the whole bottle into her hands. Shoving the anointing oil back at Amina, Serena motioned for the men of valor to hold the woman upright.

Whimpers could be heard from the lady who had stopped jerking and bouncing around. "Please help me," she begged.

Serena felt the lights find her in the crowd, and they were in the spotlight. She was glad that the lady wanted help and to be free because if that were not the case, Serena didn't need to waste her time. "Are you ready to be free of the demonic influence you have been dabbling in?" Serena asked.

"I don't mess around with that stuff. I don't know how," the unknown lady said.

"Listen to me. If you weren't involved with practicing witchcraft, God wouldn't have shown it to me. God wants to set you free so you can live for Him. I can't make you come out of sin; you have to want it. You have to denounce sin and repent to God for opening the door to witchcraft. Do you want to be free?" Serena waited for a response from the woman as Amina held the microphone up to her mouth.

"I want to be free, but they won't leave me alone," the lady cried.

"Do you believe that God is all powerful?"

"Yes."

"How bad do you want to close the door on self-destruction?"

"Bad! I want to do right and I want the Lord to forgive me."

"Repeat after me, Father, I've sinned against you. Please forgive me for worshipping idol gods. I denounce the workings of the rulers of darkness, principalities, and wickedness in high places. I repent of my sin and close the door on witchcraft and sorcery."

The woman didn't open her mouth; instead, she became limp and fell from the grasps of the intercessors and slid to the floor. They got down on the floor surrounding her, praying and calling out demons by name. Serena allowed them to pray with the woman while she instructed those standing near.

"Women of God," she called into the microphone, "if you have no training in spiritual warfare and are fearful of what you see going on before you, I advise you to leave now. The enemy operates in fear and right now, that ol' slew foot is afraid. By the authority that God has given me to tread upon serpents and scorpions, he's coming outta there," Serena hollered pointing to the woman who still lay on the floor being worked on by the spiritual doctor.

Women who understood what was taking place gathered closer and pointed their hands toward the group on the floor while praying for deliverance. The space was packed tightly and there wasn't anywhere else for the ladies to go but out into the hallway. Many others who stayed would soon find out if they could handle the magnitude of demonic activity going on.

"Pray, pray in your heavenly language. If you can pray in tongues, do it now and don't stop. We aren't leaving this place until this woman is delivered," Serena declared.

The air seemed to stop moving and humidity set in as the women travailed for the deliverance of the unknown woman in their midst. Serena revisited the second woman, confident that she was ready to receive. Two men of valor pulled the unknown woman up from her prostrate position on the floor and held on to her arms as they guided her into an upright position.

Serena grabbed the woman by the sides of her head and began to prophesy to her. "Can you hear me, baby?"

The young woman only nodded.

"Satan, I command you to release this vessel. She doesn't belong to you, but to God. I speak peace to her mind and restoration to her body." The woman was sweaty and her hair stood at its ends; however, she was lucid and faintly smiling.

"Woman of God, I need for you to repeat after me!"

"Yes," the woman responded, sounding more like herself this time.

"Tell God you're sorry for opening the door to witchcraft and sorcery."

"Lord, I'm sorry for practicing witchcraft and sorcery."

"Ask God to forgive you and let Him know that you are repentant of your actions that brought Him dishonor."

"Lord, please forgive me for sinning against you. I am sorry for opening the door to those things that dishonored you." She spoke now with boldness and felt her strength returning. "And Lord, I repent from my disobedience. Please wash me clean."

"I speak life over you, daughter. Your sins have been forgiven thee. Sin no more."

The musicians took that as their cue to rev the music up and they played some praise music to give another shift to the atmosphere. Applause, hallelujah shouts, and amens rang out in the sanctuary. The woman began to dance and shout up something. She was happy to be free. She hugged Serena and thanked her.

"Thank you, woman of God. I knew that I needed help, as I had gotten too deep in disobeying God. It became easier and easier to ignore His voice when He spoke. One day I was sitting at the Ouija boards waiting to feel some unction of conviction but it never came. I became afraid. I thank you for allowing God to use you to help me be free once again. He hadn't left me after all."

"Praises belong to God and God alone. Just remember what I said to you. Don't open the door again because next time you may die in that sin." Serena hugged the woman back and moved down to the front of the dome. She closed out the conference with corporate prayer and asked everyone to stop by her booth to purchase a CD or book she had written on their way out. The benediction went forth and an hour later Serena, along with her team, were whisked away to a waiting limo.

The limousine finally arrived in front of the mini-mansion located smack dab in the middle of Black Horse Run in Northern Durham. Serena's Twitter page was blowing up with tweets containing all sorts of praise reports and gratitude for the words she had deposited into the spirits of those women who had attended the conference. The smile that appeared on her face as James, the limo driver, pulled into the circular driveway that led up to her house was twofold. One, she was dog tired and she had been holding her bladder for the last two hours. On the flight from Atlanta she had two cups of hot tea with honey and lemon. Instead of going to the restroom after getting to the Raleigh-Durham airport, she declared she could make it home. Serena detested public restrooms and the filth that could be found in there. To make matters worse, she had two additional pints of Gatorade to drink on the way home.

Serena tweeted, Home sweet home and hit SEND. "James, please hurry up and unlock the door. I really need to use the bathroom."

He hit the unlock button and Serena jumped out of the back of the limousine as quickly as she could, racing Amina to the front door. Serena was glad she had the opportunity to shower and change into a sweat suit before leaving the Marriott in Georgia. She wanted to relax on her way home. "Amina, come on, I have to get inside before I have an accident in this Versace sweat suit. James, you can begin bringing the bags up to the house." Serena spoke over her shoulder with her head turned to the door.

"Yes, ma'am. You know you really shouldn't have had so much to drink on the way home. You could have at least allowed me to stop so that you could empty your bladder at some point," James said.

"I didn't want anything keeping me away from home longer. I can't wait to sleep in my own bed. Don't get me wrong, I love the nice hotels with the VIP treatment, however, there is no place like home."

"Excuse me, Auntie." Amina sidled up next to Serena, maneuvering around her to open the door. She secretly thanked the motion lights for coming on. The extra lighting helped to get Serena into the house quicker. Amina wouldn't have to fight with the keys and security system that was pitched right on the other side of the wall. No sooner than the door swung open, Serena bolted toward the nearest bathroom, while Amina punched in the code to the alarm system to squelch the horrendous sound that echoed throughout the house.

Amina sashayed into the living room and flipped light switches on as she went. She was still on high from the mountaintop experience, but thrilled to be home as well. Amina had a habit of walking through the house after each ministry assignment in prayer. She was not new to ministry or the tricks of the enemy.

Amina navigated a clear path around James as he carried luggage into the living room and placed them down. He had learned not to bother Amina as she consecrated the dwelling place of her mentor. She almost chuckled out loud at the thought of the first time James came into the house and inquired of where the bags should be put.

She was in the middle of praying. His interruption had broken her concentration and she let him have it. That happened five years ago, and Amina never had to tell him again not to ask about anything until the prayer was done.

Amina watched him out of the corner of her eye as he went in and out of the house with their suitcases. Her attraction to him had been growing the last year or so, but she never let on. She tried focusing on her task, but found it nearly impossible to stay focused while James's muscles flexed with the rise and fall of his thick arms. Shivers ran up and down her body and goose bumps popped out, making themselves visible. *What a man, what a man,* she thought. *Oh Lord, help me to redirect my focus to prayer. Ugh, he's fine. Mmph, look at him. Close fade with waves on top, mocha chocolate fine. Right height, just tall enough to have to bend down slightly to kiss me. Abs are tight. He must work out. The brother is saved; or is he?* Amina heard a record scratching and snapped out of her daydream.

"Are you okay, Amina? You look perplexed about something." James was concerned.

"Um, yeah, I was just thinking about you. I mean something. That's all," Amina replied.

James was unsure about what had just happened; however, he let the comment slide for the time being. "All right, if you're sure, then I'll be on my way. Everything should be here since the trunk is now empty." He gestured toward the row of bags neatly sitting in the corner of the room.

"Okay, let me give you the check." Amina was grateful for the opportunity to turn away and get herself together before facing James again. She retrieved the cashier's check for James's services and stood with her back to him for a moment before turning around.

"Amina, are you sure that you're okay?" James quietly walked into her personal space.

"Oh, I didn't hear you approach." Amina turned around and nearly bumped into James.

She jumped, startled, feeling the heat of her breath bounce off of his chest and hit her in the face.

"I'm fine. Just tired, that's all. Here's your check." Amina moved away slightly and stretched her arm forward with an envelope in her hand.

"Okay, I understand. It's been a long three days for you gals. Thanks for this." James played along. He popped the check against his palm and smiled at Amina. Something was off because Amina's hand was shaking. Not sure what was going on, James decided not to dwell on it. "Well, I'd better get going. I will see you real soon," he said.

"Thanks for everything, James. You know, for being available and considerate of our needs. I hope you get home or wherever you are headed safely." Amina walked over to the door, ready for James to leave. She couldn't let on what she was really feeling because she wasn't sure herself.

"Anytime. I love driving you ladies around. It's good for my résumé and I also like being in your company. I tell ya, it gets crazy sometimes since I drive for rappers and ballplayers also. It blesses me to be in the company of likeminded individuals who don't mind me listening to my gospel jams. Well, let me get on outta here. Good night, Amina." James winked at her and walked out.

Chapter 2

Serena exhaled as she stood in front of the mirror once she had emptied her bladder. "Oh, what a relief it is," she said to the reflection staring back at her in the mirror. She held on to the caramel-stained marble countertop and studied her neck. She turned from side to side in order to see the structure and coloring of her skin around her throat. She rubbed her neck, checking for lumps or abnormalities. Serena fretted over what could have been. Even though she hadn't found anything out of order, her only consolation was that her face looked normal. Serena lifted her right arm from the stability of the cool marble counter and grabbed her throat, which was becoming sore; and her voice was hoarse.

"Amina, come here," Serena croaked, barely recognizing her own voice.

"I'll be there momentarily. James just left and I need to make sure that the house is locked up for the night." Amina's mind was in chaos as she thought about the thing that had awakened in her that she had never experienced before. She had never been in a relationship with anyone and wasn't sure what, if anything, James felt about her. She was wondering what if as she made her rounds throughout the house, making sure that the windows were locked and the alarm system was activated.

Fear interrupted Amina's confused psyche as Serena's beckon was two octaves higher than normal. It gave her pause, but not for long. However, she needed the unwanted intrusion so that she could refocus on her purpose for the moment. Amina took comfort in her sweep of the house to defect any spiritual attacks and other demonic mischief that would be waiting to manifest. The warrior in her took the forefront of her mind and she was ready for whatever ailed her spiritual mentor.

Moments later, Amina looked on as her mentor continued stretching her neck upward and rolling her head around from both sides. Her first thought was to wait until Serena was finished with what looked like a mini workout. She second-guessed the slight increased pitch she thought she heard from when Serena had beckoned unto her minutes prior. Amina quietly did an about-face but before she could put her right foot in front of the other, her name was called.

"Amina, where are you going? Didn't you hear me call you?" Serena's anxiety gave an air of attitude in her tone.

Amina turned her head around and answered Serena. "Yes, Auntie, but you seemed to be okay when I walked by, so I thought maybe you didn't need me after all," Amina replied meekly.

"Well yes, that's why I called you. I need you; so please follow me into the kitchen where the lighting is better. By the way, has everything been locked up? Alarm set?" Serena wearily tossed the questions over her shoulder as she continued walking into the kitchen.

Amina followed behind Serena, feeling somewhat anxious. She didn't know if her spiritual mother was okay, considering that she could have just met Amina in the kitchen. She felt like she was going in circles. Serena seemed to be shaken by something, because fear wasn't a part of her vocabulary. Amina began to pray again for clarity because something was amiss.

***

Three days had passed and Serena's room remained darkened. No sunlight had passed through the room from where the massive hunter green drapes spanned from one wall to the other. Gloom held the room hostage, as no sunrays could get in to fill it with warmth. Serena slept constantly since she had returned home from the conference.

Every waking moment Serena popped Cepacol and Halls throat drops to get relief for her tender throat. Still tired from the women's conference, Serena believed that on the third day, she would be totally healed. Cups of tea that were once hot and tasty were now cold and bitter. The saucers of lemons and a bottle of honey were overflowing the nightstands that encircled her Queen Victorian sleigh bed.

The sixty-inch flat screen state-of-the-art television with surround sound was set to turn on at the same time every morning. Serena was awakened by the sounds of her favorite preacher's voice, Dr. Cynthia Trindle. Although her eyes were still crusty with sleep, her ears didn't betray her. She heard the woman of God say, "Wherever you are in Television Land, touch yourself and command your healing. Speak it out of your mouth and believe it by faith." The next voice that came from the speakers was a commercial.

Serena rolled over onto her stomach and pushed herself up to her knees, and then she rolled back down onto her backside. Sitting upright, she placed her hand on her throat and began to prophecy to herself. "Jesus." Nothing came out but a hoarse sound. She tried again, refusing to be defeated. When Serena called upon the name of Jesus, it sounded as if she were whispering.

She focused on swallowing but her throat felt swollen on the left side. Scooting over to the edge of her bed, Serena leaned over to the nightstand and grabbed the closest cup of tea. Frowning at the cup holding the bitter liquid, she had to force herself to drink a little more to wet her throat. "Ugh, this tastes horrible." She spat the bitter drink from her mouth. Fear threatened to annihilate Serena's mustard-sized seed of faith for healing. She choked back a sob and timidly placed her right hand on the left side of her neck. Her thyroid gland felt bigger than before.

"Amina, please come here." She called out and closed her eyes while she waited for the sound of Dr. Trimble's voice. "Speak to me again, Preacher," Serena whispered. She tried to concentrate on the declaration given by the preacher. Ignoring the knot on her neck, Serena decided that she would prophesy to herself as she had done for thousands of others. Before she opened her mouth her tight facial muscles pulled her jaws back together, causing her to bite her tongue instead.

Serena winced from the sharp pain that pierced her tongue. "Amina, what's the hold up?" She shrieked at the froggy sound in her voice and the foul taste of blood. Serena looked in the mirror with a crazed look on her face and couldn't seem to pull herself away from the vision looking back at her. Serena didn't recognize the woman she saw giving her the screw face. Her facial expression stated that she had no clue of what was wrong. She was confused as to why she could believe God for everyone else's healing and deliverance. Now that she was the one with the issue, she was acting like a punk who didn't know her lineage. Serena's head snapped back as if God had illuminated new revelation. She jumped up from the spot she was sitting in and nearly fell face first off of her bed onto the floor.

She screamed, "Oh, oh, oh," while trying to grab ahold of her comforter in efforts to remain on her bed and not crash to the floor. Amina barged into her aunt's dark room and snatched her up before her arms hit the floor. Serena huffed and puffed as she struggled to hold on to Amina as she pulled Serena's torso back to safety on the bed.

"Auntie, are you okay? You scared me." Amina reached over to the wall and flipped the light switch on near the door to get a better look at Serena.

"I called you minutes ago. Didn't you hear me?" Serena laughed at herself. "Of course you didn't hear me; I could barely hear myself. I was just trying to look in the mirror at my throat." Serena momentarily forgot why she was straining to see her reflection until then.

"No, ma'am, I didn't hear you. I thought you were still asleep. I was straightening up my bedroom and unpacking, getting the clothes ready for the wash. Now, why are you trying to look in the mirror at your throat?" Amina asked with concern.

"Oh, it's nothing. I don't feel too bad, just a little weak from being in bed for three days. Well, who am I kidding? I feel like processed meat. I don't have any energy and my throat is still bothering me. To be quite frank with you, I am very concerned that none of these medicines worked for me. Do you hear my voice? I surely don't sound like the world renowned prophet Serena Sampson. My throat still feels scratchy and it itches all up in through here." Serena rubbed her hands on her jaws down to her esophagus and frowned.

"Auntie, it's been three days and I have purchased everything we thought would work on your throat. Let's see, you have been taking the best-brand name throat lozenges and drinking honey menthol tea every two hours. Since you are still feeling this way, we need to take your care to the next level." Amina scratched her head in wonder.

"It's time that we call Dr. Shotten, so she can get a work up on you to find out if there are any serious issues with your throat. Oh, and let's not forget about that knot on your neck," Amina reminded Serena as if she needed any reminding at all.

"What knot?" Serena rubbed her hand around it and blinked back a tear. She hadn't realized that there was a mini flood waiting for the dam to break. The pressure behind her lids pushed the tears down her face. Her hand stopped moving and remained on the lump on the left side of her neck as she tried to no avail to hide it. Serena closed her eyes and the tears escaped by slithering down the sides of her face.

"Auntie, everything will be okay. You know that God tells us when we are weak then He is our strength."Amina held on to her aunt and Serena clung to her niece as if their lives depended on it. She waited patiently while Serena cried until she had nothing left to be purged of.

Serena looked at her niece as her love for Amina showed on her face. A flicker of shame crossed over her delicate features as she felt ashamed for being vulnerable in front of her. Amina detected this in her mentor and smiled.

"Auntie, I love you and am here for you. What would I do without you? You have practically raised me my whole life. Now that I'm eighteen, besides God, I owe who I am today to you and to Gran-Gran."

"I know you love me, baby, and you know I love you. Sometimes I have a hard time keeping the lines drawn and not going over them. I am your auntie and your mentor. You are in training to be the best prophet in the nation, and how can you be if I allow you to see me broken this way? I'm supposed to be the strong one. You know, the one who operates in the Spirit one hundred percent of the time." Serena dropped her head onto Amina's shoulder.

Amina laughed at Serena. "Auntie, really now, come on. We aren't in church, so right now you are not my mentor, but my aunt. No one but Jesus accomplished sowing to the spirit one hundred percent of the time. I hate to burst your bubble, but if you were that good, then you would have your wings by now. I am not that naive to be thinking that the saints of God never go through anything. You don't have any reason to be ashamed, woman of God," Amina assured Serena.

Amina stood up without looking back at Serena and walked over to the sound system. She began turning and twisting the knob until the dial rested on the compact disc. Amina changed the tuner to song number three, which was titled, "No Looking Back." No sooner than the artist began to sing, Serena chimed in and felt strength supersede the spirit of weakness that threatened to hold her captive.

Serena had such a beautiful voice, even if she sounded like a frog. It depended on which notes she hit if the croaking could be heard or the clarity that she was known for. The "woe is me" mentality had all but left her and she was determined not to be in bondage to an invisible demonic influence. Serena had declared that her mind was made up and she would not look back. And that fear would not keep her from going forth and completing the mandate God had placed on her life. She knew that everything she possessed spiritually and naturally all belonged to God, and she wouldn't give it up without a fight.

Amina watched Serena in silence. She witnessed a prophet unto the nations be renewed and restored. She loved to play gospel songs of encouragement because not only was it one of her auntie's favorite songs, but more importantly, the words ministered to her mind. Once she became strengthened in her mind, she would begin to command her body to line up with God's living word of healing. She didn't leave the room until Serena had gone up into a full worship with the next song called "Every Prayer."

Refreshed after a cup of hot tea, Serena went into her study to check her flashing voice mail. It had been nearly a week since the last time she was able to spend any time in her office. Serena was the head of a twenty-four-hour prayer line and was thankful for her team of seasoned intercessors. They worked the prayer line faithfully and, most of the time, without obstacles or issues. In the beginning she ran into many hurdles and there were bumps in the road, but with extra patience, prayer, and tender loving care, Serena was able to weed out those who really wanted to be a part of the ministry and for the right reasons.

Her mother, Pastor Crystal Sampson, told her that it was mighty strange that so many people showed interest in the ministry when it was first announced six years ago. She had great insight and cautioned Serena on how to handle the group without causing offense to them. She let Serena know up front that it didn't take a little bit of nothing to make folks leave the church.

The phone rang before Serena could hit the button on the voice mail to play back her messages. The red light blinked on and off furiously, but the messages would have to wait.

"Praise the Lord, Prophetess Sampson speaking." Serena had to concentrate on the pronunciation of her words to keep from straining her voice as her throat was still sore.

"Serena, child, is that you?" Crystal sounded worried.

"Yes, Pastor, it's me." Serena rolled her eyes up into her head. She had answered the phone too quickly, and if she had a chance to think about it before answering, she would have let it roll over to the already full voice mail.

"What in the world is going on with your voice? I've been calling you since after church on Sunday to see how the conference in Atlanta went, but Amina kept telling me that you weren't available, or were in the shower, or sleeping. Are you two okay over there?" Serena's mother's voice boomed through Serena's earpiece.

"Mommy, it is well. I'm just really tired and I appreciate the wisdom that Amina possesses to know that I need rest and peace. The last thing I want to do is have a conversation, plus my throat has been bothering me. You know how taxing it can be to minister three nights in a row. It's an exhilarating yet draining assignment. Women were delivered and set free, so mission accomplished. Mother, the atmosphere changed immediately upon the heartfelt worship of the people." Serena gave Crystal the quick version.

"Are you feeling better today? God really must have used you because I can hear it in your voice. Girl, I know you inside and out and you sound like you're sick. You musta overdosed on the Holy Ghost down there in Atlanta." Crystal laughed at herself. "Mama always knows when something ain't right with her children. The intercessors had also been trying to get into contact with you. I guess they grew tired of trying to reach you and resorted to calling Sister Edna. Evangelist Curry didn't hesitate to let her know that she'd left numerous messages on your voice mail, but you hadn't returned any of her calls. You know Sister Edna is ill equipped at handling matters of the spirit, and you know what she does when she can't handle an issue. She buzzed me in my office up to fifty times a day. It didn't matter that I had counseling sessions booked every hour on the hour. She doesn't have any problem reminding folks that she is just the administrative assistant, you know?" Crystal droned on and on in Serena's ear.

"Mommy, please." Serena didn't feel like hearing all of the issues that she was sure awaited her on the busy voice mail. "What was the issue they were having?" Serena asked.

"Oh, child, it was something about someone joining the ministry. I can't remember the young woman's name, but I reminded Evangelist Curry that she would just have to wait until you return to church. That's the reason I placed you over that ministry, so folks can stop coming to me seeking direction on everything," Crystal fussed.

Serena felt a sermon coming on, so she spoke up before Crystal came back with more to say. "Tell me about the service, did any souls get saved Sunday? I will deal with the intercessors and the prayer line before the day is out. I may need for Evangelist Curry to stay on call the rest of this week." Serena wished that she could just crawl back into her bed, pull the covers over her head, and go to sleep.

"Oh my, God showed up and showed out today, daughter. Judah Praise Team was in full effect and it didn't take long for the anointing of God to saturate the place. The Holy Spirit showed up and showed out, like always. It just blesses my soul to see God's people free in Him."

Serena's mother went off on a tangent, and she knew there would be no stopping her mother until she got tired.

"Mommy, did anyone get saved today? It seems like that would be the case since the Spirit was so high." Cutting her mother off from replying, Serena continued talking. "How could the anointing be that strong and no one get saved?" Serena was aggravated as her passion was seeing folks saved. The highlight of the service for her was someone surrendering their life to Christ.

"Serena, you know you can't make people give their lives to Christ. So to answer your question: no. No one received salvation today," Crystal said in a huff.

Serena listened to her mother go on and on about everything from Sister Tasha's short dress and how she wished the child would put on more clothes, to Mother Jenkins hollering and crying throughout the service because her baby boy, Jody, had gotten shot hanging out with the gang.

Serena had to put her mother on mute for a moment, happy not to have needed to respond to anything she was saying. She called out for Amina to bring her two aspirin and another hot cup of tea. She tried to stay focused on the conversation on the other end of the phone, but realized her mother was on mute when she called Serena's name to make sure she was still on the line.

"Serena? Are you still there? Did you hear what I said? Child, you must be tired. I hope you can get it together before Friday night prayer because we need you there," Crystal said.

Serena unmuted the phone with her chin. "Mommy, I'm sorry, my mind is really full and I am trying to nurse my throat." Serena wished she would have let Crystal know that she wasn't feeling well at the beginning of the call. "Can I call you back tomorrow evening to let you know if I will be able to make it for prayer on Friday evening?" She hoped that her mother would be okay with that.

Crystal didn't like the idea of her daughter not feeling well, but couldn't act as if she was too concerned because that would cause Serena to shut down. It was no secret for those who knew them that their relationship was strained, but Crystal hoped that would change before it was too late. She was also concerned about Amina, who was being groomed and trained in the prophetic ministry.

The two of them stuck together like Frick and Frack. When you saw one, you saw the other. When one was absent, the other would be also. They were like Siamese twins joined at the hip. Crystal knew that the ministry would feel the prolonged absence of the two most effective and anointed intercessors at Abiding Savior Christian Community Center. "All right, sweetie, please let me know as soon as you are feeling better. We have missed you in your absence. I will put you on the prayer list and also will solicit prayers from the pulpit. I love you and I'm here if you need me, ya hear?"

Serena agreed to anything her mother said because she was more than ready for the phone call to end. "Yes, I promise that I will call to let you know either way." Before releasing the phone call, Serena had one burning question. "Um, Mommy, has Brother Nathaniel Jackson been in service this past week? I haven't heard from him since before I left town for the conference." Serena waited, hoping her mother would tell her something about the man who had been unsuccessfully trying to court her for the last three months. They'd gone on a few dates and she liked him more than she would admit to anyone.

"Brother Nathaniel? Hmm, let me think. You know we have so many new members that I am not good with names." Crystal laughed out loud; however, Serena didn't find any humor in what she said.

"Mommy, he's the nice looking brother who stands six feet seven inches. He kind of puts you in the mindset of Idris Elba. You can't miss him. Nathaniel is such a distinguished-looking brother with the smooth bald head that looks like he has it spit shined before church each Sunday." Serena felt her temperature rising as she leaned back and sighed softly.

"Oh yes, Brother Nathaniel. Now I remember him. He's the new member who has women swarming around him like bees on a honeycomb." Crystal laughed. "Serena, are you sweet on him or something?" Crystal asked her daughter in surprise.

"Why would you ask that?" Serena closed her eyes, wishing she hadn't brought him up.

"I'm asking because if you have any interest in that brother, you had better keep your eyes open. Yes, he's been at church since you left, but trust me when I tell you that all of your single sisters haven't been delivered from the ideology that church is the spot for a hookup. The difference is that they think it's okay, as long as it's done within the confines of the church walls. Humph, a holy hookup is what I hear it's called nowadays, but back when I was a little girl, it was called pimpin' in the church," Crystal said with her tone laced with disgust.

"Pastor, don't be so dramatic. I was just wondering if Nathaniel had been in church while I was away. God showed me that He has greatness in store for him. The Lord also revealed to me that there are wolves in sheep's clothing on assignment to destroy his destiny. Women who are operating in the spirit of Jezebel are trying to blindside him by flaunting themselves in his presence." Serena felt the energy she had on reserve zapped from her just by talking about Nathaniel. She felt the spirit of jealousy and desire rising up in her flesh, so she took that as her cue to end the conversation before her carnal nature betrayed her heart.

Serena finally said her good-byes to her mother and dropped her head on her desk. Her temples throbbed as she heard her mother's voice in her head telling her to watch out for Nathaniel if she wanted a future with him. Serena had become complacent, believing that he would just follow her around and sniff up under her forever. Serena admitted to herself that she'd been acting standoffish. She tried pretending that she wasn't as into Nathaniel as she was to protect her heart from having to possibly repeat the past pain she barely got over.

Serena reminisced on the past and her ex-boyfriend, Carlos Sams. He'd promised to always love her and had even grown up in her mother's church. He was in training to be a deacon at the time and she had been called to preach. It didn't take long for Serena to find out that her man couldn't handle the favor of God on her life.

They would argue about whether God wanted both of them serving in ministry. Carlos felt that Serena should stay by his side and be a deaconess. She let him know that there was no God-ordained office titled as such and that she would preach God's Word. Slowly but surely, Carlos started avoiding her at church, and then he started breaking their dates.

The rumor mill had begun that he was a single man; however, Serena seemed to be the last to know. Eventually, Carlos left the ministry and the city without officially breaking up with her. Emotionally distraught by the breakup, Serena battled depression and she had shut down her heart. She had declared that she wouldn't fall in love again, until now.

Serena didn't give too much thought to Nathaniel being wooed by any of the other single women in the church. She called out their names and why she believed they weren't good enough for Nathaniel in alphabetical order. "Dara Ennis has two kids by different baby daddies; she is still young and wet behind the ears. Felisha Green has recently gotten saved and is said to still be seen in the clubs getting her drink on. Hmm," Serena asked herself, "what's the other woman's name who just joined Abiding Savior?"

Serena scratched her cropped hair and instantly, it seemed as if the lightbulb clicked on. "Melissa Wright. How could I forget about her? Hmm." She tried to relax, but she found no peace. Serena needed a distraction, quickly forgetting the flashing lights on the answering machine. She exited her office and went to find Amina in the master bathroom, which was reserved for Serena.

The aroma of apple cinnamon bubble bath permeated the atmosphere. Amina pointed the remote control in the direction of the Bose Wave music system mounted on the wall and powered on the compact disc player. Amina popped in the gospel group the Quiet Time Players as the melodies of their most recent single, "Sunday Morning Jam," caressed the room.

Amina made sure the temperature of the bathwater was not tepid by adjusting the thermostat to add extra heat to the liquid mix. Scented bubbles sat high upon the water and added to the ambiance Amina created for her aunt.

Serena walked in as Amina applied the finishing touches to the bathroom turned sanctuary. Apple cinnamon candles were lit and body oils of a variety of musk scents were the blame for the busy yet tranquil moments that were about to take place. Inhaling deeply, Serena smiled as Amina stood aside to allow her to enter the temporary paradise. The strong smell of apples tantalized Serena's senses, which caused her stomach to growl.

Serena smiled and nodded her head in approval of the setup that Amina had so carefully prepared for her. Amina returned Serena's smile and turned to leave, but not before dimming the lights and turning the music up. She closed the door softly behind her, leaving Serena to temporary paradise. On the other side of the door, Amina prayed that supernatural healing would take place where the enemy was on assignment to steal from her aunt.

The music permeated the air and soothed Serena's psyche. She disrobed and slid down into the water until only her chin rested on the bubbles that floated in the water. "Complete peace, come unto me now!" Serena commanded. She closed her eyes and listened as the trumpet player lulled her into a light sleep. A smile played around the edges of her mouth as her mind replayed images of her first date with Nathaniel. She'd allowed him to come to her home to pick her up but not before doing a background check on him.

Serena's arched eyebrow furrowed as her mind was attacked with images of Nathaniel and the ladies from the church who she'd named just minutes ago. Then she thought about the absence of Nathaniel's voice and who he could be with.

The smooth jazz became irritating to Serena as an uneasy feeling came over her. Her eyes popped open as she wondered if her mother was right for her to watch out for them. "Nathaniel Jackson, get out of my head," she whispered angrily, closing her eyes again and releasing a breath of hot air.

Nathaniel Jackson was good looking and he knew it too. Every time he entered a room, he was always dressed in his Sunday's best. The ladies from the church's eyes would gaze over at him, while the look of joy would cause their hands to fold daintily in their laps, their legs to cross, their backs to become straight, and necks to crook, straining to hear him say anything.

Serena remembered the first time she bumped into him in the vestibule area of Abiding Savior. Even she was taken aback by his distinct look of being a boss. Thinking back on their first meeting, her cheeks burned with embarrassment. She had literally bumped into Nathaniel by falling into the door of the church after stumbling on the oversized welcome mat.

The ushers dived in, trying to catch Serena to no avail. They landed in a heap but Serena landed perfectly into Nathaniel's arms. He steadied her to her feet that day and she saw something in his eyes that connected with her spirit. The warm and fuzzy feeling she had experienced at the moment she lay vulnerable in his strong arms was indescribable. Slightly embarrassed, Serena tried to play it off by giving him a light thank you, but the words never came out. She gave him a full-body smile, the kind that started at the top of her head and exploded throughout her being, sending a rippling effect to the tips of her toes. Breaking their intense stare, Serena felt self-conscious

again and fervently looked around for Amina. She was relieved to see Amina scurrying up the steps to the church,
and in the nick of time, they rushed into the building.
One minute from being late, they donned their coats to
the ushers and hurried into the sanctuary together as the
service praise and worship started.

Serena relaxed in the Jacuzzi and rested her head
on the back of it. Beneath closed eyelids she pictured a
wedding reception where the groom was throwing the
garter belt and one of his homeboys dove in to catch it.
She released a small laugh and began choking on the
scented water that had snaked its way to her throat the
wrong way. Flailing her arms, Serena slid on the slippery
bottom and slipped fully under the water. Serena knew
she was on her own and her effort of trying to grasp the
two side handles wasn't going too well.

The music continued to play and the saxophone blasted
through the radio system, letting Serena know that she
couldn't out-yell the song. Her throat burned like an
inferno due to swallowing water and bubble mix that was
supposed to bring about serenity but ended up causing her
more discomfort than when she'd entered the tub. At last,
Serena reached out with her left arm and felt around for
the handle. She splashed water over the sides of the tub
and grabbed ahold of the handle. Her heart was beating in
her ears at what sounded like a hundred miles per minute.
She pulled her midsection and legs up into a sitting
position and rubbed her face to clear the dripping water
with her right hand.

Forgetting that her hair was drenched, exhausted, she
turned her body and flopped both arms over the side of the
tub and rested her chin on them. It was at that moment
that Serena had an epiphany. She knew in her heart that
she didn't want to be without Nathaniel in her life on a
permanent basis.

Chapter 3

Amina pulled into the reserved parking spot that read PROPHETESS SERENA SAMPSON. Serena's was situated right outside of the door to the church beside her mother's. Amina loved driving her auntie's 2013 Buick LaCrosse. It was painted silver with a sunroof, leather seats with heating controls, and seat adjustment controls. The car could be cranked, locked, or the security code could be entered by speaking into an inconspicuous voice recorder attached to the keychain.

Serena pulled the visor down and the lighted mirrors immediately lit up and cast a glow around her face. She peered from side to side, nonchalantly searching for Nathaniel's car. She feigned making sure her makeup was flawless. She hoped that no one would be able to detect the mini bags of heaviness that hung from her tired eyes. Amina busied herself on the driver's side, placing the window protectors in the windshield since it was going to be a humid ninety-five degrees outside that day.

Serena wasn't feeling as sure of herself as she usually did. She didn't make it to prayer service on Friday night and had to admit that her emotions were in turmoil. She still hadn't heard from Nathaniel and a chill came over her at the thought of him being enticed by some other woman. She entertained visions of him and other single women in the church and she almost wanted to go back home. Serena blamed her extended absence on her throat not being up to par, although she sounded better than she had a week ago.

She pretended to be busy with her black Coach case as she forced herself from her comfort zone and got out of the car. Serena chastised herself for behaving so childishly. She frowned at her own actions and scolded herself further internally. Amina saw her mentor struggling more with herself than the bags she was getting out of the car and went to assist her.

"Auntie, are you all right?"

Serena looked sideways from up under her large hat at her niece and said, "I'm fine. Why do you ask?"

"You are acting strangely and it looks like your face is sweating. You only break out in a sweat when you are nervous about something or you don't feel well," Amina said.

Serena became agitated at that moment because her niece was always in her business. She just wanted to be left alone with her thoughts and stank spirit. God's Word was stirred up in her spirit, but the umpire of her soul went unheard and unheeded. She snapped at Amina, "Here take my Bible and iPad please." She forced the items into Amina's hand. Serena got out of the car with her knees knocking from aggravation and slammed the car door shut. She strutted off toward the opened doors of the church in a huff, with her heavy shawl tied up to her neck.

Amina pressed the door lock button to make sure the car was secure, but couldn't help but wonder if Nathaniel Jackson had anything to do with her auntie's weird conduct. She saw him out of the corner of her eye and noticed that he was oblivious to everything around him, as his eyes bored into Serena's backside. She didn't miss the twinkle in his eyes as he focused on the sway of Serena's full hips. Amina didn't say a word, but smiled to herself knowingly as she made her way into the church.

The dance team was lined up in the vestibule as Serena zipped by in a hurry. She was late and was on program to be worship leader that morning. Amina finally caught up with her as she skipped down the middle aisle behind Serena and reached the front pew. They looked up momentarily, quickly dropping their eyes as Crystal cut her eyes at them, knowing that they would hear about it sooner or later because she didn't tolerate tardiness from her leaders. Just as she approached the pulpit area, Minister Turrentine, the lead minister, held the microphone out to her as if passing the baton for the next leg of a race.

"Praise the Lord, saints. I said praise the Lord. If God has done anything for you lately, you should be standing on your feet, telling Him thank you. See, I don't know about you, but I know how to give honor to the Creator and not the creature. Can I go a little further?" Serena didn't wait for a reply from the congregants. She had been under spiritual attack every since she gave the benediction in Atlanta and she was ready to give Satan hell for all of the trouble he was trying to plant into her life.

Her eyes roamed the sanctuary then up in the balcony. Then she turned around and looked into the choir stand and gave a directive for the minister of music to play a song. "Beloved, when we enter into the courts of the most high God, He commands that we enter with thanksgiving in our hearts and a praise on our lips. I don't know how you can come in here and act like you're doing God a favor," Serena ministered.

"The enemy has sent out a spirit of deception and the falling away of the saints from the church have already begun to take place." Serena paused for effect. The musicians played their next song, which was a soft rendition of "Lord Make Me Over," as Serena continued.

It was a good thing that the healthcare ministry was on duty and cognizant of what was going on. Some of the members broke out in a shout. What were once worship songs changed when the atmosphere shifted into an atmosphere of total praise. The music ministry was always on point with one of the baddest and most anointed musical leaders in the land. Serena was high in the spirit and was happy being at home. Serena moved from the pulpit to the floor with the help of Brother Marcus. She prophesied as she moved through the church, and the more she heard the sounds of praise the harder she ministered.

Nathaniel watched in awe as the prophet seemed to wow the members. His steady gaze followed her every move and that gave him chills how she commanded the audience with such grace. He was mesmerized by her beauty. Nathaniel rubbed his chin as he stood erect on the third row. He found it nearly impossible to be so free in the spirit as his sisters in Christ. He took note of some of the men who were constrained. Most of the men just stood clapping their hands, while others sat and tapped their feet with glazed smiles on their faces.

Nathaniel closed his eyes and listened to the sound of Serena's voice. He noticed that something was quite different about it, but he wasn't thrown off. The power that usually rested on her through the glory of God could be seen and felt in every word she spoke. The church was on fire and the dance team had appeared out of nowhere with colorful flags. They waved them back and forth, ushering in the spirit of worship. Now that the fire had been lit, the eight hundred-member war cry had gone forth.

Serena wasn't sure where the sudden burst of energy came from or the physical strength she displayed minutes prior, but suddenly, she felt extremely drained. Her throat had begun bothering her again. As if on cue, Amina was right by her side, seeing that she was coming down from the spiritual pentacle she had taken the others to.

Something unexpected happened. Even though the spirit of the Lord was present in the place, Serena's knees buckled with weakness and began to shake uncontrollably. She was dressed in her robe over her Versace suit. As she grasped for air, she grappled with the silk scarf tied to her neck.

"Can we get some water over here please?" Amina saw that something was terribly wrong with Serena. She had to peel her aunt's fingers from around the microphone due to the tight hold she had on it. Sweat glistened on her knuckles as the veins stood at attention. Amina shoved the microphone into the empty hand of Deacon Jones and he passed the bottled water to Amina. She fumbled in haste to loosen the top off of the bottle of water for Serena to drink.

Serena felt the bottle pressed to her lips and struggled to open her mouth to drink. She hoped the drink would relieve the burning sensation in her throat. However, she collapsed against Amina who strained to remain kneeling. She motioned for the men of valor to help her keep from toppling over on top of Serena. Nathaniel didn't miss a beat. He sprang into action when he noticed Serena looking around as if something was wrong prior to her collapsing. He pushed through the throngs of dancing people and bodies stretched out on the floor. Nathaniel dodged at least three white sheets that were airborne for the ladies who were underdressed, but full of the spirit. Crystal, who had shed herself of her shoes and getting her shout on, was tapped on the shoulder by Elder Shaw.

"Pastor, Serena passed out." Elder Shaw's eyes were teary.

Crystal's dancing ended abruptly. She had to balance herself on the podium in the pulpit area to get her bearings. "Where is she? Where is Nurse Loreatha?"

Panic had overtaken Crystal and the spirit of celebration had become a shadow of what it was. Her mind raced and she wished she wouldn't have pushed her daughter to get back to church so soon.

"Pastor, Nurse Loreatha is attending to Serena." Elder Shaw pointed to the crowd of people beginning to gather around where Serena lay.

Crystal didn't bother putting her shoes back on. She made haste in getting to her baby. Calvin, the minister of music, held up his fist as a sign to the rest of the band and choir to end. Gasps and shrieks rang out in the congregation as everyone prepared to come to order. Most realized that a medical emergency was taking place. By the time Crystal had reached the group huddled around Serena, they made a hole so that she could maneuver through it. She didn't speak, but kneeled down alongside Amina and laid hands on her daughter while her armor bearer, Jalisa, covered her in prayer.

Amina poured the thick golden oil into the palms of her shepherds' hands. Crystal ordered all of the people who were crowded around to move back. She called the ministers and intercessors to the altar to pray and intercede for Serena. Looking around, satisfied that her team had her back, she led the prayer. Everyone in the circle prayed in their spiritual language. Amina remained by Serena's side, reassuring her that they wouldn't leave her.

Nathaniel stood back in obedience to the woman of God. He didn't go too far, as he wanted to keep an eye on Serena. His heart beat wildly inside his chest as fear entered. Feelings of helplessness overwhelmed him and it didn't take long for the devil to speak. Guilt set in the more he watched. "No, devil, she won't die, but she will live and proclaim the works of the Lord." He could've kicked himself for not calling her the whole time she was away.

Nathaniel knew Serena's schedule and knew when she would be returning. He barely gave it a second thought when she didn't return to church services as usual. Realization set in that he was being bullheaded and arrogant by refusing to call her just because he couldn't get her to commit to him.

The congregation remained hushed and prayerful until the paramedics arrived. Head Nurse Loreatha led the way to the group who were still huddled and praying. She tapped Minister Torrey on his back and when he didn't turn around right then, she tapped more urgently. She saw the agitation on his face; however, Nurse Loreatha wasn't moved as she stepped aside to allow one of the transit workers through the opening of the circle. Once the paramedics were done checking Serena's vital signs, they loaded her up on a stretcher and left the building.

Amina and Nathaniel followed the paramedics out as the church erupted with a war cry of love, adoration, shouts, and cries of victory for Serena. Crystal turned the service over to Minister Turrentine, as she prepared to leave for the hospital as well. Jalisa followed her leader back into the pulpit and grabbed her shoes along with her travel bag, which held her essentials. She trusted that the leaders of the church would make sure the rest of the service went off without a hitch.

Jalisa led the way out of the back of the church and around to Crystal's car. Before they reached the door, Jalisa had already popped the lock and the trunk at the same time. She ushered Crystal into the car and ran back around to the driver's side and pulled up behind the ambulance. Amina didn't know if she should get into the back of the ambulance with her auntie, or what.

Crystal sat in her car with a stoic look on her face and Nathaniel looked worried as he kept running his hand over his smooth bald head. He shuffled one black snakeskin boot in front of the other. No one said a word until the double doors in back of the ambulance snapped shut and the driver of the emergency service stepped up to them.

"Ma'am, sir, will either of you be riding with the patient? If so, we will need to know which of you will be riding with her. Please let us know your decision, as we need to get the young lady to the hospital for a thorough checkup. Would you prefer Duke or UNC Hospital?"

Amina looked at Nathaniel and spoke up. "Her name is Serena Sampson, and for the sake of time, UNC Hospital will be where she will go. I believe that Nathaniel will be riding with her to the hospital." She gestured toward the double doors as they were opened for the passenger.

She could tell that Nathaniel was more worried than she was and she knew the power of prayer. "Nathaniel, please accompany my aunt to the hospital and I'll ride with my grandmother. I believe it will do her some good to see you," Amina said.

Nathaniel snapped out of his reverie and caught on to what Amina was saying to him. He rubbed his chin, wasted no time, and jumped into the back of the ambulance. "I'll take care of her," Nathaniel said before disappearing into the cab of the ambulance.

Jalisa waited until Amina was in the car before hitting the hazard lights switch and pulling out of the church lot behind the ambulance. There was complete silence on the way to UNC Hospital in Chapel Hill, North Carolina. The doctors there usually provided the best care, and while they could have opted to go to Duke Hospital, that was second best in their book, and Amina decided the ride to UNC may be quicker. The traffic on the highway was minimal and before they knew it, they had reached the emergency room.

Chapter 4

Crystal, Jalisa, Amina, and Nathaniel gathered together in the hospital room Serena was assigned. The room was extremely small and didn't hold many visitors comfortably. Serena had gone down to the second floor for a CAT scan with imaging contrast.

"Amina, did Serena say she wasn't feeling well before you all left to go to the conference? Did she dress appropriately? You know this weather can be fickle. One day it's warm and then the next you don't even want to get out of bed because it can get so cold outside," Crystal said while she smoothed the wrinkles from her skirt to no avail. Crystal was nervous and in order to remain calm, she rocked back and forth in the chair.

"Gran, there weren't any clues that Auntie was sick or in pain before the conference. She complained of a sore throat and became hoarse the night we returned from the conference. We chalked it up to being fatigued and thought that Auntie would be better by now. I'm surprised that this is happening," Amina said.

"I wish that you would have told me that all the times that I called." Crystal smacked her teeth in anger.

"She had begun to distance herself from me before she left, or I would have told her to see a doctor." Nathaniel paced the floor, rubbing his head and smacking his legs as if he could reverse the outcome of that day.

"I'm sorry. You know how Auntie is. She doesn't want anyone fussing over her. We thought it was just some bug that would run its course." Amina dropped her eyes to the floor, feeling overwhelmed with guilt.

"Baby, I'm not blaming you. There's no way you could have foreseen what was going on in Serena's body. This unknown illness is just worrying me, but we will all have to adjust to whatever is needed to help Serena." Crystal rubbed her granddaughter's hands.

Amina jumped up and walked in small circles around the room. Everyone sat, drinking cups of coffee, but Amina didn't need any since she was about to jump off the walls with the adrenaline rushing through her veins. "I've told you everything I know. I'm sorry that I didn't let anyone know before all of this occurred. Auntie is here because of me," she whined and broke down sobbing.

"Amina, you are not the reason this is happening. I need for you to calm down." Crystal pulled Amina into her arms and hugged her.

"Gran, we had an appointment scheduled for Auntie for this week, but it wasn't soon enough."

Amina allowed her grandmother's soothing hum to calm her fears and stop her thoughts from wilding out on her.

"We have to believe that God has it all under control. He orchestrated things His way because He already knows the outcome. We need to stand on our faith and get through this together," Crystal said.

"Serena has the biggest test of all of us. So we need to strive to be strong for her. She doesn't need to see us with sad faces, because she's going to be on an emotional rollercoaster herself."

Crystal pulled her Bible out of her satchel and began to read aloud, "'But He was wounded for our transgressions, He was bruised for our iniquities, the chastisement of our peace was upon Him; and with His stripes we are healed.' That is what it says in the book of Isaiah, chapter

Fifty-three. I don't know about you all, but I will stand on this scripture." Crystal was positive that God would show up and give them the outcome they petitioned Him for.

"This is a great hospital." Nathaniel nodded his head in approval. "I've heard that the staff and the doctors alike are knowledgeable and they take great care of their patients. I had a friend here once and his team exemplified the patience of Job while he was inpatient. Upon his release, he wrote a check for five thousand dollars and donated it to clinical research. I'm confident that Serena will get the best care here. I'm prayerful that the more information we have, the better equipped we'll be to handle whatever the outcome of this may be."

Due to the size of her room, they all rotated spending time with Serena through the night. They were considerate of one another by staying no longer than ten to fifteen minutes at a time, excluding Crystal. She only moved long enough to go to the bathroom or stretch her legs, but she never left the room. The lack of sleep the last twenty-four hours was evident in their tired faces and wrinkled clothing. They wore it as badges of honor, as nothing was more important to them than making sure Serena knew that she wasn't alone.

"Brother Nathaniel, I just want to thank you for being here. You don't have to stay, you know," Crystal said. "This is a family affair and while I'm sure that your presence has greatly encouraged Serena, we wouldn't want you to neglect your personal affairs." Crystal knew that her daughter was smitten with the young man, but she wasn't too sure of what his intentions were with her daughter. She wouldn't stand by and let her daughter be led on by this debonair brother while she was in such a helpless state.

"Pastor, with all due respect, I intend to stay here with you ladies, if you don't mind. I am just as anxious to see

what needs to be done for your daughter as you all are. I
have already let my staff know that I won't be in for the
next few days. They know how to reach me if there is an
emergency. So unless you are kicking me out, I will be
here just in case you ladies need anything. One more
thing, Pastor Sampson: I am very fond of your daughter
and my intentions toward her are nothing less than
honorable." Nathaniel smiled in hopes of being allowed
to stay.

Jalisa took that moment to ask, "Now that's over, shall
we go to God in prayer before Serena gets back?" They
held hands as Jalisa led a moving petition to God for His
divine favor in that situation. She even prayed for God to
anoint those who would come into contact with Serena
for any reason.

Amens erupted along with shouts of hallelujahs that
filled the room. Serena was being wheeled down the hall
and she could hear the sound of triumph coming from
her room. She couldn't wait to get back there so that she
could give God praise too. The door to room 212 swung
open and the transporter pushed Serena's hospital bed in
and situated her in the center of the floor and locked the
wheels in place.

The transporter made sure Serena was okay and inquired
about her needs. The group stood around smiling. They
were visibly happy to see that she was smiling and looking a
little more like herself than the previous day.

He turned toward the group. "Hi, I'm Tremaine Whitted, Ms. Sampson's transporter. I'm in awe of the jubilant
sounds of victory we heard in the hall. I'm a believer that
God is able."

He extended his hand to shake each of their hands.
Tremaine held on to Crystal's hand, liking the satiny feel
of her skin. He believed that he'd found love again.

"I'm Pastor Crystal Sampson, the shepherd at Abiding Savior Christian Community Center, located in Bahama, North Carolina," Crystal addressed the stranger sternly. "Sir, if you were to die tonight, do you know where you would spend eternity?"

"Gran-Gran, that's inappropriate to ask someone as soon as you meet him," Amina said.

"Chile, hush up now. Grown folks are talking. The Lord's work is never done," she snapped, turning her attention back to Tremaine, waiting in anticipation of his reply.

"Oh, it's fine. Yes, ma'am. I was saved at an early age, but haven't been as faithful to God as He has been to me." Tremaine dropped his head in shame, but only for a moment. "I believe that I would spend eternity with God." He exhaled loudly. Tremaine's mind had switched tracks as he tried to mentally etch Crystal's smile and beautiful gray eyes into his mind. He noticed that her dress matched her eyes, which added to her exquisiteness. Admiring the glow that surrounded Crystal like a halo gave him chills.

Crystal ignored her granddaughter and looked the man over not once, not twice, but three times. He was an older gentleman who had silvery gray hair that streaked his goatee. His hands were strong and his firm grip electrified her. There was something about the man that made Crystal feel like a giddy schoolgirl inside. She couldn't let him know that since she barely even knew the man.

"I'm very pleased to meet you, Ms., I mean Pastor Sampson. I just need to relay a message from the doctor before I go. He said that the results of the test would be available within thirty-six to forty-eight hours."

"Thank you kindly, Mr. Whitted," Crystal said in the sweetest voice she could muster up. "Oh let me give you my card." She reached around into her pocketbook and pulled out a stack of cards. Flicking through each until she found what she was looking for, she handed Tremaine a church business card. "Please come and join us for service when you are able. The service times are on the back." Crystal smiled.

"Please call me Tremaine. All of my friends do. Thank you for this. I'll definitely keep you, well, your ministry in mind. I live in Roxboro and haven't found a church home there yet. I need to be in a church where I can be fed and used by God. You all be blessed now." Tremaine turned toward Serena. "I will be praying for you, little lady. I've seen you on television and know you to be a powerful woman of God. Watch, God is going to turn this around, you'll see. I'll see you around. It was nice meeting you all, especially you, Pastor Sampson." He tipped his head as if he were wearing a hat and smiled as he exited the room.

"Ooh, Gran's got a man." Amina smiled and hugged her grandmother. Nathaniel and Jalisa laughed at the joke.

"Well, I may be a cougar, but I still got it, I guess." The group laughed. "Don't pay me no mind. I'm too old and set in my ways to settle down with any man," Crystal declared.

"Serena, how are you feeling? How was the test?" Nathaniel walked toward the bed and grabbed Serena's free hand. He didn't want to disturb the dressing on her right arm. The sight of the intravenous tubes made him nauseated. He stared into her eyes waiting for a response.

"Nathaniel, what are you still doing here? I thought you had left a while ago." Serena was happy inside and her stomach felt the tingle of butterflies. That's what he did to her and even more so now that she could see tears in his eyes. In that instant, she wondered if he really was the man for her. It wasn't as if he hadn't tried over and over again.

"Erhmm, did you two forget you weren't alone? Serena, baby, you didn't answer Brother Nathaniel's questions."

Crystal was just as interested in her daughter's health and state of mind.

"Mommy, I'm fine. You know there is no rest for the weary in this place. Every five minutes that door is swinging open with someone coming in to check my temperature, blood pressure, to empty my urine bottle, or to give me medication to relieve my discomfort." Serena rubbed her throat and although her voice was scratchy and her neck a little swollen, she felt okay.

The group laughed, knowing that she was telling the truth about hospital stays. Each of them, with the exception of Nathaniel, had visited many members who had been hospitalized at one time or another and that was their testimony also. Serena looked around at the people who loved her and all she could do was smile. She trusted God and she trusted those in the room but she wondered if she could trust Nathaniel with her innermost fears or insecurities. She wondered if he would walk away when the pressure was on. Her thoughts were broken when another visitor entered the room.

All eyes were fixed on the young lady dressed in burgundy scrubs. Smiling, she directed her attention to Serena before speaking. "Hi, my name is Dr. Sinclair and I just wanted to stop by to introduce myself to you. I'm working on the team with Dr. Mason and Dr. Noel. I know you were informed that your test results would be back within the next day or so, but I wanted to speak with you about the most recent findings that I can relay right now. Is that okay?" Dr. Sinclair looked around the room as if asking for privacy, yet no one moved.

Serena felt a chill travel from her face to her feet. She wasn't sure if she wanted her family to stay or leave for what could be bad news. Crystal had no issue speaking up on the matter. "Doctor, I'm Serena's mother and this here is her niece, Amina. Jalisa here is a close friend to the family, and this is Brother Nathaniel Jackson, Serena's friend." Crystal moved her arm in an upward swing and then rested her hand at her side. "If you don't mind, we would like to be here to support my daughter with whatever news you have for her, just in case she forgets something or something is misunderstood by the patient." Crystal stood flatfooted on the dingy tiled floor.

Serena knew that her mother's mind was made up by the look of determination on her face. She had seen that look many times before and she knew it meant that nothing would change her mind. Serena nodded her head in agreement to let Dr. Sinclair know it was okay for her to share whatever news she had.

"I came straightaway from the onsite lab to inform you that Dr. Mason was on to something when he ordered the head, neck, and chest scans. He had already spoken to the team about the concerns of swollen thyroid glands in your neck. While we haven't gotten back the actual results, we believe with a ninety-nine percent surety that our goliath is going to be to attack spreading cells of cancer in your throat. The knot detected on the side of your neck is believed to be a tumor." Dr. Sinclair became quiet until she was sure that what she said had been received.

"Dr. Sinclair, how bad is the cancer? What is the prognosis?" Crystal asked.

"We should have more information as early as tomorrow morning. I don't want to scare you, but it's my mantra to keep it real with my patients. Are there any more questions? I will be happy to have the nurse bring some pamphlets by about possible treatment options and more information on the disease itself," Dr. Sinclair said.

Serena nodded her head to the news she had just received. Although tears welled up in her eyes, she declared in resignation, "By Jesus' stripes I am healed."

Amina didn't care to hear what the doctor was talking about because she trusted in God.

While they talked among one another, she had gone into the tiny bathroom, leaned against the sink, and prayed to her Heavenly Father on behalf of her aunt. A knock on the door startled Amina who wept as she sat on the closed toilet seat.

Nathaniel's face paled at the discovery. A wave of nausea washed over him and he needed to escape quickly. The nearest getaway was the bathroom and Nathaniel remembered that Amina was still inside. He told himself to get it together before he gave himself away. "Amina, are you okay in there?" Nathaniel asked selfishly, more concerned about the fears that had arose in him and rocked him to the core of his being when he'd heard the potential cancer diagnosis. No one was aware that his mother had died from cervical cancer after he was born. He never got the chance to know her and he had gotten used to crying in the dark because of the void in his life. Nathaniel had accepted Jesus Christ for the remission of his sins, but he was still holding on to bitterness at God for destroying any chance of him having a mother's love.

On the other side of the door, Amina turned on the sink faucet and splashed water over her face in attempts to freshen up. It didn't really matter because her eyes told the real story. She opened the door to allow Nathaniel to take her place in the tiny room. "I'm sorry for taking as long as I did. I hope that I didn't inconvenience you." Amina looked down at the floor because she didn't want to get emotional again.

Nathaniel didn't reply, but moved to allow her enough room to exit the bathroom and then went inside, moving his large frame into the quiet place. He locked the door and fell against it. He exhaled long and hard, hoping to feel the release of his pent up frustration.

Nathaniel had lots of natural qualities, but he was not as spiritual as he needed to be right now. He rubbed his head and wiped his eyes with his large hands. His father, Jeremy Jackson, had been a respectable man, God rest his soul. He had singlehandedly raised Nathaniel after his mother passed and he never married again. Nathaniel relaxed his stance and turned the water of the sink on and just let it run. He sat on the toilet and watched the water run out of the faucet nonstop.

Nathaniel couldn't hold his tears hostage any longer. He allowed them to fall, realizing the old saying that men do cry in the dark was true. His father never cried around him and Nathaniel believed that if he had cried in front of his father that he would be deemed weak by his father.

Waves of confusion washed over him as he tried to decipher if the purpose of his breakdown was from memories of his deceased mother or for the woman he wanted to spend the rest of his life with.

Nathaniel mused over the second time he had visited Abiding Savior not long ago.

He had gotten there late as Serena was ending her sermon, but he felt as if he was on time. His eyes beheld the most beautiful woman he had ever seen. The Sunday before, he had been there to catch her before she had a terrible fall. He wasn't able to speak with her after the service because he had to leave due to an emergency at the detention center for at-risk youth that he ran.

Nathaniel was convinced that she was an angel because he felt like he had died and gone to heaven. She wore her hair in shoulder-length brown and gold streaked tresses that hung above her neckline. Serena's caramel complexion was clear and without blemish. He imagined towering over her five-foot-three-inch frame as he easily stood six and a half feet tall standing straight up. Serena's image was etched in his mind and he loved how the gold preaching robe fit her body like a glove. It wasn't tight or distasteful, but it fit snugly and clung in all of the right places. That's when he knew that he must get into the presence again of the beautiful woman who graced the pulpit.

After the benediction had been given and the dismissal had taken place, Nathaniel waited patiently in line to shake the woman of God's hand. The line grew shorter and shorter and he finally saw Serena at the end of the line near the door. The thought of looking into her eyes again made him nervous. When it was finally his turn, he was at a loss for words. Nathaniel touched Serena's hands and they felt as smooth as silk. He held her petite, ringless left hand in his right one and gave thanks to God. Nathaniel introduced himself to her and thanked her for being a vision of perfection and promised her that he would be back.

Serena was humble and appeared to blush when he stared deeply into her eyes. Serena's hand trembled in his, as if she knew what her eyes revealed to the semi-stranger. She pulled her hand out of his and tucked it down by her side and thanked him for coming. Nathaniel saw her out of the corner of his eye as she pulled her personalized handkerchief out and patted her face in preparation to receive the last of the members.

Nathaniel had become comfortable hanging out in the hospital bathroom. No one bothered to knock on the door to check on him and he was fine with that. He needed that time to be alone with his thoughts. In doing so, he hoped that he would draw strength from someplace deep within to show Serena that he wasn't going anywhere, no matter how bad things were.

At last, Nathaniel stood up and looked in the small mirror, seeing how red his eyes were. Splashing the running water on his face, he hoped that his eyes wouldn't betray him. Knowing that he couldn't hide out in the bathroom forever, he murmured a quick prayer, rinsed his hands, dried them, and exited the bathroom.

Chapter 5

Nathaniel helped Serena to reassign her duties effective immediately and indefinitely. She had missed two more Sundays of service and midweek services due to her hospital stay. Doctors Mason, Noel, and Sinclair entered her room on Tuesday morning as promised. She pushed the food tray away, since she wasn't really impressed with the liquid diet she was on. Dr. Mason spoke up on behalf of the team.

"Ms. Sampson, test results showed severe swelling in your lymph nodes on your thyroid glands. We believe it's due to the cancer cells spreading through the jaw to the vocal box." He spoke slowly and deliberately as to not confuse Serena. Amina and Nathaniel were with her as they had stayed with her overnight. It was no easy feat convincing Crystal to go home and that everything would be fine. Amina had to constantly remind her that she had a blossoming ministry waiting on her return.

"We performed a needle aspiration and we biopsied the cells captured. It looks that my thoughts on the possibility of throat cancer were correct," Dr. Noel explained. "It has progressed from being localized to regional and has been staged at level three." They discussed the plan of treatment that Serena would take.

The first thing on Serena's treatment plan was to have the tumor and both thyroid glands removed surgically. The procedure would make it necessary for her to spend another two or three days inpatient at UNC Hospital.

Serena had mixed emotions once she was released from the hospital. She couldn't believe that her God would allow the enemy to get at her this way. Her life had been dedicated to serving God and the people of God for the last twelve years. She had lost out on the love of her life because he couldn't handle the demands that ministry had on her.

Crystal had been calling every morning, noon, and night since Serena was released from the hospital. Serena knew her mother meant well, but she needed time to digest the information. She'd been trapped on the emotional rollercoaster, aimlessly riding since the week before.

During one of the quiet moments while she was in the hospital, Nathaniel pulled his chair up beside Serena's bed while she watched Dr. Trindle bring forth a Word full of wisdom on Black Entertainment Television. In his mind, he had rehearsed over and over again what he wanted to say to Serena. He grabbed her hand, rubbed it gently, and watched her in silence.

Serena's eyes were glued to the television screen. She was enthralled by Dr. Trindle's message on going into the enemy's camp and taking back all that he had stolen from the people of God. She struggled to focus on what she was saying; however, heat rose to her cheeks as she felt Nathaniel staring at her. Serena glared through the television screen mounted on the wall. It was as if she were hypnotized by the words being sown into her weakened spirit. Tears once again slid down Serena's pretty face and landed on her dull blue and white gown.

Nathaniel let Serena's hand go and reached up to wipe the stream of tears from her delicate skin. Picking up her hand again, he felt the courage he needed to let Serena know how sorry he was for ignoring her and not keeping in contact with her when she, left for the conference.

"Serena, baby, I'm sorry for not keeping up with you once you left for the conference. My ego was crushed when we last met. You knew that I wanted to begin a committed relationship with you, but you denied me. It's nothing for me to get a woman; however, the first time I laid eyes on you, I knew that you were the only one for me. I called myself getting back at you for leaving me hanging and refusing to let me know if you wanted to be with me, so I went out with Melissa." He watched for Serena's reaction to his confession before proceeding.

"Nathaniel, please, you don't have to apologize. I'm wrong too. I'm sorry," Serena whispered. She loved the way his hands felt against her skin. She felt secure as his large hands covered her smaller ones. She didn't want to look into his eyes because she didn't want his pity.

"No, let me finish," Nathaniel said. "I didn't want you to feel like you were in total control of the situation. Melissa saw me after church one evening and inquired how I was doing. I was vulnerable and appreciated the fact that she paid enough attention to me to ask. She was pretty, so I invited her out to dinner." Nathaniel felt Serena's hand tense up as he blurted the rest before he lost his bravado.

"I went out with Melissa for selfish reasons. I had hoped to run into someone we knew from church so they would inform you, but my plan backfired. I had hoped that you would call me at some point during your absence, but you never did." Nathaniel paused for effect before continuing.

"I didn't think you cared if I went out with someone else, since you didn't take the time to make sure that I was okay after our last date." Nathaniel's eyes were filled with sadness as he saw the same sadness in Serena's eyes. He was sure that she wouldn't want to hear that he had planned to move on, but he had to be honest with her. "Serena, you bruised me by not taking me seriously. I have told you before and now I'm telling you again that you are my soul mate." He paused to allow the words to sink in. "I don't want to lose you, Serena. Not like I lost my mother. Baby, I need for you to believe me when I say that I'm here for you. If you want me, I will be right here every step of the way."

Nathaniel went on to share how his mother passed away and then he apologized again.

Serena listened intently to what Nathaniel was saying but the images of him and Sister Melissa flashed through her mind. Her only concern was what was going on between them now. Her stomach was in knots as she whispered, "What about her?" She was afraid of the answer, but she wouldn't be able to move forward with him if there was anything going on between them.

"Serena, Melissa means absolutely nothing to me. I hate to admit this, but I used her to get through nights of you being gone. I took her out a couple of times when she admitted that she was looking for something permanent with me. Serena, I knew that I couldn't reciprocate because my motives for dating her were wrong. She was disappointed when I told her that I wasn't looking to take our friendship any further. I let her know that she wasn't the woman for me; you are," Nathaniel said.

"Are you sure? The timing is just so jacked up. I may not make it," Serena whispered.

"Will you be my lady? Will you allow me to be the man to you I desire to be?" Nathaniel refused to listen to the seeds of doubt that Serena spoke. "We are only going to think and speak positively." Nathaniel smiled at the thought.

Serena was tired from the little bit of conversation they had, but she was thrilled to know that Nathaniel still wanted to be with her. She had run from love long enough and had finally accepted the fact that she wanted someone to love as well. She could only hope that Nathaniel wouldn't have a change of heart if the storm lasted too long. Doubts danced in her thoughts, but she decided to cross that bridge if it ever came to that. "Yes, I will be your lady." Serena smiled.

Chapter 6

Amina lay awake in her room. Her senses had been on high alert since the day her aunt had passed out during church service. She jumped at every sound, no matter how small. Sleep eluded her even though she was extremely exhausted. Last week, she faithfully remained at her aunt's side.

Since Serena had been home from the hospital, she didn't require as much as she usually did. Amina remained dutiful by making sure the house was tidy and quiet while Serena rested. Church members had dropped off foods from every food group in loads. Some tried to linger by making small talk; however, Amina didn't allow them to stay too long. She had her work cut out for her in figuring out where everything should go and what could be wrapped and frozen for later use. She was happy that they didn't have to worry about going hungry anytime soon. There were all types of soups, fruits, pastries, and drinks on deck.

Amina's grandmother and aunt had been there for her ever since she could remember. They had raised her when her own mother decided that she didn't want her or her father after she was born. Jonathan had plans to marry her mother, but she'd broken his heart. Her grandmother told the story time and time again, but she wanted to hear it from her father.

"Daddy said he was young and in love with the wrong girl. If it weren't for God, I would be fatherless, too."

Amina had a hard time getting him to open up, but she continued to press the issue until he gave in. He explained to her that there was no way that he could raise a child by himself once she'd left. Jonathan shared the details about her mother during one of their many video chats. Jonathan's mother and sister were his saving grace as they agreed to allow Amina to live with them and they had been together ever since.

Growing up, Amina would wonder if various women she saw in passing were her mother. She would never know if the lady who had given birth to her had any regrets about leaving her. Sadness weighed on Amina's heart as the thoughts of never having a traditional family caused a void in her life. She shook her mind clear of the remnants of her past.

Amina made sure that Serena was well taken care of. Selflessly, Amina had thrown herself into making sure that Serena had her daily baths, hot or cold meals each day, depending on what she thought she wanted. Sometimes, Amina would make two or three different meals for Serena because she couldn't make up her mind about what she wanted. Amina had begun to lose weight as a result of worrying and from the lack of eating regularly.

Rolling over onto her side, Amina dreaded having to get up out of the bed. She looked warily out of her window at the darkened sky. The gloominess outside had infiltrated the mind-sets of the occupants of their house while it watched and waited for the opportunity to unleash its fury. Although, she was unsure of what the future had in store for them, one thing Amina knew without a shadow of a doubt was that God's Word promised that no weapon formed against them would prosper.

Amina tossed and turned in her twisted bed sheets, kicking and fighting for her freedom. She looked around her bedroom and gave God thanks. She stood, shaking her legs so that she could get rid of the feelings of pins and needles stabbing her. Her feet sank into the purple shag carpet and she stretched her tired bones by reaching up to the ceiling until she stood on tiptoes. "Thank you, Lord, for another day."

Feeling invigorated, Amina was ready to command her day. She started by making her bed, which was almost like Serena's but smaller in size. Her favorite color was anything in the purple family. Her wallpaper color, her carpet, her curtains, her bedspreads and pillows, to her pillowcases, and even her bathroom were adorned in lavender and different shades of purple. She looked satisfied with her mini cleaning spree and headed into her bathroom to get cleaned up.

An hour later, Amina had almost completed two loads of wash and was in the kitchen listening to her new favorite gospel recording star, Cashyra. She particularly loved the track titled "Come Home." She recalled the gospel release party at the end of the summer. The hype was past the roof about the gospel sensation with the golden voice. Smiling to herself, she remembered her skepticism, but was pleasantly surprised when Cashyra hit all of her emotions with her music.

Amina snapped her fingers as the music played and the atmosphere was changed. No longer was the kitchen just where you came to eat, but there was a brightness that overshadowed the gloom that had taken up residence on the other side of the house. Amina turned the music up loud enough to block any negative thoughts that were trying to gain a foothold in her mind. Amina felt the power of the words building her up and she sang along.

Tears streamed down Amina's face as the song ministered to her. She thought about how she could have been the one someone was praying for. It could have been her who needed to come back home and surrender her all to

Jesus. She cried for those who didn't want Jesus, for those who didn't know Him but wanted to, and even more so, she cried for her mother, whom she didn't have one solid memory of.

The ringing phone irritated her because she rarely had any quiet time. "Sampson residence. How can I help you?" Amina's nasal sound made her sound sickly.

"Amina, it's Gran-Gran; what's the matter? You getting sick too? Lord, I need to know what's going on around here," Crystal bellowed.

"Good morning, Gran-Gran. I was just having a moment, that's all. Really, I'm fine. I'm actually thinking about coming to church this morning," Amina said.

"It would be good to see you this morning, sugar. I don't want you to overdo it since you are taking care of your auntie and all. How is Serena this morning? I thought it would be best that I give her some time to fully digest all that has happened and embrace what is to come." Crystal twirled her long mustard-colored phone cord around her fingers.

"Gran, Auntie is doing as well as can be expected as I'm sure you know. She hasn't been her usual vibrant self because she's tired from what she's been through. I pray she isn't settling into a state of depression. When are you coming by? It would be good for you to come as much as possible so that she won't start in again about not having your attention in health or in sickness."

"I know that Serena and I have had our differences, but sometimes I just don't know how to communicate effectively with her. She may be right in her thinking and I have no excuse for my lack of nurturing through the years. I've made myself available to her, but she never calls me or reaches out to me for anything," Crystal rambled on.

The beeping intercom interrupted the conversation Amina was having with her grandmother. Startled, she jumped from the noise coupled with anxiety and secretly wished that the intercom system was never built, but Serena would have it no other way. She wanted to be able to reach Amina at any and all times when she needed her. Agitated, Amina suppressed the negativity she was feeling and inhaled deeply. She released the hot air, put Crystal on hold, and cleared her throat before speaking.

"Auntie, I'm here. What can I do for you?" Amina did her best to sound chipper.

"Amina, hey it's me, Nathaniel. I was wondering if you wouldn't mind bringing your aunt a bottle of water and a banana to her room? Oh, and if it's not too much trouble, can you bring me a bottled water as well?" Nathaniel chirped into the speaker.

"Sure, is there anything else I can get for either of you?" Amina offered.

"Thanks and no. I believe that will do it," Nathaniel answered on behalf of Serena and himself.

"Nathaniel, will you be able to stay with Auntie for a couple of hours? I would like to go to church this morning. It's been a minute and I need to be recharged," Amina said, desperate to get away.

"Sure, that won't be a problem. I'm planning on sticking around most of the day anyhow. I know you are in need of a break from the monotony of what's been going on, so say a word of prayer for me and Serena too," Nathaniel said.

"I'm on it. I will go ahead and take some things out just in case either of you get hungry before I get back." Amina disconnected the intercom. "Hello? Gran, are you still there?" Amina had clicked back over to resume talking with Crystal; however, she had already hung up.

Amina took out one of the many bowls of soup and placed it on the counter in case Serena got hungry. She

Lachá M. Scott

had labeled them by the kind of soup it was and the date it was received.

Fresh fruit baskets lined the marble-stained island that was in the middle of the kitchen. She eyed one of the baskets, making sure there were bananas inside before grabbing the basket and bottles of water and sauntering out of the kitchen.

The feelings of heaviness had returned and Amina had to shake the feelings of sadness off before using her elbow to knock on the door to Serena's bedroom. Exhaling, Amina used her elbow to knock on the door to deliver the items requested.

"Come on in, Amina," Nathaniel welcomed her into the room. Seeing that her hands were full, he jumped up from where he had been sitting to assist her. "Here, let me help you out."

He took the fruit basket from Amina's arms as she placed the water bottles and napkins down.

"Thanks, I almost didn't make it." Amina laughed and placed the items on the dresser.

Amina eyed Serena lying there as if the bed were swallowing her up. She didn't look like herself, having lost eighteen pounds and she slept on and off throughout the day.

Serena nodded her head with a smile. She looked worn out and her skin had paled considerably. As an afterthought, Amina asked over her shoulder, "Do you mind me driving your car this morning?" She waited for any acknowledgment from her aunt. "I promise to take good care of it."

Nathaniel spoke up on behalf of Serena. "I'm sure that she won't mind you taking her car. You drive it more than she does, anyhow, and you will be the only one driving for a while."

Amina watched her aunt while Nathaniel made decisions for her and spoke on her behalf. She didn't flinch so it must have been okay. She smiled at Nathaniel, noticing how he was taking charge and seeing how Serena was relaxed enough to allow him to take control of the situation.

A wave of sadness hit her as she went to her bedroom to prepare for service. It wasn't the norm for her to be going to church alone. Amina swung open her closet doors and stood still, looking up and down the racks of suits, mentally trying on a couple. She'd decided on a black and pink pinstriped three-piece suit. Upon trying the pants on, she noticed that they were considerably larger than the last time she'd worn them. Amina walked over to her floor-length mirror and turned around slowly in the mirror while holding on to the waist of her pants. She finally decided to wear a black knit dress that nearly swept the floor. She hurried to shower and dress before running out of the door to church.

Amina arrived at church later than she expected, but was happy that she'd made it in time to see her grandmother take the pulpit. She tried to shake off the uneasy feeling weighing down on her shoulders. She was determined to leave her cares at the door. Amina smiled at the usher and took a program before giving her a slight hug and followed her down to the front of the church. The usher pointed to the front pew for Amina to sit, which was reserved for family only.

"Saints of God, let's honor God today. I mean really honor Him by our praise offering and servanthood," Crystal commanded from the pulpit. "As children of God, sometimes we forget why we assemble here every week, but I pray that you will examine yourselves to make sure that you aren't one of the ones who's forgotten. There are many who would love to be here in your place, but for some reason or another, they can't be." Crystal struggled internally to remain the pillar of strength in the faces of the people, although she felt like crying.

"Amen, you can say that again." The pulpit committee cheered their leader on.

The shouts of love and encouragement gave Crystal the jolt of recharging that she needed. Since Serena's diagnosis was given, she had been an emotional wreck. "Serena was released from the hospital until her surgery is scheduled for her biopsy. It doesn't matter what it looks like, I believe that God is able," Crystal declared.

"It's all right, Pastor," someone cried out.

"We love you, Pastor," others said in unison.

Crystal felt her help coming on and said, "I love you all too. I declare you all are the best flock in all this side of the earth. I trust that God is going to turn this around. Even though the devil is speaking, God's voice is louder and He has the last say so." One tear fell and then another, but Crystal charged on. Jalisa handed her a handkerchief and Crystal dabbed her eyes a couple of times before continuing.

"I'll be preaching this morning if I can." Crystal felt a praise in her belly and started shaking her hands. "I feel like the prophet Jeremiah when he said that he felt like he had fire shut up in his bones. Thanks to you all, my iron is being sharpened by your iron of love and encouragement. I have to take a moment, if you don't mind, just to give my God some praise."

Crystal handed the microphone to Elder Shaw and danced like David danced. The musicians took their cue from Crystal and the music started. The people got up on their feet and began to praise God too. Amina sat there immobile and watched what was going on around her, unaffected. Her eyes glazed over and she did nothing to stop them, as tears spilled onto her cheeks, bringing liberty with them. Next, she began to cry out to God and then gave Him praise.

Standing, Amina shouted, "Hallelujah, thank you, Jesus." She wasn't much of a shouter but she was a jumper. Up and down she jumped until she couldn't jump anymore.

Crystal had felt the release when it happened. The paradigm shift had taken place and she felt in her spirit that she could move on with the service. "God is good, ain't He?" Crystal asked, holding the microphone toward the congregation.

"Amen and amen. Yes, He is." The congregation became subdued while others continued to shout as Crystal opened with a word of prayer followed by the scripture. "You may be seated in the presence of God, if you can."

"Preach, Pastor!" members of the pulpit encouraged her. Some were still dancing in the aisles.

"Give the Lord a handclap of praise," Crystal instructed the congregation.

They acquiesced and clapped in obedience before settling down for the spiritual meal they were sure would be fulfilling. "I'd like to use as a sermon topic 'There is Power in Forgiveness.' Ahhh, let me say that again because y'all didn't hear me. I said, there is power in forgiving," Crystal bellowed to the crowd. Amens erupted from the pulpit.

Crystal waited until they quieted down before continuing: "Jesus was asked by Simon Peter how many times should he forgive his brother? 'Seven times?' he asked. Jesus' reply was seventy times seven. What was he saying, my sisters and brothers?" Crystal wasn't expecting a reply and she drove full speed ahead. "What it means is this: no matter how many times you are wronged, no matter how much folks talk about you, lie on you, or are your source of disappointment, you are expected to forgive the ones who hurt you," Crystal taught.

Crystal ignored the moans of the people. "Ah, yes, you must forgive. I know some of you all don't like what I just said, but don't get mad; get delivered," Crystal instructed. Whoops and hollers rang out among the congregation.

Walking to and fro across the pulpit, Crystal enlightened the congregation on what forgiveness really meant and how it freed up the one who had been wronged. She was compelled to preach that sermon mainly due to her own situation. "See, church, it isn't easy to forgive when the ones who hurt you the most are your own family," Crystal revealed.

"You preaching," someone in the choir stand shouted loudly, followed by clapping.

"Many times in this life, we want to hold on to the pain in order to gain sympathy from others. We want to continue to throw someone else's indiscretions in their face instead of forgiving and moving on. I've been guilty of not forgiving with pure motives thinking that my stuff didn't stink. Truth be told, we have all hurt someone at some point in our lives. Some hurts we know about and some we don't, but the moral of the lesson is that if you don't forgive, you won't be forgiven." Crystal reached for her water on the podium to wet her throat.

"Love keeps no records of wrongdoing. Jesus was the best example of that. He lived, hung, bled, and died so that we might live. Saints, you can't live the life of abundance Jesus intended when you are walking in unforgiveness. It's like spiritual poisoning and causes separation from God when you refuse to show mercy to obey His word by forgiving others. I'm a living witness that there is power in forgiveness. Giving up your right to revenge frees you up, gives you back power," Crystal drove her point home.

"Hallelujah!" Evangelist Curry spoke up.

"Yeah!" Mother Jenkins added in agreement.

"Preach, Pastor!" someone from the balcony yelled.

"Can I get an 'amen,' church?" Crystal felt freed up by obeying God and bringing forth the word He ordained.

"Amen, amen, amen." The congregation began to jump up and shout in victory.

"God's Word tells us that those who show mercy will obtain . . ." Crystal moved with the Holy Spirit.

"Mercy," the congregation yelled out.

"Don't let the sun go down on your anger. Whatever problems you have, you need to talk about it and get it right before you close your eyes for the night. No one knows the day nor the hour they will be called home. You want to make sure that when your name is called that your soul is right with God. Are there any witnesses out there, or am I just preaching to myself?" Crystal hollered.

The church grew quiet and she wondered whose toes she was stepping on with God's Word.

Deciding that her point was made, she began to give God praise. "If you believe that there is power in forgiveness, stand up on your feet and praise God for His unfailing love and grace." Crystal eyeballed the crowd as she waited to see if anyone was in agreement with her.

The choir began to sing as the members stood to their feet. Hands were raised, eyes were closed, prayers and praises were going up. Crystal gave the altar call and two people gave their lives to Christ and joined that day. The man looked familiar. "Sir, would you state your name so the congregation can welcome you." Recognition caused a smile to sneak up on Crystal as she eased down from the pulpit and thrust the microphone into his face. "Here, speak into the microphone so everyone can hear you."

"Hi, I'm Tremaine Whitted." He smiled sheepishly.

"Put your hands together for Brother Tremaine, church," Crystal commanded, and the congregation began to clap.

"This brother I met over at UNC Hospital. He works there and has been helping take care of Prophetess Serena," Crystal said.

The clapping grew louder and some were yelling thank you to the man.

"Tremaine, we give God praise for your presence today. I didn't think you were going to come, but God does work, don't He?" Crystal asked.

"I told you I was coming, Pastor Sampson. I'd just like to say thank you for inviting me. I could feel the love as soon as I got here and I thought to myself, if this is what heaven feels like then I don't want to miss out. The Word helped me and my heart is lighter. I won't leave here the same as I came," Tremaine declared with boldness.

"Praise the Lord. We are all happy that you decided to come and worship with us. We need to work on getting you baptized and usher you through new members' orientation." Crystal felt giddy inside about the possibility of seeing him more often.

The members laughed and others shouted in agreement with Crystal. She turned her attention to the young lady who had also given her life to Christ and joined the ministry. "I haven't forgotten about you, baby. I was just saving the best for last. Can you tell us your name, sweetie, and how old you are?" Crystal looked into the young girl's eyes.

"I'm Anissa and I'm fourteen years old." She rocked back and forth on the balls of her feet.

"Are you nervous?" Crystal hugged her for comfort.

"A little."Anissa shrugged as tears came out of nowhere and rolled down her face.

"I haven't seen you before. Is this your first time here?" Crystal probed while scanning the crowd to see if anyone who knew her would come forward to support the young girl. A young fellow, who looked to be the same age as

Anissa made his way to the end of his row and down toward the altar. Anissa smiled at the young man in appreciation.

Crystal stood off to the side to allow the young boy to support Anissa. "Church, let's give the Lord praise for what He has done by the moving of His spirit today."

Shouts of praise could be heard all through the sanctuary. Crystal motioned for one of the intercessors to come and take the new members to the back to minister, pray, and give them some information about the body of believers they decided to join. "Church, you all know what we do here at this church. I declare we need to give God some real praise. The angels in heaven rejoice when one soul comes into the Kingdom and we have doubled that," Crystal urged.

The church followed through with their leader's request. She waited until the church had quieted down before making her last announcement. Seeing as though the members had begun to have their own side discussions, Crystal decided to intervene before she lost them altogether.

"Can I have your attention before we have the benediction?" Crystal bellowed into the microphone. The authority that boomed from her request caught everyone off guard, although they knew the order of service and they hadn't been released yet. "Did you all forget where you are?" Crystal reprimanded the members and visitors alike.

"That's more like it," she said. The rolling of eyes from some of the younger members didn't escape Crystal's stern glare, but she pressed on, speaking as if everyone was all right with being called on the carpet. "Now, if you don't want me to have to make it rain in here, then remember where you are and how to conduct yourself. Now on to other news in this Christian community. I want to remind you to make sure that you're not only keeping Prophetess Serena lifted in prayer, but we need to keep all of our members who are sick or going through some other troubling times lifted in prayer," Crystal said.

Instead of Crystal attempting to bring them back one more time in order to give the benediction, she released the microphone to Jalisa. Everyone heaped to themselves or other groups talking, laughing, and acting rowdy, so Crystal left them to themselves. She didn't have the energy to do anything but walk away at that point. She heard the continual praises going up and the animated voices that followed her down the hall to her office, where she retreated and sat down. Jalisa followed on her heels, but Crystal sent her away. She needed some one-on-one time with God. She hadn't been able to tell them that Serena was in the battle of her life.

Not long after the benediction was done and the high praises had dwindled, there was a light knock on the door. Crystal snatched the mirror that sat on her desk up and peered into it. Her eyes were red, swollen, and still wet with tears from petitioning God for a miracle.

"Hmm, I wonder who that is." She stood up and straightened out her suit before walking over to the door. Whoever it was had stopped knocking, but curiosity got the best of Crystal. She hurried to the door, unlocking it. Pulling the door open, Crystal was shocked to see that it was Tremaine.

Crystal's breath caught in her throat as she admired the swag in Tremaine's step. Afraid to open her mouth, she cleared her throat loudly instead. "Erhmmm." Crystal held the hum until Tremaine turned around.

Hearing the door open, Tremaine was positive that she stood watching him. What she didn't know was that he'd intentionally walked heavily, so that the clacking of his Armani shoes would cover up his thumping heartbeat. He'd heard her clearing her throat, but acted as if he didn't just to see if she would invite him back down the hall. He smiled when she did.

"Brother Tremaine, is there something I can do for you?" Crystal asked. She wondered how he found her office or who led him to her door.

Tremaine took his time turning around due to him having a serious case of nervous energy. His palms were sweaty and his stomach started to bubble. Checking his surroundings, he turned on his heels and faced his new pastor with a big smile. "Pastor, I hope I wasn't intruding. One of the ushers escorted me back here and asked me if I would be okay before leaving me here," Tremaine explained.

"Brother Tremaine, you're not interrupting anything important. It's good to see you again." Crystal closed the door behind her. Walking toward him, Crystal didn't give him the standard church hug. She hugged him tighter than she had any other male church member. She inhaled his clean scent. Forgetting momentarily that she was still holding on to the man, she let him go abruptly. Making no apologies for her strange behavior, she asked, "Shall we talk in the sanctuary?" Crystal gestured for Tremaine to follow her as she led the way back toward the front of the church.

"Thank you, Pastor Sampson. Your church is really beautiful." Tremaine, still shocked about how close Crystal held him, couldn't focus on anything but the way she felt in his arms. He tried to shake off the warm feelings that settled into the pit of his stomach. Silently, he looked around the edifice before taking his seat. Tremaine was impressed by the intricate carving of the cross above the choir stand behind the pulpit. He wondered how this all came about, but figured this wasn't the time to inquire. Trying not to stare, he basked in Crystal's beauty.

Closing his eyes briefly, he envisioned them standing at the altar, switching vows.

He heard tapping and opened his eyes, remembering where he was. "I'm sorry, I was just reflecting on how much I enjoyed the sermon today. I haven't really heard too many women preachers, but I can honestly say that you are awesome at what you do up there," Tremaine admitted.

Smiling nonstop as Tremaine talked, Crystal found her voice. "Aw, you're too kind. I can't take credit for what happens in this house; it's God's house." Crystal threw her hands up and circled them around. "He gets the glory. I'm just happy that He allows me to carry His Word. I love being used by the Lord. So you're new to women pastors or preachers?" Crystal wondered how this would turn out.

"Growing up, I was taught that only men were called to preach, but I have a different outlook today. I want to thank you again for reintroducing me to Jesus. I have lots to learn and lots of growing to do, but this time I'm in it to win it. How is your daughter doing, Pastor? I've been out of the loop the last few days since I've been on vacation and wanted to let you know that I'm thinking of her." Tremaine did his best to kept the conversation going in effort to stay in the presence of his future wife.

"Thank you for your concern. Serena's doing as well as can be expected at this time. We have a long road ahead of us." Crystal rubbed her hands together and dropped her eyes because she felt herself becoming emotional all over again. Then it happened: the tears fell, and there was nothing that she could do about it.

Tremaine didn't know what to do. He looked around the sanctuary for someone to walk by, but there was no one. He reached over and pulled her head to lay on his shoulder then placed his large hands over Crystal's and rubbed them. He opened his mouth and began to sing. The smooth melody of his voice made him sound like the original singer of the gospel hit "Never Would Have Made It." Tremaine closed his eyes and belted out the chorus, getting lost in the words.

Crystal lay her head on Tremaine's shoulder, allowing him to caress her hand while she had her second good cry within one hour. She had gotten pretty comfortable, almost forgetting where she was. She heard the creaking door as it closed, which meant that someone saw them."Oh, I'm sorry." Crystal sat up, snatching her hands back, alarmed. Crystal dabbed at her eyes the best she could without smearing her makeup any worse than she had.

"What are you sorry for? I hope I'm not being too forward, but are you worried about what people would say if they saw you with me?" Tremaine asked.

"Brother Tremaine, I don't know you very well. It would be awkward if any of my members came through here and saw us sitting here together with my head on your shoulder, you singing and holding my hands. How would that look? The rumor mill would be buzzing with speculations and accusations. I can't afford to have a scandal break out in the church. I'm sure that there are many standing by waiting for me to fail. I'm sorry, but that's just not who I am. I have an image to uphold," Crystal said.

"I understand and I hope I didn't imply that you were anything other than a virtuous woman."

Tremaine's cheeks burned while trying not to be offended. He got up from his sitting position and rubbed his gray slacks to free them of any wrinkles. "I guess I should be going now. Please tell Miss Sampson that I will be sure to check on her if she's there when I go back to work. I will say a prayer for you all in the meantime." Tremaine tipped his imaginary hat again as a farewell, giving Crystal a lazy smile.

"Brother Tremaine, I have just one question, if you don't mind." Crystal didn't want him to leave, but felt that she needed to set some boundaries before someone started sowing seeds of deceit.

"Yes, ma'am." Tremaine stopped short of leaving the sanctuary. Even in her sad state, Tremaine was in awe of her beauty and strength.

"When I met you at the hospital that day, I asked if you were a believer. You said that you were saved, but you came up today to receive salvation?" Crystal straightened up to finish up her conversation with Tremaine. She needed to see his eyes because that's where the truth lay. She hoped that the pain she felt in her feet would be alleviated with some Epsom salt and warm bathwater later that afternoon.

"I received salvation when I was a teenager. Granted, at that time, my parents kept me in church, but I had other things on my mind. I was young and wild. Do you mind if I sit again? This will take a while and I promise to keep my hands to myself." Tremaine held up his hand in innocent surrender.

Crystal gestured to the pews. "Take your pick." She turned away from Tremaine for a split second and looked upward and exhaled. Turning back around, Crystal noticed he'd already taken a seat. She smiled at him as she sat back down beside him, having forgotten all about the noise that had startled her minutes before. She twisted her body in her seat, giving him her undivided attention.

"Well, as I was saying, I was young; my only desire was to make my parents happy. So when Pastor White gave the altar call one Sunday before church ended, I walked down to the altar alone. I was afraid because I didn't see my mother or my father, who were sitting up in the balcony, but I couldn't turn back. The applause from the congregation escorted me down the aisle until I met the pastor and shook his hand. I was baptized the same day, but I didn't really have a clue of what I had done. I felt like I was the same little boy I always was. I still walked the same, talked the same, and had the same selfish desires. I had the zeal to follow Christ, but I didn't want to give up my desires. I've lived a reckless life, but am thankful that I heard you all praising God in Ms. Sampson's room that day. It stirred up something in here." Tremaine pointed at his heart. "And I figured that God must have still loved me to allow me to feel the tug to come back to Him."

Amina walked into the sanctuary and was surprised to see Jalisa sitting over to the left. She continued walking toward Crystal and Tremaine. "Excuse me, Pastor, I'm sorry to interrupt. Do you know how much longer you will be? I know that you wanted to check on Auntie today and you need to eat something." Amina turned to Tremaine. "Hello, Brother Tremaine. It's so good to see you again." She held her hand out for him to shake it.

"Hi, it's nice seeing you again as well. It looks like we will be seeing a lot more of each other, now that I'm a member here." Tremaine stood and shook Amina's hand.

"Yes, Brother Tremaine, you are family now," Amina confirmed, shaking his hand.

Having lost track of time, Crystal stood as well and turned to see Jalisa approaching. "Jalisa, I didn't know you were still here. Why didn't you come to me about the time? I'm sorry, Brother Tremaine, but we do need to get on out of here. I'm sure that the trustees are ready to kick us out so that they can lock the church up and go home to their own families." Crystal tapped Tremaine on the arm and laughed nervously.

"Pastor, I didn't realize you were on a time schedule today." Jalisa smiled and shrugged her shoulders for the added effect. "I'll go to your office to retrieve your things and we can get going when you're ready." She addressed the church's newest member. "Welcome, Brother Tremaine; it's good to see you again." Jalisa hurried out of the sanctuary.

"Amina, darling, I will be with you in a moment. Let me wrap things up with Brother Tremaine, and I will see you at the car momentarily," Crystal said.

"Yes, ma'am, I'll see you shortly and once again, Brother Tremaine, we are so happy that you decided to join our ministry." Amina went back toward the direction she came from and exited the church.

Jalisa saw Amina when she came out of the church. "I've put Pastor's belongings in the car and I'm going to get going if the two of you will be all right getting home." Jalisa put Crystal's things into the trunk of Serena's car.

"Thanks, Jalisa. If I can get her to come out of the church then I'm sure that we will be just fine. Between you and me, I believe that Pastor Sampson is smitten with Brother Tremaine."

Amina was happy about that as she had never witnessed the sugary way that her grandmother spoke or the way her eyes lit up when she looked at him.

"You know, I think you're on to something. Not that I was eavesdropping or anything, but Pastor seemed pretty relaxed with the brother and she usually doesn't laugh that much when having a spiritual conversation. Oh, and keep this just between us; I saw the two of them looking mighty cozy when I passed through the sanctuary. Now get this, Brother Tremaine was singing to Pastor, and she seemed to enjoy it." Jalisa crossed her arms and leaned back onto the car.

"Yes, now that I know that, I will be keeping an eye on those two. Who knows? Love is in the air. First it was Auntie Serena and Nathaniel, Gran-Gran and Brother Tremaine, and . . ." Amina dropped her gaze bashfully.

"And?" Jalisa pressed. "Is there love in the air for you as well?" She stood erect and put her hand on her slender hip.

"You know that I'm new at all of this relationship stuff. I don't really know what it is, but I'm finding that James, Auntie's driver, is someone I'd like to kick it with. Just to see where his head is at, ya know?" Amina admitted. "I'm beginning to see him in a way I never have before. There's still so much that I don't know about him, but I'm interested in finding out. James may be a reformed bad boy, and I'm attracted to him." Amina sighed.

"Pray and seek God before making any moves or commitments that may be temporary. Take your time and remember, I'm always here if you need to talk. Now back to Pastor and Brother Tremaine, I'm hoping that God has sent him here to be a blessing to the ministry and to Pastor. She's been alone for a long time, so it would be nice to see her be able to sit back and allow someone to take care of her," Jalisa said.

"Um, what about you, missy?" Amina put the ball of romance back in Jalisa's court.

Jalisa smiled and tooted her lips up in the air. "To answer your question about my love life, I'm good right now. I haven't been able to get out much, with school and all. I have had my eye on that cutie who joined the church about a month ago. His name is Todd, but I can't remember his last name. We are also in the same physiology class over at NCCU, so I'm sure he's seen me, but I don't believe that he's noticed me," Jalisa said.

"I hear ya, but practice what you preach. Pray and seek God. You're a beautiful young woman who has a lot to offer. Let me know if I can do anything to help get the ball rolling." Amina winked at her friend and confidante. "I'm pretty sure we can be there for one another as we try to keep one another sane as we travail through this season of life," Amina promised.

They laughed and hugged one another. Hearing the giddy laughter from behind them, they turned to see

Tremaine holding the door as Crystal exited the church. The grin she wore covered her whole face and he looked just as happy to be in her company.

"You have my number; if you need any more encouraging call me." Crystal stepped to the side while Tremaine opened the car door on the passenger side of Serena's car for her to get in. Before getting in, she leaned over and gave Tremaine a short hug. "It's good to know that chivalry isn't dead after all." Crystal waved.

"Thanks for your time and yes, I have your number. I'll try not to wear out my welcome." Tremaine waved to the three of them and walked across the empty parking lot to his own car.

Amina and Jalisa looked on as Crystal watched Tremaine walk away. The ladies gave each other a high five, hugged, and went to their separate cars. Amina opened the door to the driver side of the car and Crystal jumped. "Gran, did I startle you? You look like you've seen a ghost."Amina laughed at herself, knowing that her grandmother would try to deny that she was smitten with Brother Tremaine.

"My mind was someplace else, that's all. Isn't Brother Tremaine a nice fellow? Humph, he's not too hard on the eyes either," Crystal acknowledged with her heart racing and butterflies flittering around in her belly. She knew there was chemistry between her and Tremaine, but she wasn't sure what she would do about it.

"Remember that day at the hospital when I joked that you were in love or something like that?"

"Ah, yes, how could I not remember? I forgot you are a prophet and you called it that day, but how would I look by falling out over some man I barely know?" Crystal asked. "Baby, I neglected all of the wrong people for the sake of carrying on your grandfather's legacy. Abiding Savior was everything to your granddad and I was right there in the trenches with him until he passed away. I knew that he would have wanted me to carry on in his steed as the ministry was young," Crystal explained.

"Gran-Gran, come on. You've done a great job with Abiding Savior and I'm sure that Granddaddy would have been proud." Amina reached out to hug her grandmother over the armrest. "It's time that love found you again. I don't believe that God would allow you to be alone during your golden years," Amina said.

"Well, we will just have to wait and see what God is going to do about my love life or lack thereof." Crystal adjusted her chair and put her seat belt on.

Amina reflected on the scene between her grandmother and Tremaine and got teary eyed. Crystal had worked hard for the kingdom of God and had toiled in the vineyards even after many other churches had closed their doors. She glanced over at her grandmother, who seemed to be caught up in her feelings because she had a goofy look on her face.

Amina turned on the radio to the smooth jazz station by pushing buttons on the steering wheel.

She pulled out of the church parking lot into the traffic. Connecting her Bluetooth, Amina called James, but disconnected the call as soon as she thought about it. Her phone rang and she answered it immediately. "Hello, this is Amina," she said.

"Hey, what's wrong? Did you change your mind about wanting to talk to me?" James laughed.

"Hi, um, did the phone ring on your end?" Amina blushed, knowing she had just called his phone and hung up. She didn't want him to know that she just wanted to hear his voice. She almost started to lie to him about calling him mistakenly, but after hearing his excitement, his voice calmed her and motivated her all at the same time.

"Laugh out loud. Why would you ask me that? I called back as soon as I checked my phone. Is everything all right? Has something happened? You sound as if you've lost your best friend." James frowned slightly as his heart rate skipped a beat while anxiously waiting to hear her reply.

"All is well. Actually, I was just calling you back since I missed your calls." She pepped up. "I'm with Gran and we're just getting out of church service. We are heading to our house now. Brother Nathaniel is staying with Auntie until I get back." Amina smiled as she drove along.

"Ah okay, that's good to hear," James said. He was excited about what was happening between him and Amina. "Well, I'm glad you called because I was actually going to call you to check on you ladies and to let you know that I'm on my way out of town for work." James checked his bag to make sure that he had his toiletries.

"Oh, where are you heading to this time?" Amina perked up even though she wasn't really happy about his leaving again.

"I'm heading to Philadelphia." James pulled at some lint on his bedcovers, not sure of what else to say.

"Well, please pray before getting on the road and drive safely." Mindless chatter had begun in Amina's head. Distracted, Amina almost hit a car from behind. She swerved into the opposite lane to avoid hitting the car. "Ughh!" She slammed her fist on the steering wheel. The force from the sharp turn caused her to lurch forward and her heart beat wildly. "Gran, are you okay?" Crystal hadn't moved an inch and she didn't respond. "Gran?" Amina touched her arm and Crystal smiled before opening her eyes.

"Yes, baby, did I miss anything?" Crystal yawned.

"Amina?" James paced his bedroom. He wasn't sure what was going on, but he hoped that they were okay.

Amina had forgotten that James was still on the phone. "I lost my focus and almost rear-ended the car in front of me. I barely missed it, but was able to switch lanes." Amina knew that there was no way that she would be able to repay Serena if something happened to her car. "Whew, that was scary." Amina exhaled.

"Okay, maybe I should let you go?" James clicked on the speakerphone and headed into the bathroom. He examined his face in the mirror for stubble and decided that he should shave before hitting the road.

"Yes, okay." Amina didn't want their conversation to end, but she needed to pay attention to the road.

"I'm only a phone call away if you need me for anything or nothing at all," James said.

"As always, thanks for being so thoughtful. I will let Auntie know that you called to see how she's doing." Smiling, she looked over at Crystal, who was wide awake and gazing out of the window.

"Text me to let me know that you made it home safely," James said.

"I will do that as soon as I get in. Hey, maybe next time you are off on the weekend, you can go to church with me." Amina envisioned them strolling into church arm in arm, while the debaters and the haters gawked at the new couple walking by.

"If my schedule allows, I would love to go with you. I know I need more of the gospel in my life than just when I hang out with you and Prophetess Serena. I hear a lot over the radio since I spend most of my time in a car, driving the stars around," James admitted.

"Well, I know you are more of a worldly man and have been places and seen things that I never have nor do I have the desire to. I am sure that God can take your worldly desires away and replace them with spiritual," Amina said innocently.

"What do you mean by worldly? Yes, I've been to many places and have been privy to various situations in my line of work. However, I don't party, drink, or do drugs, but I don't claim to be perfect. I've given my life to Christ, but I can't just quit my job. I can't beat the folks down who sign my paychecks with the Word of God. All I can do is be a witness and share what I know about God and that's it. So if that is what you mean by worldly, I'm not that dude." James shut down.

"James, I'm sorry. I didn't mean to offend you. I was speaking in ignorance, and for that I apologize. I really wasn't trying to judge you. I was just saying . . ." Amina tried to explain.

"I get what you're saying. I don't want to talk about that anymore. I've said my piece about it and I have some more packing to do for work. I didn't want to end this conversation on a sour note, but I need to have a moment to calm down and get the rest of my things together. I'll talk to you later." James didn't give Amina a chance to reply; he clicked his cell phone off.

"James, please call me before you get on the road and again, I'm sor—" She heard the phone disconnect in her ear. Her mouth hung open in shock that James had just disconnected the call without allowing her to fix what she'd said. Although Crystal wasn't paying her any attention, her cheeks burned with embarrassment. She closed her mouth and drove the rest of the way home in a daze.

Amina could have kicked herself for implying that James was worldly. She didn't have enough information about him to have made the assumption. She was worried that she had ruined something good before she had a chance to experience it. Parking the car, Amina dreaded going into the house, knowing that she would be expected to join her family for tea.

Chapter 7

The last two weeks were a blur for Serena. Serena had given thanks to God for each day of waking up, but that day was different. She woke up that morning with an attitude of gratitude. She pulled the draperies back and tied them to their designated areas. Serena leaned into the windowpane and tried to soak in the warmth of the sun, praying for it to overpower her sudden chills.

Serena wished that God would give her two wings to flail her face and two wings to fly away. She didn't want to have to go through the test. She had trusted the prophetic words from God that she had sown into the lives of thousands of others about His healing power. She had even been the catalyst used to bring forth healing in ailing women time and time again. Serena was disappointed in herself because she struggled to believe God's scriptures on healing for her own wilderness experience.

Amina knocked on Serena's bedroom door and then pushed it open to see Serena soaking in the sun pouring into her windows. She was pleased to see Serena up, but figured she would be since it was the day of her surgery. Amina wanted to pray with Serena before her grandmother or Nathaniel had arrived. "Good morning, Auntie. How did you sleep last night? How are you feeling this morning? It's such a beautiful day outside, isn't it?" Amina curtsied in front of Serena.

"Oh, sleep is so overrated. Who has time to sleep?" Serena was still feeling weak, but she sauntered over to her bay-sized window again and peeked between the curtains. "My focus is on how my Lord will show up and show out in the operating room this morning." Serena smiled at her niece and hoped her show of bravado was enough to convince Amina that she wasn't afraid about the idea of being cut open. Serena moved away from the window and walked over to her bed, which was still unmade. She busied herself by working to untie the sheets that were balled up.

"Auntie, I will get those for you. I need to throw them in the washing machine and change your bed linen. I also plan to vacuum and dust in here before you are released from the hospital." The thought alone made Amina sad. She shivered as she heard the prognosis replaying in her mind and wished that it was only a dream.

"Baby, are you going to be okay with this?" Serena asked Amina, pulling her into an embrace.

"Yes, ma'am. I'm more concerned about you than myself." Amina laughed nervously. Her mind was bombarded with visions of what could go wrong in the operating room.

"Talk to me, baby." Serena prodded Amina to open up to her because she sensed that Amina was hiding something. It took longer than Serena had expected, but eventually, she was able to pull the source of anxiety out of her niece.

"Auntie, I'm scared. I mean, what if something happens and, you know? What would I do without you?" Amina allowed her fallen tears to drench her face.

Serena wiped the tears from Amina's face and looked her in the eyes. "Sweetie, you don't have to be afraid for me. I trust that God is going to see me through and when He delivers me from the fiery furnace, there will not even be the smell of smoke on me. I won't try to convince you that I don't have any concerns about the what ifs, but I will say that today has enough worries in it for me," Serena declared.

"God knows the plans He has for my life and His will must be done. I can't be consumed with thoughts about what tomorrow or the next day holds. I speak life and I'm commanding the angels of God to keep my charge until His will for this season in my life has been fulfilled." Serena felt strengthened by her proclamation.

Amina leaned in to give Serena a hug. She held on to her for a few minutes as she cried over her shoulder. She pulled back to see that her aunt had also been crying. They smiled at one another and Amina went to the dresser top and pulled the bottle of anointing oil down. She anointed her aunt's forehead and then her own and they prayed for the surgery to be a success.

James got out of the car, walked up to the house, and rang the doorbell. He had already gone by to pick up Crystal and she waited in the car. Amina opened the door for him and they exchanged strained hellos. A few minutes later, James came outside for the second time, rolling two bags. Serena came out after him, clad in a black jogging suit, a baseball cap, and donned a pair of oversized shades. James popped the trunk and began putting the bags in.

Amina appeared from inside of the house then stepped back in to make sure she had set the security system. Satisfied that all was secure, Amina headed to the car, dragging another bag behind her.

"Hey, James, how are you today?" Amina handed him the bag to place inside the trunk. She hadn't talked to him since that Sunday and she wasn't sure if he hated her, or what. Her heart skipped a beat as she stood near him. Amina admired how sharp of a dresser he was. His blue shorts, blue checkered shirt, and blue Nikes were on point. He obviously took good care in how he looked before going out and it turned Amina on. She hoped that he had forgiven her, but couldn't be sure just yet.

"Miss Amina, I'm blessed, and how are you holding up?" Grinning, James looked around to make sure that no one was looking. He caught her by surprise by pulling her into his arms.

Her desire to be close to him dictated her next move and before she thought about who could be watching, she returned his embrace and held on to him as tightly as she could. His arms tightened around her waist followed by a slow peck on her lips.

"Whew, God sure does know what you need when you need it. He even answers unspoken prayer. I was so afraid that you would blow me off when you saw me. Thank you for turning my worst fear into a woosah moment. Thank you. Initially, I didn't know what to expect because our last conversation went left. When you didn't call me back before you went out of town, my fears were confirmed," Amina admitted.

"Well, I thought about what you said and I also prayed about it. After I calmed down, I realized that I could see why you said what you said. I can't blame you for that, but now that we have discussed it, we can leave it alone, right?" James looked at her with all seriousness.

"Yes, I've definitely learned my lesson and will be slow to speak from here on out. This way I won't put my foot in my mouth again. I'm happy that we are all right."Amina smiled, feeling happier than she had been lately. "I guess we should get Auntie to the hospital because Auntie has to check in soon."

"Come on, sweetie. Let's get you in the car so I can lock up the trunk." James turned around and gasped for air. He felt as if the wind had been knocked from him as he wondered how much of their exchange Serena had witnessed. He finally found his voice and spoke up. "Oh, Prophetess Serena, I didn't realize that you weren't seated comfortably in the car. Please accept my apologies for the delay." Not wanting to allow another moment to slip past them, James opened the door for them both and Serena quietly entered the back seat followed by Amina.

Amina leaned back and closed her eyes. She didn't want to talk, just wanted to think about James and how his strong arms felt wrapped around her. The double surprise came when he had pecked her on the lips. Her eyes snapped open and she greeted Crystal. "Good morning. How are you this morning, Gran?" Amina asked with a smirk on her face.

"I'm doing as well as can be expected in light of what's going on. You seem to be doing good after what I just witnessed. Is it safe to assume that I would be correct?" Crystal asked.

"I'm better now." She knew then that James and she were busted. If the chair had an eject button, Amina would have gladly pushed it to be free of the hot seat she found herself in. Instead, Amina chose to relish the moments she had shared with James and was excited about what was next.

Serena sat quietly in the car, looking out of the window the whole trip to the hospital. She was thinking about Nathaniel and marveled at how close they had grown in such a short amount of time. It was no secret that she had played hard to get in the beginning, but when she found out that she was sick, she wanted someone to be there to catch her in case she fell.

Twenty minutes later, James pulled up in front of the UNC Hospital entrance after taking the scenic route. Once all the bags were sitting curbside, he went around and opened the doors for the ladies to exit the car. "Okay, I guess this is it until after your procedure, huh, Miss Serena? I wish you the very best. If you ladies need me for anything, don't hesitate to call. I mean that." He looked directly into Amina's eyes and winked.

"James, you are the best driver a woman could ask for. Thank you for your words of kindness." Serena reached out to hug James. She paid him well, but she really valued him as more than someone who drove her around when needed. Serena saw ministry in the young man and felt an urge in her spirit to give him a word from the Lord. "James, my brother, God wanted me to tell you that if you would go all the way with Him, you will never see lack a day in your life. I hear Him saying that your heart isn't like many because He has given you a heart of flesh. He knows the plans He has for your life, my brother."

Serena felt the release in her belly as she held on to James. She held him at arm's length and blew him a kiss. Releasing him, she looked at her family, inhaled deeply, and then exhaled. The next thing everyone saw was Serena's jacket flapping in the wind as she entered the hospital.

James was in awe of what had just taken place and felt a move in his spirit. He wanted to let her know, so he yelled out to her but she never turned around.

"Thanks again for all that you do, James. I'm sure that everything will be fine, but if you think about it, please pray for us. It's always good to know that someone is praying when you can't." Amina spoke up on behalf of Serena. She smiled at James and hugged him again before he dipped into the car.

He rolled the window down and told her, "All I will do is think of you all while I'm gone. Remember, I'm just a phone call away. Take care, Pastor Sampson." He winked at Amina and pulled away from the curb.

Tremaine was back on duty and he was happy to see the Sampsons coming into the hospital in spite of the crisis they were involved in. He had called Crystal to let her know again how much he was blessed at the service at the church. "Good morning, Ms. Sampson," he greeted

Serena just as her hospital bracelet was being fastened around her thin wrist.

"Good morning, sir. How are you, uh, Tremaine?" Serena remembered him from the time before.

"I'm blessed and happy to be at your service. I hope that you have been recouping okay, and I've been praying for you. I'm sure that you won't be surprised by what I'm going to say, but I would like for you to know you have a very supportive group of people standing in the gap for you." Tremaine winked at Crystal before pushing her to the elevator.

He pushed the elevator door button number six. Without delay, the elevator popped to a stop on each of the designated floors and people filed out like flies, heading into different directions. Finally, reaching the sixth floor, Tremaine made small talk with Serena as he transported her to her assigned room.

Amina and Crystal walked together into the hospital. They went over to the registration desk and Crystal used Serena's name. The administration okayed her getting Serena registered due to her notoriety. They went to the waiting room and sat down, both preoccupied with their own thoughts.

"I see that Brother Tremaine is here today. I will just wait here with you since Auntie has already gone up to her room. I'm sure that she could use some time alone, so hopefully she will be in bed by the time we get up there." Amina tried to engage her grandmother in conversation.

"That's fine, baby, I could use some company right now." Crystal prepared herself by pulling out Serena's health insurance card and waited for her name to be called. Her thoughts were temporarily diverted back to Tremaine. He had a sophisticated swag, even when he was wearing his work scrubs.

"Ms. Sampson?" Someone from patient service associates came to the front and read from a clipboard she was holding.

"Hi, I'm Ms. Sampson." Crystal stood with Amina at her side.

"Hi, I'm Tina; if you will follow me this way, I will get you all set." Tina smiled warmly. "Come on in and have a seat." She gestured to the two additional chairs in the cramped office. She sat down and went to work on her computer. "Ms. Sampson, I was informed that you would be handling the registration for the patient, Serena Sampson. Is it safe for me to assume that no information is to be disclosed if anyone was to call and inquire about the status of Miss Sampson or inquire if she's a patient here?" Tina peered over her horn-rimmed glasses.

Crystal pushed forward to the edge of the cushioned chair and her knees knocked on the wooden desk before she responded. She leaned in as close to the woman's face as she could and spoke with as much sternness that she could muster and said, "Absolutely not. There will be all kinds of folks calling here trying to get the latest on Serena and I won't have her being the talk of the hospital or this city," Crystal said. "In case you don't know, Serena Sampson is a widely respected evangelist of the gospel. She's been on television and holds the largest women's conferences all over the world. The media would love to get ahold of the fact that she's battling such a horrible illness. They'll have her dead and in the grave before she hits the operating table," Crystal said.

Crystal was in mothering mode and was ready to protect her child. "Everyone who needs to know about Serena is aware of what's going on." Crystal sat back and waited for Tina to finish up so they could get upstairs to Serena. She hoped that Tremaine would still be around when she got upstairs.

"Ms. Sampson, okay, I just need for you to sign here and I will mark her as private in the computer." Tina handed the disclosure form and insurance forms to Crystal for her signature. She finished up the paperwork. "I have already given Miss Sampson's identification band to the nurse. She had it on before leaving the floor. Other than that, if you have no other questions, our business is all done. Do you need an escort?"

"Thanks for your assistance and I hope I wasn't too aggressive." Crystal stood and gathered the paperwork before placing her satchel on her shoulder. "No, my granddaughter and I can make it." Crystal shook the lady's hand and Amina did the same before heading silently to the elevators.

"Sweetie, can you make it with those bags? I will be up shortly," Crystal said.

"Yes, I can make it. Take your time." Amina welcomed the quiet once she stepped into the elevator. Happy that the elevator went straight to the sixth floor without stopping, Amina was anxious to get to Serena's room. She prayed internally as she walked to the nurses' station.

"Hi, I need the room number for Serena Sampson, please," she told the nurse sitting at the desk.

"Hold one moment please." After checking, the nurse informed Amina of the room number. "It's room six thousand twelve." The nurse smiled at Amina.

"Thank you, ma'am," Amina replied politely and then walked away.

Crystal walked the halls, praying for each patient room she passed. Moseying through the hallways of each floor, she touched each door, made a cross sign, and murmured words of prayer in her heavenly language and then moved on to the next room.

Crystal wished that Jonathan was in town already. He had let her know that he needed to wrap some things up at work. She recalled the conversation, and something was definitely amiss. She heard it in his voice. She couldn't understand why he sounded calm about the terrible news he had received about his sister.

Crystal believed that Jonathan was always wrapped up in this or that with his business. She knew that she had raised her children right, but when it came to being sympathetic and sensitive, Jonathan must have been sleeping when God passed out those attributes. Crystal smacked her teeth as she made her way up to the second floor. She'd decided to take the stairs because she didn't trust public elevators.

Finally reaching her destination, the first person Crystal saw was Nathaniel. She stood by quietly and watched the interaction between her daughter and Nathaniel. The twinkle in Serena's eyes could be seen from where she stood. It dawned on Crystal that there was more to the story than Serena had revealed initially. The sight itself warmed her heart to know that this young brother was serious about her daughter.

Crystal moved around and walked straightaway into the room toward her daughter.

"Mommy, what took you so long to get up here? Oh, don't tell me you were walking the halls and praying for those on the floor?" Serena looked at her mother knowingly.

"Nathaniel, good morning, how are you feeling today?" Crystal asked, ignoring Serena's questions for the moment.

"I'm blessed, Pastor Sampson, and how are you this fine morning? I was just trying to cheer Serena up and take her mind off of things until the doctors come for her." Nathaniel moved around to make room for Crystal at Serena's bedside. Just then his cell phone rang and the sounds of "Here I Am" burst through the speaker of the phone.

Crystal's hands flew up in the air as she began to worship God. "Whew, is that who I think it is? He's my favorite gospel artist. The man is anointed and preaches while he sings. I'm hoping that one day I can get him to come to our church and bless us. It's a shame that his wife passed on, isn't it?" Crystal shook her head, talking to herself.

"To answer your question, yes, that's what I'm supposed to do, pray for others, or have you forgotten?" Crystal held her hand to her hip while her pocketbook dangled on her wrist and her Bible was in the other hand.

"Pastor, Mommy, I'm just saying, can't I have a moment? A day of prayer, all of your attention, ever?" Serena poked her lips out and rolled her eyes.

Crystal looked dumbfounded. The anger behind the words echoed in her eardrums and she was caught off guard by Serena's belligerent tone. Her head swung around as if she had been struck in the face. It wasn't as if Serena had never said it throughout the years, but it was obvious that her words had fallen upon deaf ears, until then. The cards in Crystal's mental Rolodex began flipping.

Serena's comment played like a scratched record over and over. Serena's words resonated with the core of her being and she prayed that God would redeem time for her to right her wrongs. Instead of being the best mother she could have been by giving more to her daughter, she was out of order and had given more to the church: her second ministry.

"Baby, I'm sorry." The tears fell from Crystal's eyes and dropped to her face.

Serena felt guilty for behaving like a child. It wasn't the right time or place for her to berate her mother. She berated herself as she looked at her mother and saw her differently for the first time. Usually, Serena saw a stern woman who was always shaking her finger in Serena's face for this or that she had done wrong. Chastisement was always on her lips. But today, Serena saw something else, without all her splendor, a woman who did the best she could with what she had. Nathaniel moved to comfort Crystal, but she would not be consoled. Uncontrollably, her shoulders jerked up and down as she struggled to catch her breath. She managed to steady herself on the bedrail and the tears continued to flow.

Serena didn't mean to make her mother cry. Crystal seemed to retreat to a time when she and Serena were at odds. Serena had accused her mother of putting everything before Jonathan and her. She wondered where the instant jealousy came from and wished she could have eaten her words, but God knew her thoughts, so she knew that she may as well have said it.

"I'm sorry. Baby, I tried my best to be a good mother to you and your brother. It wasn't easy being a single mother. I was always taught that the parent is right, no matter what, but the little girl in you spoke up today and I finally heard what you said. I was brought up that you do as you are told, period. I wasn't allowed to think for myself or live and you know your grandparents were a strict pair, but as I grew, I was convinced they were that way because they really did love me. I realize now that I blamed you for a lot of things that I am partly responsible for. Please forgive me."

Serena looked from Nathaniel to Amina and then to her mother. She didn't know what to say, so she didn't say anything. She couldn't think of anything else except for the fact that within the hour, she would be heading into surgery.

Doctors Noel and Sinclair entered the triage room with their scrubs on. Dr. Sinclair spoke first. "Good morning. How is everyone today? I'm Dr. Sinclair. I believe I met you all when Serena was here a couple of weeks prior." She smiled at each person upon making eye contact. When Dr. Sinclair saw the look on Crystal's face, her smile fell slowly from her face. "Are you okay, Ms. Sampson? Everything is going to be okay." Dr. Sinclair moved over to the medium-height, stocky woman with skin the color of brown sugar and rubbed her arm in efforts to comfort her.

Everyone in the room watched and waited silently for Crystal to speak up and say something. Moments later, she picked her head up from her arm and straightened her posture. Mother Sampson said, "Good morning, Doctor. I'm fine, thank you. I was just having a heart to heart with my daughter before she goes into surgery." She wiped the remnant of tears from her face and smiled. "You take good care of my baby, you hear?" Crystal didn't wait for a response before she kissed Serena's forehead and peered into her eyes for an answer to her question.

"Good morning, Dr. Sinclair." Serena stretched her arm forward to shake the hand of the lady who would be a catalyst in saving her life. "I'm ready to get this over with while I'm still able to hold on to a measure of my sanity." Serena laughed out loud but not loud enough to shake the fear of going under the knife.

"Serena, everything will be okay. You watch and see. The operating room is being prepped now. If it's okay, I would like to say a prayer with you before we go in. I don't ever go into surgery without first seeking God for His divine wisdom and healing power," Dr. Sinclair stated.

The revelation alone had everyone smiling in approval. Prayers were already being answered. Everyone seemed more confident, except for Crystal, who stood as still as a statue. Amina reached out to Crystal, who ignored their pleas to join them in prayer. Nathaniel followed suit and called out to her; she shifted one foot in front of the other, but never moved. The group joined hands as Dr. Sinclair petitioned God on Serena's behalf. She even touched on the rift in Serena and Crystal's relationship, asking God to work it out.

Chapter 8

Jonathan was still having a hard time believing that his baby sister was sick. He had promised his mother that he would be home within the week. He was actually looking forward to getting out of New York.

"Hey, lover," Sedric said happily.

"I've asked you not to call me that," Jonathan responded dryly. He could have kicked himself for falling into Sedric's arms again. He slapped his forehead in frustration. *When I go to do good, evil is always present.*

"You don't have to be so harsh. Remember, I'm here because you called me blubbering like some drunken fool. So don't be standing there acting all self-righteous now, suga." The man was dressed only in briefs, pouting while standing with his hands on his hips.

"I wish I would have never called you, Sedric. I hate this lifestyle and my mother taught me better than to be some strumpet with any man. I've changed my mind and want you to leave." Jonathan kept his back to Sedric as the tears streamed down his face. He recalled his mother's reason for the call, and once she had finished explaining to him what was going on, guilt struck him like lightning hitting its intended target. The call still had him pretty shook up.

"I love you, Jonathan, but I refuse to keep making myself available for your every whim. You say you don't want to be in a relationship with me, but you keep calling my phone. I've tried moving on, and each time I feel like

I can, here you come calling me. Like a fool, I continue to do flips for you, but you're only using me and this is it. Don't call me anymore; lose my number, Jack," Sedric whined.

Jonathan never looked back as Sedric's words broke into his mental and brought him back to his current situation. "It's done. We are not getting together again. I really believe that God has a godly woman out there for me and I don't want to miss out on her when she comes."

"Ha! You're gay, Jonathan. You will never be happy with a woman, not after what your baby's mama did to you. Remember that, Jonathan; that's why you ran away from home and came here. I want to marry you, but your ego won't allow it. I want to meet your family, but you're afraid to come out of the closet. You'll never be happy with a woman, but I know I can make you happy if you just let me."

Jonathan's jaws flinched in anger. "That's enough," he roared.

"Please don't do this. You would be crazy to throw away ten years of our relationship. You made me believe you wanted me and needed me. I understand that you're upset about your sister right now, but once things calm down then you will want to pick up where we left off. I will call you to see how you're doing." Sedric was near tears.

"This is it. I know that I will have to struggle to be free of this perverted spirit that has me bound, but I'm sure that I will get the strength I need once I get home. If you love me, then let me go," Jonathan pleaded.

"Your life will be a lie. You know you can't change who you are. God created you this way." Sedric cried and stomped around the living room like a spoiled brat.

"You fool! I know that God didn't create me this way and He didn't create you this way. I turned to this ridiculous lifestyle due to pain and disappointment. I hate the night I ever lay down in that bed of sin. God didn't make the mistake; I did."

"Say what you want to say about it. I know who I am and happily gay is the only way I'll ever be. I know that God intended for me to be this way. Look at me, damaged goods. He sat up there on His throne in heaven and watched while my virginity was taken by that ol' nasty babysitter. She hurt me night after night and you know what hurt the most?" Sedric rocked back and forth on the balls of his feet. Getting no response from Jonathan, he said, "The killer was when I told my mama and she didn't even believe me. From that moment on I have never trusted a female to protect me. I believe that God created me to find happiness any way I can and you are my happiness," Sedric explained.

Jonathan felt a twinge of emotion himself, thinking back to the night he tried to outrun his pain and ended up doing things that had plagued him ever since. He turned around and looked Sedric in the eyes and pointed to the door. "Good-bye, Sedric."

"I don't want things to end badly for us. I can understand that you are upset, so I will leave you alone. I hope she gets better." Sedric left.

The next few days went by in a blur for Jonathan. He stood patiently in line to have his bags checked. The airport attendant called out for the next person in line; however, Jonathan didn't hear her. Someone tapped his shoulder from behind and that brought him back to reality. He barely turned around when he heard the call again.

"Will the next person please bring your bags up for check-in?" the customer service agent requested.

Jonathan detected the irritation in her voice. He moved on ahead and placed his bags on the scale one by one. "Good morning." Jonathan smiled warily at the skinny

Caucasian woman who looked like she would rather be anywhere else.

"Good morning. May I see your identification please?"

Jonathan handed over his electronic ticket and his driver's license for verification. He still had a hangover from drinking every night since he'd broken things off with Sedric. It was obvious that he was still having a hard time with the news about Serena. He didn't have the patience to sit at the computer and make the arrangements to get to North Carolina. After drinking a few glasses of rum and Coke, against his better judgment, he called Sedric and asked him to make his flight arrangements. Sedric said he had no problems making the arrangements for Jonathan, until the conversation took a turn down the wrong path. Sedric asked if the phone call meant that Jonathan had changed his mind about them being together on a permanent basis. Jonathan tried to make Sedric understand that he just needed someone to talk to and it was by no means a call for reconciliation.

"Mr. Sampson!" the desk attendant yelled in her thick New York accent, clearly agitated.

Jonathan, who had gotten caught up again, snapped back to the present, not really sure why the woman was acting so testy. "Yes, ma'am." He wanted to snatch the woman by her multicolored scarf that hung around her neck for hollering at him. Instead, he remembered what his mother taught him and humbled himself.

"Wow, something really has you upset. You haven't been an active participant of this exchange since I saw you standing in line." Her voice softened and she seemed sympathetic.

"You're right. I have a lot going on right now and I apologize for holding up the line."

"Sir, I hate to tell you this but the name on the ID doesn't match your name on the ticket."

"Huh? I don't understand what you mean. Of course it matches."

"No, sir, Mr. Sampson. See here." She read the name on his driver's license and leaned forward for Jonathan to see his license and plane ticket.

"Oh Lord, what have I done?" Jonathan dropped his head, perplexed about why Sedric would do such a horrible thing to him. It was at that moment, when the attendant told him about the name difference, that he'd figured it out. "Ahhh!" Jonathan slapped his forehead.

Embarrassment set in as Jonathan acknowledged that Jonathan Bronson was printed on the e-ticket. Sedric had used his own last name in order to get back at him for not taking him back. "Miss, I can explain. I got a call from my mother earlier this week with some bad news about my sister. I've been distraught over her illness and had so much on my mind that I didn't realize that the wrong last name was typed on my e-ticket. I need to get home as soon as possible. How can we fix this?" Fuming inside, Jonathan made a mental note to call Sedric and handle him for jacking up his ticket. He knew that a new ticket at this late hour would cost him about a grand.

"I'm sorry, Mr. Sampson, but you're going to have to purchase another ticket. There's no way security will allow you to go any farther without a ticket bearing the correct name. Let me check to see when the next flight to North Carolina will be leaving." She typed furiously on her computer.

Jonathan remained silent. He was tired and ready to sit down somewhere. He heard the grumbling of the others waiting in line to be serviced. Looking around, Jonathan noticed that there was only one other desk that was open and the lines were getting congested. "Whatever you can do would be greatly appreciated. I really need to get home as soon as possible," Jonathan said.

"It looks like our next available flight leaves at four o'clock this afternoon." The attendant furrowed her eyebrows as a pained look creased her features.

"What is it, ma'am? Can I get on the next flight?" Jonathan was concerned.

"Sir, it looks like that flight is full. Do you mind me checking for another time frame this evening?" the attendant asked.

Jonathan had reached his boiling point but didn't want to take his mounting frustrations out on the lady who was trying to assist him. He glanced at her nametag and said, "Nancy, I have a medical emergency occurring right now. Is there anything you can do to get me on the next flight?"

"Sir, I apologize, but I can't make any promises. The only way you will be allowed on the next flight is if someone cancels their flight. If you will have a seat right over there then I will call you back up within the hour and let you know if any cancellations occur." Nancy cleared her screen, dismissing Jonathan, and called up the next passenger waiting.

Jonathan felt dejected as he moved for the next person behind him to be granted access to the departing gates. Jonathan pulled out his cell phone. He angrily tapped the touch tone buttons, waiting for an answer while tapping his foot impatiently on the hardwood floor.

"Hello?" Sedric's feminine voice sang through Jonathan's earpiece.

"What did you go and screw up my ticket for?" Jonathan demanded.

"Ha, ha, ha I got you. You have reached the voice mail of Sedric. I'm not available to accept your call right now. Please leave a message after the tone and do have a nice day."

After waiting for the tone to sound, Jonathan left his message. "You fool, I promise you that if I ever see you again, you are one dead gay man." Jonathan hissed into the receiver of his cell and pressed the end call button. Anger coursed through his veins as he threw the Apple iPhone against the wall not far from where he sat. It cracked and glass went flying everywhere. Jonathan no longer cared who may have been watching his tirade as he broke down and cried.

Chapter 9

When they reached Serena's room, Crystal forced a smile onto her face as she walked into her daughter's hospital room. She tried masking the worry by directing her attention toward Amina and Jalisa as they hovered in conversation. Crystal placed her pocketbook down and walked over to the sink to wash her hands. She tried shutting everyone else out as she dwelled on the information that Dr. Sinclair had recently shared with her. She also let Crystal know that although the procedure itself was successful, Serena's fight was just beginning. Dr. Sinclair was optimistic about Serena's recovery, but she hesitated to promise anything in case God had other plans. They would know more once the results came in.

"Gran-Gran, are you okay?" Amina knew that when her grandmother took to the task of straightening around the room and washing her hands constantly, she was nervous.

Crystal nervously rubbed her hands on her skirt and smiled weakly. "Everything will be all right, baby. I'm just thinking, that's all." Crystal acknowledged her armor bearer. "Hey, Sister Jalisa, when did you arrive, and have you girls eaten?"

"Pastor, Amina and I went to the cafeteria to get a little something while Serena was in surgery. Where did you go? It's been two hours since we have seen you." Jalisa's concern grew for her pastor, knowing that the situation couldn't be easy for her. Jalisa got up and hugged her spiritual mother before sitting back down in one of the hard chairs provided for visitors.

"Honey, I was just here and there. Needed to have a little talk with Jesus and didn't feel like being around anyone," Crystal said with a hint of sadness in her eyes. "I think I'd better eat a little something because I'm feeling weak." Crystal's heart was broken and she couldn't stand to see her daughter lying in that hospital bed with tubes coming from her. The scene was one she never imagined that her own child would ever have to endure. She glimpsed at Serena one more time and then cast her eyes downward as her head weighed heavily on her shoulders and hung down before walking out of the door.

Amina looked over at her aunt, who was sleeping and had been since the nurses brought her back from surgery. Amina had watched silently, hating to see her aunt in so much pain. She witnessed the nurse asking Serena what her pain level was and held up a chart of one to ten. Serena held up both hands, so the nurse gave her a shot of morphine in her IV.

Nathaniel dozed in the recliner chair on the other side of Serena while she slept. When asked to leave the room and wait in the waiting room, Nathaniel was hesitant and requested to be alerted when a room had been assigned for Serena. He made it clear that he wanted to be in the room when she arrived back. The two hours it took for him to see Serena again felt like an eternity.

During their separation, Nathaniel knew that he didn't want to spend a day without her because he wanted to be there to protect and love her. During the time Serena was in the operating room, he separated himself from the group but not before making sure the ladies would be okay. He'd gone to the hospital chapel at the end of the hall to pray for Serena. He was happy to have made it back just in time to see Serena being wheeled back into the room.

Dr. Sinclair didn't want to disturb Serena, so she moved around her bed quietly and checked her vital signs and wrote her findings in her medical chart. Feeling like all eyes were on her, Dr. Sinclair was more than certain that everyone watched every movement she made. The only noises that could be heard in Serena's room were the incessant beeping of the monitors and machines hooked up to her and the whispers from the television. Amina looked over at Jalisa and then over to Nathaniel, who had begun to snore lightly. Dr. Sinclair was about to leave the room.

"Is there anything that you ladies need? I can have the nurse make sure you are comfortable. Would you like a pillow or a blanket? I apologize that the chairs are so small and hard, but due to the size of the room, that's about all we could fit in here." Dr. Sinclair looked at them apologetically.

"No, thank you, we're fine," Amina said, looking at Jalisa to confirm. She glanced sideways at the doctor and shook her head.

"Thank you, Dr. Sinclair. I'm fine too. We understand about hospital rooms. I'm usually here with Pastor Sampson when our members and family of members take ill," Jalisa replied.

"Well, if you need anything, please go to the nurses' station and someone should be able to assist you. I will come back by before my shift ends to see how Miss Sampson's doing." She smiled and exited the room.

Amina waited until the door closed behind the doctor and she drew the curtain around to give them more privacy. She reached out to hold her aunt's hand. Rubbing her hair, Amina hummed a song she had heard on the radio a few times. The song was a testament of one going through trials in their life and although Amina didn't know the words, she knew the melody well.

The song grew in her belly and it resonated into the atmosphere and before she knew it, Jalisa was by her side, singing the words. Jalisa sang with such grace and authority. The anointing she carried in her words caused a spiritual shift of the mood in the room.

Serena, who had been sleeping soundly, stirred slightly with a frown, marring the once peaceful look on her face. She seemed to be in great pain and this alarmed Amina, who had stopped humming and began to pray. Jalisa continued to sing the words now with her head held back and really feeling the song. She was oblivious to the drama taking place at Serena's bedside.

Amina grabbed the suction tube and placed the small plastic opening at the corners of Serena's mouth and the saliva disappeared as it was being sucked into the machine. She delicately wiped the spittle from her lips with a washcloth. It was a wonder that Nathaniel never woke up, nor did he stir.

The singing had stopped and Amina turned to see why. She saw her grandmother returning from wherever she had come from and the note Jalisa belted out prior to Crystal's return seemed to be caught in her throat. The look on Crystal's face couldn't be described in one word.

"Is she all right?" Crystal seemed to lose her will to walk closer to the bed. She stood blocking the doorway with tears pouring from her bloodshot eyes.

"Gran, she is fine," Amina answered.

"You're sure she's okay? I wouldn't be able to handle it if she were suffering," Crystal said.

"Gran, see, Auntie's fine and she's sleeping soundly," Amina assured Crystal. She looked over at Jalisa and asked, "Isn't that right, Jalisa?" Amina's eyes begged for Jalisa to go along with her on the matter. Amina didn't want her grandmother to worry any more than she already was.

"Pastor, all is well. Why don't you come and rest yourself. Do you need anything? I would be happy to go down to the café to get you something," Jalisa asked. The bags hanging underneath her eyelids were visible and they made Crystal's eyes appear to drag her facial features downward. Jalisa pointed to the chair she had recently vacated. "Come and sit down," Jalisa coaxed. When Crystal didn't move, Jalisa walked over to her and led her to the chair like a little child.

"No, that's okay. I don't have much of an appetite. Why don't you get ready to go on home. I believe that with everyone else here, I will be okay." Crystal stood up and hugged Jalisa then flopped back down into the chair.

"Are you sure, Pastor? I don't mind staying, really I don't," Jalisa said.

"Yes, I'm sure, sweetie. I will call you if anything changes," Crystal replied.

"Okay, if you are certain that you won't need me; I'll be heading home. Please keep me updated on how Prophetess Serena is doing." Jalisa spoke more to the atmosphere than to anyone in particular.

"See ya, Jalisa." Amina walked over and gave her friend a big hug.

"I'll talk with you all soon. Take care." Jalisa blew a kiss to the group and left.

Amina wanted desperately to change the subject to anything other than Serena's condition. "Granny, everything is going to be okay. God is going to see us through this storm just like He has time and time again. We must not forget the benefits of being a child of the King." Amina wanted the revelation to resonate in her grandmother's mind and heart before speaking again.

Crystal didn't respond right away to her granddaughter. She knew in her heart that God's Word was true; although she found it hard to believe that her Lord had given Satan permission to try her family that way again. She was taken back to when she had received a phone call from someone at the church almost twenty years ago. Hearing the words that her husband had a heart attack and had been rushed to Duke University broke her heart and her spirit.

Crystal remembered questioning God the whole ride. The sounds of the machines beeping and binging could be heard out in the hallway of the hospital floor. Her husband, Herbert, lay there in the hospital bed with tubes running everywhere. Crystal was too afraid to go anywhere near her husband's bedside.

The room was dark except the bright greenish lights that functioned as what they were designed for. Herbert remained unaware of what was going on as his life slipped away. Crystal stayed in the room and talked to him like she would have if they were sitting down at the dinner table. Her heart felt like it would burst at any moment, but she refused to leave him there to die alone. Finally, after midnight, Crystal had grown accustomed to hearing the machines. She drifted in and out of light sleep.

The tears flowed from her eyes as the memories were as clear as if it happened yesterday. She wasn't sure if she had been dreaming, but she could almost bet her life on it that Pastor Herbert Sampson had told her that he loved her moments before he flatlined. Crystal thought she was all cried out, but sitting there watching her daughter lay in her sickbed brought back painful memories. She had been an emotional wreck since she woke earlier that morning and she didn't have the energy to fight. She laid her head onto Amina's shoulder and allowed her emotions free will.

Amina threw her arms around her grandmother and rocked her like a mother does a baby. She knew that she would have to be strong for the three of them.

"Gran, have you talked to my father?" The words rushed out of Amina's mouth before she could fully process her own words.

Crystal took a moment and wiped her tears before looking at Amina. She smiled at her granddaughter, who looked like her daddy had given birth to her instead of her mama. "Baby, I meant to tell you I talked to him again. With everything going on, I forgot to tell you that your father will be here this evening," she said and smiled at Amina.

"Wow, Gran-Gran, I can't believe he is really coming," she said excitedly. "He must be a busy man. I thought that he would have been here by now. Do you know how long he will be here?" Amina asked.

"He said he was able to get a three-month leave of absence. He explained the situation to his boss and, after, went to his human resources department and gave them the documentation he needed me to send to him. Once they saw the serious nature of the matter, they signed off on his leave. Once he gets here, he will stay with me. That way he can drive my other car to get around." She patted Amina's knee. "Of course you will have unlimited access to your dad. I'm praying that you both will be able to catch up on some of the lost time you've missed. It's time for our family to come together and bond again." Crystal had a faraway look in her eyes.

Chapter 10

"Daddy!" Amina ran like a little girl up to her father and hugged his neck tightly. She let the floodgates of tears loose as she inhaled the scent of the man who was half responsible for giving her life. She held on to him as if her life depended on it.

"Hey, baby girl." Jonathan tried to match her enthusiasm. He hugged her back, noticing how much she had grown. He was tired and had a few drinks while he waited the day out to get home. Tears filled his eyes as he held his now grown-up daughter as his mind raced back to when she was a little girl. He'd missed out on each phase of Amina's life and guilt came rushing in. Their hug lingered and when they finally departed, it was evident that the emotional side of him had surfaced due to the tears sliding down his cheeks.

"It's good to see you," Jonathan said, clinging to Amina a little longer before releasing her and walking over to Crystal who was already standing.

"Mama," Jonathan said, rushing into his mother's arms. He cried tears of relief of seeing her again after so many years. "I'm so happy to see you, Mama. Look at you," Jonathan said, touching Crystal's graying edges.

"Let me look at you, son." Crystal pushed Jonathan away from her and the first thing she noticed was his bloodshot eyes and his sunken cheeks. "How are you? How was your flight? Now that we finally got you home, I got a mind to lock you away someplace just to keep you here. Son, I sure have missed ya and I know Serena is going to be happy to see you," Crystal said. "I'm sure that you have lots of stories to share about the Big Apple. New York is a big city; how you living up there by yourself? Or is there a special lady you keeping away from us up there?" She smiled with tear-filled eyes.

"Mama, I'm good, but jet-lagged. I had some issues at the airport and that threw me off schedule big time. As soon as I get some rest, I will be sure to fill you all in on big-city living," Jonathan promised. Looking at Crystal, he asked, "How's Serena?"

Crystal didn't speak right away. She watched his body movement, especially the way he was acting. She could smell the alcohol on his breath and it didn't smell like he'd only had one beer or two; he'd been drinking heavy alcohol. The stench was in his skin and even though she could smell traces of mint, it couldn't kill the potent smell coming from his pores. He had been drinking.

Crystal made a mental note to find out about this alcohol problem. She thanked the Lord for the confirmation of what the Holy Spirit had revealed to her in a vision not long ago. Crystal was calling out different issues that her parishioners could have been dealing with. She heard alcoholic in the spirit realm, but wasn't sure who God was talking about. When Crystal continued with the altar call, she didn't obey the spirit of God and neglected to call out the spirit. Standing there looking at her son, Crystal repented in her spirit for being disobedient.

Using her right hand, she turned him around so that she could check him out from the backside. "Humph, you're looking a little skinny from the backside. I guess that girlfriend of yours isn't as good a cook as your mama." Crystal forced a laugh.

"Well, what can I say? I was never able to find a woman who would stand with me and not get cold feet after their curiosity was satiated of how I would treat them, versus the other dogs in the street they always complain about. Once they realized I was a real man who needed a good woman who didn't run at the first sign of accountability in the relationship, they were the ones who left me hanging. So much for the quote all black women love to use loosely about a good man being hard to find. Needless to say, Mama, I've missed you and the meals you cooked for me as a growing boy." He hoped he didn't sound like the liar he was.

Laughter filled the room and then dissipated as Jonathan conjured up the courage to walk over to his sister's bedside. When he first came in, he purposely shifted his attention from her to those in the room he could possibly draw strength from before he laid eyes on his beloved sister and friend. Serena stirred at his touch, but continued resting peacefully. Tears welled up in his eyes as he watched her facial features to see if he could detect anything other than what his natural eye could see.

Jonathan reached into his pockets in search of the mints he kept on hand. Knowing that his breath wasn't the freshest with all of the alcohol he'd consumed before getting there, he popped a few mints into his mouth. He had to make a quick stop to the corner store before calling for the cab to pick him up and give him a ride to the hospital. His nerves were bad during the plane descent because he'd feared returning to the place he'd run away from all of those years ago. Eventually, he would have to face his demons, but he would keep them at bay for as long as possible. Jonathan could only hope that his skeletons wouldn't find him out and expose him.

"Sis, you can relax, baby. I'm sorry, I should have come sooner, but I'm here now and I ain't going nowhere until I know that you're going to be okay. You hear me, girl?" Jonathan rubbed her hair as the tears fell from his face. "Big bro will be right here when you wake up."

Jonathan bent down and nuzzled Serena's nose, and he gave her a wet kiss on the side of her face. He looked back at his family with deep regrets of abandoning them long ago. "Despite my prolonged absence, I love this girl. This is my baby; if something ever happened to her, I would never be able to get over it. I owe her my life." Jonathan broke down crying and fell into Crystal's arms.

There wasn't a dry eye in the room. Amina walked over to her family and nudged her way into the embrace, not wanting to lose out on the moment. No one saw Serena as tears slid down each side of her face. Although she couldn't move her neck, her hearing was perfect and something inside of her leaped when she heard her brother's voice. She wished that she could get out of the bed to be an active partaker in the family reunion.

She didn't know what God had in store for them, but she knew it had to be all good. The pain was excruciating and Serena was tired. She used her free hand to pat the mattress, searching for the morphine pump. When she grasped it, she pushed the button and the machine beeped in acknowledgment that the painkiller had been released. She closed her eyes and went back to sleep.

The nurse noticed that the room was overcrowded upon entering the room. She made a mental note to request one of the rooms on the end to accommodate the traffic to and from the room. When she was able to get a clear view of Serena, she gasped in awe. She was totally star struck because she had watched the woman of God many times on television. It was an honor to be asked to be in care of such an awesome warrior for the Lord; that's why it was no hassle when Dr. Sinclair, approached her and asked her to take care of Serena for the night.

"Hi, my name is Ariane and I will be Ms. Sampson's nurse for the next twelve hours. Pastor Sampson," she said, reaching out for the pastor's hand to shake it. She waited until Crystal stood and noticed that her eyes looked tired. Dark circles made themselves at home, sitting on her cheekbones. Ariane was not shocked to see the strength abound in the woman of God in spite of the condition her daughter was in.

"It's a pleasure to meet you, Ariane. This here is my granddaughter, Amina, my son, Jonathan, and my daughter's friend, Nathaniel." Crystal made the introductions.

"Hi," they said in unison to the nurse and went back to standing around.

"Okay, well, I'm going to check on our patient now. Don't hesitate to call on me throughout the night if you need anything at all," Ariane advised the group. "If she wakes, please let me know right away. I would love to be able to come in and introduce myself to her when she is coherent," Ariane instructed as she checked Serena's vital signs and recorded the findings in her medical chart. She checked Serena's Foley bag to check for urine levels and then she proceeded to record the information.

"Nurse, how is she?" James walked in with a huge bouquet of roses, totally consumed by what he saw as his eyes zoned in on the woman of God whom he'd served faithfully as her driver for the last three years.

"Hi, I'm Ariane, Ms. Sampson's nurse, and you are?" Ariane looked at the tired-looking man who stood two inches taller than her five foot seven frame.

"James, James Jones. I'm Prophetess Serena's driver," James introduced himself. "Where can I put these flowers?" James looked around for an empty space.

"Hey, James. It's good to see you." Amina sensed his apprehension for being there. She went to stand beside him.

"Hey, beautiful. Please forgive me for not speaking when I first came in. My mind was a little preoccupied on seeing that Prophetess Serena was okay. Good afternoon, Pastor Sampson, folks." James whirled around almost dropping the vase. He smiled at Amina.

"Here, let me get those for you." Amina was happy that James was there. She had missed him while he was away.

"Thank you kindly," James said. He handed the vase to her and winked at her, smiling before turning back to Serena. He rubbed the back of his head, which was full of satiny coal black curls.

Amina looked at James and her stomach knotted. She barely felt the tips of his fingers in the exchange but she didn't miss the electricity that came with the touch. Placing the vase of flowers on the windowsill, she admired him from the backside. She liked the way his strong shoulders dipped onto his lean back and thin waist. Even though it was hard working with him in the beginning, Amina felt something move through her that she hadn't experienced before. She was afraid and excited at the same time about what was happening between them. James Jones had flipped a switch on inside her and she was really excited to go to the next level with him.

She shook herself as if chastising her thoughts but it was too late. She began to wonder what their real first kiss would be like and if it would be the fireworks she got with the little peck James had planted on her unexpectedly before. She stood there with a dreamy look on her face.

"Miss Sampson seems to be resting well and her vitals are stable." Ariane spoke to the group and they hung on to each word she said. "It was nice meeting all of you. Oh, by the way, visiting hours are over at nine and one person is allowed to stay overnight. Miss Sampson will have a new room assignment by midday tomorrow. We wanted to afford her more room for visitors because I believe we have already outgrown this room." Ariane gestured around the room and laughed. She wrote her name on the dry erase board and exited the room.

"Daddy, this is James." She stood between the two men. "Jonathan Sampson, meet James Jones. He's Auntie's driver and well, he's my driver too since I'm practically with her wherever she goes." She smiled and moved out of the way so the two men could shake hands.

"It's nice to finally meet you, sir. Amina's a really sweet girl." James shook Jonathan's hand.

"Girl? I would like to have you know that I am nineteen going on twenty. That classifies me as a young woman," Amina defended herself from behind the two men.

"I guess your little girl isn't so little after all." Crystal laughed.

James smiled and said, "I've gotta get going. I just wanted to stop in since I'm just getting off the highway to come and check on you all." James turned back toward Jonathan and said, "Mr. Sampson, it was great meeting you. I would love to take you to lunch just to chat before you leave town."

"It was nice meeting you as well. Lunch, heh? I think that can be arranged," Jonathan said to James, looking at Amina with raised eyebrows.

"See you all later." James bid farewell to his extended family and Amina followed him out.

"Mom, you need to go on home and get some rest. I'm here now and I don't mind hanging out overnight." Jonathan didn't want to have to ride home with his mother because he knew the barrage of questions would begin before they could get out of the hospital parking lot.

"I just want to be here if she wakes up or needs anything. She needs to know I'm here," Crystal insisted by crossing her arms over her chest, clutching her satchel to her chest.

"Pastor Sampson, you need your rest. You've been cooped up here all day, so please take this opportunity to go home and relax. I had planned on staying here with Serena anyhow," Nathaniel pleaded.

"Yeah, Mama, we got this. We are in the hospital, ya know? If Serena needs anything, there are doctors and nurses here who will have what she needs and plus she has us," Jonathan said.

"Okay, I'm going. Let us pray so I can get on outta here. I've got some things to check on at the affairs at the church anyhow. Amina, it's nice that you decided to rejoin us. I will need a ride home shortly, but first we are going to intercede in prayer for Serena." Crystal asked, "Son, will you lead us in prayer?"

"Well, to tell you the truth, I'm a little rusty in the prayer department. Can I get a pass this go around?" Jonathan shuffled his feet like he always did when he was nervous. He hadn't felt the presence of God in his life for a long time. He was sure that God wouldn't hear anything he had to say.

"Nonsense. You are a child of the King. Are you insinuating that you can't get a prayer through on behalf of your sister who's lying in her sickbed?" Crystal was perturbed.

"Mama, please don't pressure me now. Have someone else pray." Jonathan's tone suggested that he didn't want to discuss it any further.

"Very well, son; however, we will be sitting down at some point and having a heart-to-heart. Remember, God and I are on first-name basis and He will advise me concerning you. Let us pray," Crystal said.

Chapter 11

The diagnosis wasn't a shock for the team of doctors working to help Serena. When they revealed the biopsy results to Serena and her family, no one reacted to the diagnosis. It was to be expected that this would be the case until the initial shock wore off. Peace had cloaked itself around Serena and it could be seen on her face.

"Are there any questions?" Dr. Mason asked, looking from one face to another before proceeding with any further prognosis.

Nathaniel raised his free hand while he rubbed the back of Crystal who leaned loosely on his left arm. "Since you had to remove part of Serena's vocal cord during the biopsy, does this mean that she should be able to recover fully?"

All eyes were on the team of doctors as they waited for someone to answer the question to their satisfaction. Dr. Mason looked to Dr. Sinclair to give the prognosis. When she didn't speak up quickly enough for his liking, he cleared his throat and called out to her, "Dr. Sinclair, do you care to expound for the family?"

"Uh, yes." Dr. Sinclair was feeling some kind of way about the news she was getting ready to share with the family. "Miss Sampson was diagnosed with stage three throat cancer. This means that while Dr. Mason didn't have to remove both of her vocal cords, Selena still has a long way to go as far as a prognosis. We are happy to see that she's breathing on her own now."

"Will my daughter need to have any additional types of treatment?" Crystal looked directly into Dr. Sinclair's eyes.

Dr. Noel jumped in. "Well, let's just put it this way. Ms. Sampson has a sixty percent survival rate. With that being said, she will need to undergo radiation therapy and chemotherapy. Our plan is to fight the cancer aggressively and, well, we'll keep our fingers crossed for the best outcome. The good news is that although the cancer has advanced or spread to her thyroid glands, they have already been removed to keep Ms. Serena from having to endure another surgery. One of the down sides of having the thyroid removed at such an early age is that Miss Sampson will more than likely need to receive hormone treatments for the rest of her life. If her vitals remain stable, she will be released in a couple of days with a treatment map in place."

Serena was able to sit up in bed by day two and she had progressed to being able to move around. She sat up straight in the recliner padded with pillows and a thin sheet, flipping from channel to channel on the remote. Serena was happy to have the tubes removed the day before. The doctors had excavated the breathing tube since Serena's oxygen intake was stable at ninety-eight percent. There was an oxygen tank and mask on standby just in case she felt winded with a drop in her oxygen levels.

Serena sat quietly, struggling to digest the diagnosis and prognosis. For the first time since being in the hospital, her stomach growled. She wanted a piece of baked chicken, but knew that was out of the question for a while. For the time being, her meals consisted of liquid substances due to her dietetic restrictions. Her mind wandered as she longed to go home and sleep in her own bed.

The silence was deafening as each person processed the information in their own way. It was evident by their facial expressions that they were still worried about the possibilities of the disease winning. Crystal eased out of the room with Amina on her tail. Nathaniel walked over to Serena and placed his hands on her shoulders and rubbed them in assurance that everything would be okay.

"I can't believe this is happening. Why does God continue to take away from our family? Ah, I've gotta get out of here." Jonathan was distraught as he left the room.

"Thank you, doctors, for explaining things to us." Nathaniel stuck his hand out for them to shake. "I'm sure that we will have more questions as time progresses. How much longer will Serena have to remain in here? I'm confident that the sooner we can get her back home, she will begin to feel like her old self. Hopefully that will make this process more bearable to endure." Nathaniel spoke on behalf of the family in their absence.

Dr. Mason jumped right in to answer. "We would like to begin chemotherapy tonight at midnight. Nurse Ariane should have given Miss Sampson a list of the drug names and their short and long-term side effects a few days ago. Do you have them on hand?" Dr. Mason directed his attention to Serena, who nodded her head in acknowledgment of having received the pamphlets.

He smiled at her and reached over to rub her knee. "Well, we will be around until seven o'clock. So if you need us for anything before then have the nurse on duty page us." Each of the doctors shook Nate's hand and then Serena's before leaving the room.

Serena nodded her head in approval to what the doctor had said. When she blinked her eyes, tears fell. Head bent, Serena gave in to her emotions. The weight lay upon her shoulders as heavy as lead, causing her to slump. She spoke to herself: "It's more than I can bear. Every time

I feel like I have a grip on things, the doctors can say one word, or look a certain way; then my faith wavers. Jesussssssss!" she cried out.

Chapter 12

Serena awakened to the sounds of Dr. Trimble preaching on television. At first, she wondered if she had been dreaming, but now, with her eyes open, she knew that it was real. Dr. Trimble was preaching again on healing just as she was the morning Serena got the courage to see what was going on with her throat. Serena turned her neck slowly so that she could see Dr. Trimble and focus on the message. Hearing the amens floating throughout the congregation on the television screen tore at Serena's heart. She missed traveling and preaching to women for their spiritual and physical breakthroughs.

Tears welled up in Serena's eyes as she envisioned herself back at the Georgia Dome and how the atmosphere was right for the women and so many lives were changed. She feared that she may never experience that again. Depression lingered.

Thoughts wandered wildly in Serena's mind as she wondered if she would ever be able to carry the mantle of God again. She didn't even realize that her current state was an assignment from God. She'd gotten caught up in her flesh and forgot that everything that the enemy meant for her bad, God meant for her good. It didn't matter to Serena that the only sounds that could be heard where the prophetic words flowing through the anointed vessel, Dr. Trimble.

The reality Serena lived in at that moment was all she could think of. No longer concerned about what anyone would say if they walked in on her having an emotional moment, she allowed the tears to run down her face. Shaking her head lightly, she beat the bed with her fists because she felt no connection with the God she had tried to serve faithfully for the last fifteen years.

Hot tears flowed down Serena's face. She was grateful to have made it through the surgery. The tubes had now been removed, but her voice was still raspy and she had to keep her throat wet by sucking on ice and Popsicles. It frightened her to think of choking on the ice or it sliding down her still tender throat. She wondered where everyone was but it didn't take her long to figure it out because the flushing of the bathroom toilet momentarily snatched her attention from herself.

Nathaniel emerged from the bathroom, looking scraggly, but in a handsome, rugged kind of way. Serena allowed her thoughts to travel and she wondered what it would be like to wake up next to him every day.

"Hey, sleepyhead," Nathaniel whispered.

Serena smiled through the salty tears that were still streaming down her face. She held her hand out to Nathaniel and he came to her. They stared into each other's eyes and Nathaniel used his free hand to wipe away the tears on Serena's face. "Baby, please don't cry. Everything will be okay." Nate's eyes became misty as his heart pounded with love for the woman he would one day propose to.

Serena's hazel eyes grew big and they asked questions she was afraid to verbalize. Instead of feeling happy, Serena wasn't sure that she would be around long enough to experience the love of Nathaniel she'd denied herself for so long. Her fears of dying from the late diagnosis became more real to her. She mentally chastised herself for being headstrong and blinded by foolish pride, deceiving herself to believe that she didn't need anyone. She turned away from Nathaniel's steady gaze and looked out of the window. She didn't want to think of what was to come and she didn't want to feel anything for Nathaniel. Her mind and heart warred against one another and her heart was winning.

Nathaniel pulled Serena's chin to guide her eyes back to his. He winked his eye at her and spoke from his heart. "Lady, you are blessed of God. I know that the situation looks bleak right now, but you have strong faith in God. You have too much work to do and many lives to reach. Hold on because I am here with you to ride the storm out together." Nathaniel wasn't sure he'd gotten through to her by the look on her face.

Serena couldn't believe what she was hearing. She hadn't heard Nathaniel speak with such authority before now. Even though her facial expressions contradicted her true feelings, she believed everything he said. Her mind stayed on his declaration to be with her through it all. Serena had long ago convinced herself that she didn't need a man. Serena was having second thoughts about the possibility of love.

Serena released his hand and said something that shocked them both. "Honey, thank you for being my knight in shining armor. I was afraid to let you in because I've been hurt before. I love you," Serena whispered to Nathaniel.

"Baby, you shouldn't be trying to talk. We can discuss all of this when you are out of here and have had a real chance to recuperate," Nathaniel said. Serena was the most beautiful woman in his world and he secretly vowed in his heart that he would love her and take care of her for the rest of their lives.

He wanted to propose to her right then, but he wasn't really prepared. Rejection was his greatest fear, but he was confident that the struggle was over. Her acceptance of him was like music to his ears and he wished he could pick her up out of her hospital bed and hold her. He knew he would cherish her forever. "Serena, you've made me the happiest man alive. To be honest with you, I was beginning to think that you wouldn't give me a chance. We have gone on quite a few dates over the last few months, but you were still keeping your distance from me by your hesitation to commit yourself to me. I will say this, lady: you stole my heart the first day I walked into your church and caught you in my arms. I felt a patter in my heart and a nervousness in my belly that I had never experienced, but I knew I would do whatever necessary to make you mine. I love you, Serena."

Serena smiled, reminiscing on that day. She still wasn't up for having long verbal conversations, but her eyes said it all. Love and fear fought for their place and fear won out. "This conversation is to be continued. I don't want to make any commitments that I am not able to follow through with, but thank you for letting me know that your feelings are the same for me as mine are for you."

Nathaniel hoped that Serena would let their love blossom into what he believed had been ordained by God. He couldn't fathom losing Serena now that things had turned in his favor. The feeling of happiness was fleeting as his mind was arrested with thoughts of Serena being overtaken by the disease. A sad look draped his countenance and he turned away from Serena in an effort to shake the dismal feelings away. He was relieved that the nurse had come in because tension had filled the air.

"Good morning, Miss Sampson. How are you feeling today?" Nurse Lisa whizzed into the room, oblivious of the cloud of heaviness that hung in the air.

"Good morning. I'm feeling a little stronger today than yesterday. Thank you for asking." Serena was in awe of the incredible care she had been receiving since arriving at the hospital. She could tell that the nurses and doctors alike were passionate about making their patients feel good in the midst of perilous times. "Nurse, am I going to be released anytime soon?" Serena asked. Serena was more than ready to get back to her life and prepare for the next step.

"I know that being here for an extended amount of time can be a bit worrisome." Nurse Lisa paused. "We're in here all times of the day and night, poking and prodding on you as if you're a pin cushion. I know your recovery would go a lot faster if you were in the comfort of your own home. I'm just going to check your vitals and I'll be speaking with the doctor about your pending discharge. Your blood pressure is great and I need to draw blood one more time, and then I will be out of your hair."

Serena crossed her arms, shaking her head no. "No more blood here," Serena said softly as she tapped her arms searching for a vein.

"Babe, did you hear that? You may get to go home today!" Nathaniel was ready to take care of her.

"Yes." Serena shook her head just a li'l bit. She tried getting out of the bed because she had the urge to go to the bathroom.

"Serena, what are you doing? It's not time to go any-where yet," Nathaniel nearly screamed.

Serena pointed to the bathroom door. He got up and she mouthed no. She needed to begin to do things on her own again. She felt the need to be alone for a little bit. She needed to get herself together. Once she was inside the bathroom and shut the door, she pulled the gauze bandages back and examined the remnants of the storm she was now in. It wasn't easy looking at the scars on her neck, but Serena continued to stare in the mirror at them.

She had flashbacks of the last few years of her life when she was in the limelight, delivering God's Word to empower women from all over the world. The fear that resided in her heart showed up in the reflection, staring back at her as she wondered if she would live to give her testimony.

Chapter 13

The first week of being home had its challenges for Serena. Amina had been working around the clock making sure that Serena's room was clean and disinfected from any germs after she was released from the hospital. Cleanliness was necessary due to Serena's compromised immune system. The chemotherapy had already begun to claim Serena's hair and rob her of any strength she had worked to regain after the surgery.

James had been a big help in between his jobs, making trips to the grocery store. He shopped with care and made sure he followed Amina's grocery list and checked it twice. Serena spent most of her time in her bedroom resting and reading the Bible.

Serena sat up in bed when she heard a knock on her door. She craned her neck to see who was on the other side of the cracked door. She saw her prayer group peeking back in at her. They didn't wait for an invitation; they just pressed their way into the room, smiling and toting their Bibles in hand. They filed in one by one. Evangelist Curry led the pack with Amina bringing up the rear. Each of the ladies lightly hugged Serena's neck and told her how much she had been missed.

Serena tried to put on her happy face and embrace the ladies who worked very closely with her in ministry. She wasn't up to having company so soon but she didn't have the heart to turn them away, although they had shown up unannounced.

"Prophetess Serena, we have all been praying for you. How are you feeling?" Evangelist Curry opened the conversation, placing a stack of cards on the dresser.

"Did you receive the arrangement of flowers sent on behalf of the Intercessory Prayer Team? Pastor Sampson told us that you didn't want too many visitors and that your hospital room was God-awful small." Sister Edna had the gift of gab and sometimes she talked too much.

The ringing of the doorbell silenced the women. Amina excused herself to go and see who was at the door. It didn't take long for the ladies to see who else had joined the visit. A light knock on the door had everyone's attention. The lady seemed hesitant to enter Serena's room. Amina followed behind her and nearly pushed the visitor into the room. Serena's eyes grew big when she caught the woman's gaze Serena hadn't forgotten that Miss Felisha Green had a thing for Nathaniel.

"Hi, everyone. I'm sorry that I'm late. I got turned around when I drove past the subdivision." She stammered before continuing to speak to Serena. "Prophetess Serena, I've been praying for you. I believe that God is going to bring you through just fine." She smiled nervously, trying not to look as uncomfortable as she felt.

"Come on in, Sister Felisha. You're right on time. Prophetess Serena, do you remember Sister Felisha?" Evangelist Curry inquired.

Serena refrained from speaking, but acknowledged Felisha Green with a curt nod. She wondered why the woman was in her home. It was no secret that she was in competition for Nathaniel's heart.

"Mmhmm." Seeing as though no one spoke up, Serena raised her eyebrows at Evangelist Curry and lightly cleared her throat. Now more than ever she wished the ladies would leave and take Miss Green with them.

"Prophetess Serena, Sister Felisha came to me during your absence and let me know that God called her to intercede on the behalf of the saints. I took the liberty of meeting with her and after seeking God on it, I invited Sister Felisha to join the prayer ministry," Evangelist Curry explained boldly.

Serena could see what no one else could: Evangelist's chest poked out, bubbling with pride.

Serena wanted to disappear underneath her bedcovers, but instead, gritted her teeth and smiled. She shook her head up and down in a manner that had everyone believing that she was on board with Sister Felisha being a part of the ministry, but she had her guard up. Making a mental note to keep an eye on Miss Green, Serena decided to relax and be cordial to the woman.

"I appreciate your prayers, Sister Felisha, and welcome to the prayer ministry. I'm excited to see what God has in store for you and even more excited to see what you will bring to the ministry." Serena didn't really have a reason not to like the pretty mocha-complexioned lady standing before her. She didn't have time for any drama with any of Nathaniel's wannabe harem and had hoped that once the word had gotten out about them having solidified their relationship, the ladies would let any thoughts of being with him go.

The room had grown quiet, but it didn't stay that way for long. Sister Edna asked the ladies to join hands so that they could pray with Serena and be on their way. It just so happened that Sister Felisha was the closest to Serena, so she grabbed Serena's hand and bowed her head to pray. Serena looked around the room and caught Amina's eyes.

Amina looked apologetic for allowing all of these women into Serena's bedroom. Sister Sherry prayed so hard that Serena was sure that heaven and earth would meet and shake hands in agreement. Serena's mind was someplace else and even though she was an intercessor at heart, she was happy to hear the word "amen." She thanked the women for coming by and exhaled when they had all gone.

The silk scarf Serena had been wearing to cover her now bald head shifted on her scalp. Her hand flew up to her head and she snatched the scarf off and flung it over her bedside to the floor. She rubbed the naked spots on her exposed scalp and anger built up in her heart. She didn't want to be angry with God, but He was the only one she could be upset with.

"Amina?" Serena called for her niece. Amina didn't come right away, so Serena called out for her again, sounding distraught.

Amina tapped on the closed bedroom door two times and entered without waiting for a response. "Yes, Auntie, what's wrong?"

"Look at me, Amina," Serena said.

"Okay, Auntie, I'm looking." Amina looked her aunt over, not understanding why her aunt was alarmed all of a sudden.

"I'm ugly. Look, look at this." Serena pointed to her pointy head that had dents and moles all over her scalp. "Can you believe that God would allow me to go through something this drastic? What do you think He wants me to get from this kind of trial?" Serena asked, horrified.

Amina didn't know how to respond to her aunt's outburst of emotion. She invited her aunt to pray with her and held her hand out to grab Serena's hand, but Serena didn't oblige. "Auntie, please don't allow the enemy to deceive you into believing that God has left you or intends to allow you to die during this season. I declare and decree that you will live and not die. You shall proclaim the works of Jesus Christ." Amina tried to encourage Serena.

"Aw, Amina, I don't want to hear scripture right now. I know all of the scriptures. I know how to speak life and believe for healing. Can we be realistic right now? Can you allow me to be transparent and vent right now?" Serena asked, becoming hysterical.

"Sure, Auntie. I was just saying—"

"Yes, you were just saying what every other Christian would say. It's your duty to encourage your sisters when they are going through it. I know the drill. This is what I do for millions of women around the world. They go through these types of things, not me. I'm a servant of God. I have been faithful to the ministry. When someone needed me, I went. When they called, I answered. So one question, why is this happening to me?" Serena pounded her fists on the bed and threw a temper tantrum. Wisps of hair that hadn't become detached from the root waved back and forth in the air. The cool air on her scalp gave her chills throughout her body.

"Auntie, please calm down. I'm not sure why this is happening to you. I believe it's to make you a stronger woman. I'm sorry for throwing Bible scriptures at you, but that's all I know to do. You're my spiritual mentor and I have emulated you for so long. I can't give you worldly wisdom because I have none." Amina picked up the hand mirror and brought it to Serena's tearstained face and held it there. "You are a beautiful woman who is loved by many. You aren't your hair and, most of all, Brother Nathaniel loves you in spite of what you are going through."

Serena looked into the mirror and tried to look past the physical deterioration staring back at her. Her feelings were out of sorts and she was tired of trying to hold it all together. She couldn't help her reaction to the situation she had been placed in. "What if I die? What if Nathaniel doesn't want to stay with me once he sees how sick and tired I am due to the effects of the chemotherapy? I don't like having dark circles under my eyes and, here, look at my fingernails." Serena thrust her fingers in front of Amina's face.

Amina looked at Serena's fingernails and saw that they were brown and had lost their luster. She couldn't imagine what her aunt was really feeling. Sympathy was all she could give due to her lack of experience in going through something like this. Amina was determined that she would be there to encourage her aunt every step of the way to her healing. She refused to give in to feelings of doubt of her aunt's total deliverance. Tears threatened to have their way, causing Amina to excuse herself from the room.

Amina heard the doorbell ringing and hoped that it wasn't anyone else from the church because if she opened the door and that was the case, she would be turning them away. Amina stood on her tiptoes in order to peer out of the peephole. She sighed with relief upon seeing Nathaniel on the other side. She jerked the door open.

"Hey, Brother Nathaniel, I'm so glad that you're here. Auntie has been wigging out for the last hour or so and I have run out of encouraging things to say to her. It's like God answered my prayer and sent you in the nick of time. I was getting ready to call Gran-Gran, but you will do," she said as she pulled Nate into the house and quickly closed and locked the door.

"I'm sure that I can get her to calm down. Don't worry; you get some rest and I will take care of Serena." Nate rubbed his hands together and went to see about his bride-to-be.

Chapter 14

Jonathan pulled into the gravel driveway of his child-hood home. He was grateful to his mother for allowing him to drive her second car while he was in town. He loved his mother, but he hoped that she was nowhere around yet. He wanted to get his drink on with no interruptions. He was guilt-ridden because of his sister's illness. He tried to rationalize in his mind what if he had turned out differently. Then he would have been man enough to take care of his own kid instead of pawning her off for someone else to raise. Then maybe his sister wouldn't be sick. He had shucked his parental responsibilities, which added undue stress to the lives of his mother and sister.

Jonathan had been in a funk ever since he arrived a month ago. He had requested an extended leave of absence. As Jonathan gazed out of the window, childhood memories that Jonathan had suppressed for many years came rushing back. He remembered playing outside with his baby sister. Forgetting where he was as the memories played in his mind like an old movie, Jonathan popped open the can of the beer that he'd purchased on the way home from the convenience store.

He was entranced by scenes from his past. Jonathan remembered the day of his father's funeral and how he'd held his sister's hand the entire day. Different faces showed up at their family home and ate up the food brought in by various church members. Fun times and not so fun times replayed through Jonathan's mind.

He couldn't believe that he had fallen so hard that he'd missed the signs. Sherry Paxton was the love of his life and there wasn't anything he wouldn't do for her. They had been dating only a year, but true love knows no limits. Sherry wasn't a churchgoer and God was just another fairytale to her, which brought disdain from his mother. Crystal had sat him down and preached time and time again about the sin of fornication.

Tears fell from Jonathan's eyes when Amina burst through Sherry's birth canal nine months later. He could never understand why Sherry showed no emotion whatsoever toward their new baby girl. She was the spitting image of her mother, with her coal black eyes and head full of satiny curls that draped her face like a veil. Six pounds and thirteen ounces of beautiful cried in her mother's arms, but whatever motherly instinct God gave to women somehow missed Sherry.

Jon whimpered and his body shuddered in pain, causing the beer can to scream from the pressure of having its sides squeezed under the grip of Jonathan's strong hands. Jonathan was in the midst of a "woe is me" marathon. He had barely made it back to his mom's house after going to the T-Mobile store to purchase another cell phone. Putting the car in park, he punched in the numbers to Sedric's office. He had memorized every number that he had for his former lover. Each time he called, Sedric's voice mail picked up and he was stuck with the option of leaving a message or hanging up altogether. The last two times he called, he decided to get some things off of his chest. "Sedric, you no-good sorry excuse for a man. You owe me six hundred dollars for screwing up my plane ticket. You knew that I would need to have every dollar spared until I return to New York, but you couldn't stand the thought of my dumping you."

Pushing the end button, Jonathan slung the phone into the passenger seat and grabbed another beer. Jonathan chugged and belched. He drank until he couldn't drink anymore. The high he was seeking wasn't as fulfilling as he had hoped. Beer sloshed around in the can and eventually, Jonathan came to himself. Anger filled his gut and he lost his desire for the beer. He slammed the can against the steering wheel, not caring that he was in his mother's car.

Overtaken by emotions of brokenness and shame, the thoughts didn't stop there but kept reeling through his mind like a movie projector. Three months after Amina was born, Sherry came to his home and told him that she wasn't going to marry him and become the family he had always hoped they would be.

Jonathan reminded Sherry that he had proposed marriage to her and she had said yes. He asked what was going to happen to the dreams they had. Sherry let him know that those were his dreams and she only agreed to marry him because she was caught up in the idea of being in love, not because she really wanted to get married. She went on to tell him that she wasn't the one for him. She was a free spirit and felt like she would be missing out on something great if she settled down at such a young age. Not long after her shocking revelation, Jonathan called her home to try to speak with her about the matter. Amina's grandmother, Ms. Paxton, told him that Sherry wasn't home and had left the night before with all of her things. He'd never heard from her again.

Jonathan's heart was broken and he was convinced that he would never love again. That night, he took the first of many drinks. His goal was to drown out the pain and forget the woman he was planning to spend the rest of his life with. That same night, he found himself at one of the house parties across town in Durham and that was where he experienced his first sexual escapade with a man.

He cursed aloud and let out a long, throaty growl. No one knew why he really left home. It wasn't because he felt incapable of being a great dad to his little girl. Jonathan realized that he needed to leave her there with his mother and sister because he liked the attention he got from his male suitor too much to declare what he'd done was an accident. Jonathan refused to bring shame to his home. He couldn't bring dishonor to his mother or his father's church that she worked so hard to maintain. Options few, Jonathan decided that he needed to leave home, run away, and that's what he did.

Coming back to himself, Jonathan realized what he had done, causing alarm to himself. The nightmare had been put on pause for the moment, but Jonathan knew it was only a matter of time before his lifestyle came back to haunt him. He looked around at the mess he had made as his nostrils filled with the stench from the wasted alcohol. He screwed his face up, tired from the events of his trip thus far. Sleep was what he needed and he decided to take the car to have it detailed as soon as he had gotten some rest. Cranking the car up and letting it sit idle for a moment, Jonathan opened the garage door and gave thanks to God that she wasn't home as he pulled the car into the space on the opposite side of the garage. His mother would appreciate the short walk from the garage to the door.

Once inside of the house, Jonathan wasted no time running through the house and jetting up the stairs to his old bedroom. He flounced onto his twin-sized bed and before he could finish his prayer in thanks, snores emanated from him. Jonathan's slumber was short-lived when he heard the house phone ringing. Drowsy and a little buzzed from the beer he drank prior to going to sleep, he was a little angry. He reached over and snatched the phone from its cradle. "Yeah?" Jonathan made sure that his caller knew that they had interrupted his nap.

"Hey, Daddy, did I wake you?" Amina's troubled voice gave Jonathan the jolt he needed to shake off the remnants of sleep and his stank attitude.

"Baby girl, I was just getting some much-needed rest. What's wrong? Is everything okay?"

"Yes and no. It's just that Auntie has been stressing again over everything for the last few days. Why haven't we heard from you? I was sure you would have stopped by before now. Auntie needs all of our support and I think if you were to come and see her then she would feel better." Amina took a swig of her sweet tea. Getting no response from Jonathan, she carried the conversation.

"She's been experiencing fits of rage over her loss of hair. One minute she's crying and refusing company and the next she's calm and quiet. I have done all that I can do. Plus Auntie has made it clear that she doesn't want me throwing Bible scriptures at her," Amina explained.

"Calm down, sweetie. I can only imagine what my sister is going through. I have never been sick, so I'm sure that her emotions are riding high and then extremely low at times. I have confidence that she will bounce back because her faith is strong in God," Jonathan encouraged Amina.

"Daddy, when are you coming by to see us? I was hoping that we would have time to reconnect. I believe that God is going to do something miraculous for our family. I am not sure how He is going to do this, but I can't let go of my faith now."

"I'm in no rush to get back to New York, baby. I'm going to make time for you and we are going to be fine. I'm still getting used to being back in the city. I've been visiting some friends from high school. I'm relaxing right now and needed the down time to just get out and about. Not to mention that I am doing all kinds of odd jobs for your grandmother. She has been leaving me to-do lists on the kitchen counter before she leaves for the church each day for me to do. You know how Gran-Gran is. She stays gone all day and when she gets home, she checks to see if I have done the tasks she assigned before leaving." Jonathan let out a lazy laugh. He knew that the time was coming for him to sit down and have a heart-to-heart with his daughter. The only problem was that he wasn't sure what he should share with her and what to keep under wraps.

"Daddy, are you still there?" Amina thought the call had been disconnected until she heard him stirring on the other end. He never answered her, so she called his name again. "Daddy, is something wrong?" Amina asked.

Jonathan cleared his throat and came back to the conversation. "I'm still here. Let me call you back, okay, sweetie?"

"You sound strange. Are you sure you are okay?"

"I'm fine. Now let me call you back in a little while, okay? I have some things to do and then I can make plans to come over to see you." Jonathan's patience was wearing thin.

"All right. Just make sure you call me back today, Daddy. I love you."

"I love you too, princess. We will talk a little later on." Jonathan didn't waste any time hitting the end button on his cell phone to release the call. Thinking back to his earlier actions, he wished that he hadn't wasted a good beer in the car. His body was calling the liquor that was his vice he used to numb his feelings. It was the only time that he felt normal and free to be himself. He needed to be able to have peace of mind for the rest of the day.

Frustration settled onto Jonathan's shoulders. No longer able to sleep, he jumped up and went to take a shower. His mind was already made up that he would take his mother's car to the detailer and have it cleaned thoroughly. Then he would stop at the store to get another beer or maybe even a six pack. He really wasn't up to facing his demons nor was he ready to sit down and discuss his life with his now grown daughter or mother. It would only be a matter of time before they demanded some much-needed conversation, but for now, he just wanted to put it out of his mind.

Guilt rained down on him and he broke out into a cold sweat. Fear clasped its fingers around his heart and squeezed. Panic chased the fear and his heartbeat raced while water ran down his back and droplets popped out on his forehead. Jonathan leaned into the shower to turn it on and before he knew what happened, he blacked out as his body crashed into the tub with the water still running.

Chapter 15

Serena heaved into the toilet. She hated vomiting but she had to admit the release made her feel better even though the relief was fleeting. Serena continued coughing and spitting the remnants of her breakfast into the toilet bowl. She was tired and her throat was still sore. The loud grunting and other undistinguishable sounds she made were wearing on her.

"Baby, are you okay?" Nathaniel had been watching from the doorway. He hated hearing the love of his life suffering. He wondered if he was really equipped to stand by his woman through the good and the bad. Tears welled up in his eyes and he slapped them away angrily.

Serena tried responding in between gasping for air and spitting up what was left on her stomach. "Am I okay? Nathaniel, I'm stooped over puking my guts out and you're asking me if I'm okay. Um, you figure it out." Serena was frustrated with the sickness and she was angry that her body betrayed her. She wiped her mouth with the damp cloth she had been clutching for the last hour.

Nathaniel fought to remain positive and patient with Serena. "Take it easy on a brother, okay? I know you're sick and I am sorry about that. If I could take away the nausea, cold sweats, vomiting, neuropathy, and fatigue that the drugs cause, I would. I understand why you are acting the way you are, but . . ." Nathaniel was running out of things to say.

"You understand? And how would that be a true statement, Nathaniel? I know that we haven't been dating that long, but are you a cancer survivor? Do you know how it feels to have your arm stuck like it's a pin cushion? Have you been so tired that you want to stay in bed for days? Have you been pumped with deadly drugs that can one day be the reason for an untimely death? Oh, do tell how you can relate to what I am going through." Serena's last statement dripped with sarcasm.

"That's enough, okay? I will have you to know that it's hurting me to see you go through the exact same thing my mother went through before God called her home. I'm here consistently and I just want you to appreciate the fact that I am. I feel helpless that I can't do anything to take away your pain. I can't take your place, or I would. Stop punishing everyone around you," Nathaniel reprimanded Serena.

Serena felt horrible. She wished that she could take back her ranting, but she couldn't. The last thing she wanted to do was run Nathaniel off. She hadn't been in a relationship in a long time and her life consisted of no one but herself. She hadn't had anyone else's feelings to consider before now. Her cheeks felt flush with embarrassment and the realization that her mother was right about something during their last conversation. She needed to be more sensitive toward those closest to her.

"I am so sorry. I feel really terrible about what I said. Look at me. How could you want to be with me? I'm angry, fly at the mouth, and my prayer life has been lacking." Serena hiccupped. "Can you forgive me, honey?" Serena promised herself that from here on out if she didn't have anything nice to say, she wouldn't say anything at all.

"Serena, I forgive you, but I must admit I don't like the person you are becoming because of the cancer. I haven't ever been disrespected by a lady and I won't start being disrespected by you. Let me say this: if you ever talk to me like that again I will walk out of this house and out of your life," Nathaniel said.

"Note taken." Serena felt like a child who had just been scolded for doing something wrong.

Serena appreciated her man taking charge. She was ashamed for the way she had been behaving.

The faces of the sisters in church who would love to be in her place when it came to Nathaniel popped into her head.

Serena was used to being her own boss; she knew that it was time for her to take a lesson in submission. Silence filled the air and finally after staring up at Nathaniel, Serena stuck her arm out for him to help her up off of the bathroom floor. She was still weak and it didn't help that her legs had fallen asleep due to her being crouched on the floor with her legs tucked under her.

He bent down and scooped Serena up from the floor and placed her on her feet. She wet her washcloth to wash her face. Then she gently brushed her teeth, taking care not to scratch her gums, which would cause bleeding. Once she was done, Nathaniel picked her up, cradling her in his arms and maneuvering sideways out of the bathroom. He imagined carrying Serena over the threshold after their wedding. Reaching the bed, he placed her ever so softly on the mattress and returned to the bathroom to disinfect the toilet. After the bathroom had been cleaned, Nathaniel leaned on the doorjamb to watch Serena sleep.

Nathaniel decided that he would leave for a while to handle some business and return later. He kissed Serena on the forehead and covered her up. He walked into the living room where Amina sat reading her Bible. "Hey, I'm going to get on out of here. I have some things that need my attention and then I'll be heading to Bible Study. Do you need anything before I leave?"

Amina was so engrossed in reading that she didn't hear Nathaniel come up behind her. She jumped at the sound of his gruff voice. "Hey, no, I'm fine. Thanks for asking. How is Auntie? Will you tell everyone we said hello and send our love to the church?" Amina asked.

"Of course I will. They will be glad to know that Serena will win the battle regardless of what the naysayers think about it. She has her next appointment in a few days, so I'm going to be handling some things at the center in order to go with her," Nathaniel said. "You know she has four more months of chemotherapy." Nathaniel sighed.

Amina stood up from the table and hugged him. "Thank you for being here. I know it's not easy watching Auntie go through this. All we can do is keep praying that God gives us the strength to walk through this valley experience with grace. Gran-Gran called before Serena was leaving for her chemo appointment and offered to go with her, but I'll be sure to let her know that you will be going with her," Amina said. "You know she's Miss Independent and she's been unusually irritable lately."

"Don't worry. I believe that your auntie and I have a new understanding." Nathaniel smiled at Amina as he thought back on the conversation he had with Serena beforehand. "I will see you ladies later and remember, I am just a phone call away. Don't hesitate to call me or text me if you need anything. She's resting now and after puking her guts out I know the nap is well deserved." He picked up his coat from the back of the dining room table chair and threw it over his arm. Amina walked him to the door and said, "See you later" before closing and locking the door.

Amina prayed after reading and glanced at the clock on the wall. Seeing that the hour was getting late, she prepared something for Serena just in case she wanted it when she woke up. She moved around the spacious kitchen where she fumbled with pans and ingredients to fix dinner. Amina wondered why she hadn't heard back from her father. He had promised to come by, but he never showed up or called to explain why. She decided that she wouldn't press him, but the more she thought about his absence the more angry she became.

The relationship between Jonathan and Amina was strained to say the least, but she still expected for the man to keep his word and come to see them. That was the only way she could silence his excuses about why he hadn't been accessible since he was supposed to be supporting the family during time of crisis.

Amina wanted to cheer Serena up, so she fixed a tray up and added softly scrambled eggs and a slice of white bread with no butter to the plate. She squeezed oranges into a container to make fresh orange juice. James slipped into her mind as she pressed and squeezed on the oranges. She took her time by rolling them on the countertop to make them soft. Then she cut the tops and the bottoms off and went to work.

Amina hadn't talked with James since the day at the hospital. Every time she thought about him, she smiled. He wasn't like the guys she hung out with from school. There was nothing to those boys, but the more she thought about James, she looked forward to their journey together.

Dripping sounds slammed onto the countertop and she heard juice splashing onto the floor. There was orange juice and pulp everywhere except in the juice container. She laughed at herself and shook her head as if to shake the thoughts out of it. Prepping the breakfast tray, she poured the juice into a midsized container instead of the large one she'd originally planned to use. She didn't look forward to cleaning up the mess she'd created. Amina dodged around the disaster in order to put the finishing touches on Serena's tray. The door stood slightly ajar so Amina used her foot to push the door all the way open and walked into the dimmed room to place the tray down to turn a light on.

"Auntie, it's time for you to eat something." Amina moved swiftly around the room, ready to serve Serena and she noticed that Serena was still buried underneath her covers. When calling out to her proved ineffective, Amina balanced the tray in the crook of her arm and used her free hand to reach down and shake Serena. She finally began to stir, sat up, and stretched.

"Mm, how long was I asleep and where is Nathaniel?" Serena was more interested in having her questions answered than eating her meal, which was getting colder by the minute.

"You've been asleep for a couple of hours and Nathaniel left not too long after you went to sleep. He said that he had some things to take care of before going to Bible Study," Amina informed her. She unveiled the food tray, seeing that the steam had gone from the food. She knew that her aunt's stomach couldn't take the smells of food cooking or hot foods. "Auntie, guess what else he said." Amina teased while preparing the dinner tray for Serena.

"What else?" Serena asked, looking at Amina sideways as she fluffed her pillows to place behind her back so she could eat comfortably.

"Nathaniel said that he's going with you to your next chemotherapy appointment." Amina held her breath, waiting for Serena to say something.

"Okay, is that what he said?" Serena laughed to herself, thinking back on their bathroom talk from earlier. "Well, what do we have here?" Serena asked, gesturing toward the tray. Seeing the food was confirmation that she was indeed hungry because her stomach rumbled.

"Scrambled eggs with no pepper, only a dash of salt, and two slices of white bread slathered with your favorite strawberry jam, and a glass of freshly squeezed orange juice."

"Mm, sounds good. Now if only my taste buds could appreciate the sweetness of the jam. I love strawberries, but of course you already know that. I truly appreciate how you have stepped up even more since I have been dealing with this, this . . ." Serena reached for the glass of orange juice.

"It's ministry for me. I just hope you can keep it down. I felt so bad that you got so ill after your last meal. You know what? I wish I could take your pain, Auntie." Amina's eyes were glued to Serena's.

"Sweetie, as long as God is on my side I'm going to be all right. God never promised me that I wouldn't have to suffer, but He did promise that He would never leave me nor forsake me. Now fix your face before you have me crying in my food."

Serena tried to be strong and brave in front of her niece, but she had her moments of doubt. She prayed over her food before eating with an added request that her food stay down. Serena picked up her fork and ate slowly. Swallowing was still laborious for Serena, but it was getting better. With each bite, she asked God to allow her to eat without gagging, which would only set off a range of reactions that started at her esophagus and ended at her stomach. She didn't really taste the food but, twenty minutes later, she had finished everything on her plate. Picking up her glass, she washed down the remnants of her meal, happy that it was finally over.

Amina sat on the other side of the bed flipping through channels, not wanting to leave Serena's side until after she had finished eating and was resting again. Her mind was on James again and she hoped that he was also thinking of her. She wanted to talk to him, but didn't want to interrupt him while he was working. Amina started talking before she realized she was getting ready to share her innermost thoughts about a man for the first time.

"Auntie, what do you think about James?"

"What do you mean what do I think about James?" Serena raised her eyebrows, trying to figure her niece out before she went any further. When Amina didn't answer quickly enough, Serena went on speaking. "Well, he's nice, humble, respectable, and older than you are, young lady," Serena said smiling.

Amina dropped her head down, wishing she hadn't brought the subject up at all. She knew she should have kept her mouth shut and just tried to figure things out on her own. The last thing she wanted was for anyone to tell her that James was too old for her because she already knew that, but it was too late. Nothing anyone said would change her mind about her blossoming love for James. She hoped that Serena would give her blessings for them to at least see where things went.

Serena smiled, knowing that Amina was smitten with James. She remembered the day James came to pick them up for her surgery. She smiled again when she thought about the look on James's face when she caught them making out. Serena knew that Amina was nervous by the way she kept picking at the silk comforter. She figured that her silence was torturing Amina, but she kept quiet a li'l longer. The more Serena thought about James, a spirit of peace settled to calm whatever fears she may have had about Amina dating. This was not only new to Amina, but to Serena as well.

The phone rang and both of the ladies jumped. They snapped out of their private thoughts as the phone rang over and over again. Serena looked over at Amina and shook her head as an indication that she didn't want to talk to anyone. Serena was feeling emotional as she paid attention to the changes and desires taking place in her niece's life. She was sure there would be many more talks about Mr. James.

Amina answered the phone and upon hearing the caller's voice, worry shadowed her facial features. Amina didn't know what was going on with Jonathan, other than him saying that his head hurt from a fall, but she could barely make out the rest of what he was saying because he slurred when he talked. The more she listened to his voice she knew that something was terribly wrong. That confirmed the need for a surprise visit to Gran-Gran's soon. The phone call was a short one. Serena watched Amina's facial expressions go from one extreme to the next, until she finally released the call and started crying.

"Sweetie, what is it? What's going on? Please stop crying. Who was that? Did they say something to upset you?" Serena was alarmed. It didn't help matters when Amina bawled like the little girl she used to be. Serena pulled Amina over to her and hugged her. She hoped that it wouldn't be long before Amina calmed down enough to let her know what was going on. She pondered on what it could be since she had talked to Crystal just the day before and she hadn't said anything out of the ordinary.

Minutes later, Amina had regained her composure and told Serena what had transpired on the phone with Jonathan. Wiping the last of her tears, she told Serena what happened. They both sat in silence, caught up in their own scenarios of what was going on with Jonathan. Serena wondered why she hadn't seen nor heard from him since he'd visited her at the hospital. She'd been so caught up in her own issues that she didn't dwell on his absence. Serena bowed her head and prayed her brother, niece, and her mother would be able to press through the process of whatever God was doing.

Amina was still afflicted by her father's voice. She tried to figure out what was going on with him. If she wasn't mistaken, he sounded like he was drunk. She chided herself, thinking that her father wasn't an alcohol drinker. Remembering that her father lived all the way up in New York, she wasn't sure how he was living. She didn't know too much about his life and what he was involved in, but her gut told her it wasn't good. That thought alone gave her more of a reason to worry about him and it made her awfully anxious to find out what was happening in his life. She wouldn't involve her grandmother by calling and causing her to worry just yet.

Chapter 16

"Good morning, son." Crystal's heart was heavy. She was in no shape to preach that morning, but it was too late for her to get one of her associates to step in. She'd failed at getting Jonathan to open up to her and she didn't understand why he wouldn't go to church.

"Mama." Jonathan bent to peer into the refrigerator, looking for something to make breakfast with. He hoped that this conversation didn't last long, relying on his short answers to win him a pass. He didn't know how wrong he would be.

"Jonathan, you have been here almost three months and aside from the hospital visits, you haven't gone to see your sister nor your daughter. You act like you don't belong to this family. I sure hope that you didn't go up to New York and forget your foundation. What are you hiding? Do I have to remind you that I'm on first-name basis with the Almighty One?" Crystal tooted her lips and pointed upward.

"Mom, I talked to Amina a few nights ago. See? I'm keeping in touch just like I said I would," Jonathan said, hoping that would be enough for his mother.

"Do you even know what's going on with your sister? When I called you to come home, it was my understanding that you would be here for your family. Instead, you are gallivanting all over the county, doing God knows what," Crystal fussed.

"Good morning to you too, Mama." Jonathan replied dryly as he walked around her to reach the cupboards in search of something to eat. His stomach growled. Jonathan didn't really care what he ate for breakfast because whatever he ate constituted his breakfast meal. He'd been known to eat steak and mashed potatoes for breakfast and eggs, ham, and toast for dinner. That was his way of living since he'd gotten away from Crystal's traditional way of cooking meals designated by the time of day it was. He'd awaken most mornings and run to Starbucks to grab something quick on his way to the office each day.

"Jonathan, if something were wrong would you confide in me?" Crystal looked directly at her son, who had dropped his eyes and fixed his cereal. "Jonathan, look at me when I'm talking to you. What's going on with you? I know it's something, but I want you to share with me. We are both adults now and I'm sure that whatever it is, God can work it out." Crystal walked over to Jonathan and lifted his chin so that she could see his eyes. "I'm here. Please let me in." She felt herself getting upset inside, but tried to keep her emotions in check.

"Pastor, please, no preaching to me this early in the morning. Save that for your eleven o'clock service, would you?" Jonathan was so over talking that he ignored his mother until she tapped him on the shoulder and yelled in his ear.

"Jonathan Sampson, don't you dare ignore me when I'm speaking to you. I will not be disrespected in my own household by you or anyone else." Crystal's blood pressure rose and she could feel her internal thermostat rising. She was prepared to knock him upside the head in two point five seconds if he didn't humble himself.

"Can't a man just eat in peace, please? If there were something going on, I am sure that God would have told you by now. You know, with you being super spiritual and all." Sarcasm dripped from Jonathan's lips.

Before Crystal knew what was happening she had a flashback from the past and she walked over to Jonathan and slapped him straight in the face. "Just who do you think you're talking to? I know you been up in New York living with no boundaries. I wasn't going to say anything, but you have stepped on my toes now, boy. I knew something was up with you before you got here and it was confirmed when you got here and instead of your favorite cologne singing to my nostrils, the stale smell of alcohol on your breath singed my nose hairs."

Jonathan kept his head low. He wished he would have stayed upstairs and waited until Crystal had left the house like usual, but today, the rubber met the road and he wished that he could get a drink. "It was only a few drinks. I'm not comfortable with flying, so to calm my nerves, I had a coupla shots of tequila and orange juice." Jonathan fidgeted in his chair, pushing the cereal around in the bowl. He'd lost his appetite.

"You know, maybe, I could have believed that had I not seen the empty beer cans in my car that I graciously allowed you to utilize during your stay. Now this is the second and the last time you will disrespect me. Something has taken a drastic turn for the worse."

"Mama, I'm not an alcoholic. I drink socially and sometimes when I'm keyed up. I can admit that I've been somewhat stressed since learning of Serena's health crisis." Jonathan hoped his half-true explanation would appease his mother. Shame colored his cheeks as the blood collected there. He could have kicked himself for not cleaning the car out before now like he'd planned to.

"It just may be time for you to come on back home. I don't know what's happened to you since you've been in New York, but I'm no fool and the drinking is only a symptom of something deeper going on with you." Crystal kept digging and picking, determined to get the truth. "Jonathan, what if someone would have seen you driving my car and drinking alcohol? Do you realize what that would have meant for the church?" Crystal hollered in disbelief.

"Come home? Why would I want to do that? You know I have terrible memories of this place." He stood and turned his back to Crystal. Dumping the cereal out, he rinsed the bowl and dropped it into the empty sink.

"And what's that supposed to mean? What would be so bad about that? What's so horrible about your childhood that would drive you away from home?" Crystal was tired of her son talking in circles.

"Mama, this is no reflection on you. Things happened here that I didn't want to have to come home and have to face. I stayed away for as long as I could not, because I don't love my family. I had to put as many miles between North Carolina and myself as I could. I guess you don't remember that home is where my heart was broken, Mama." Jonathan pressed his back up against the kitchen counter and rolled from side to side. He was too antsy to be still while baring his soul.

"Oh, Lord, please don't tell me this is about that girl, Sherry Paxton? If you would have just listened to me in the first place, you wouldn't have ever gotten caught up with that child. She wasn't good for nothing and I could see her true intentions from a mile away. She used you, son.

"Mama, don't do that. I loved Sherry with all of my heart and she is Amina's mother. We were supposed to get married and live happily ever after." Jonathan was getting emotional as he thought back to how happy he was.

"Jonathan, there is no happily ever after until you get to heaven. I had been hearing things around town about Sherry before she told you she was pregnant. Members from the church would see her out traipsing in and out of clubs at all time of night. I was trying to save you the heartache before things blew up in your face, but you didn't want to listen to me. You were always in a tizzy, thinking that I was trying to break you up," Crystal admitted.

"Well, why didn't you tell me about it instead of getting an attitude every time I brought her name up or she came by? I could have confronted her and made her tell me why she felt the need to portray being a good girl to me, but was out in the streets like that." Jonathan shuffled his feet thinking back to when he was always stuck in the house while she claimed to be out with her girlfriends.

"Son, how could I just come out and say your girlfriend is trifling? I didn't have concrete evidence but the spirit don't lie. That and the rumors, which I abhor, had to be true. I didn't want to hurt you with the truth because I knew that before it was all done and said, the truth would show up. Even though you were hurting, you had a great support system here with me."

"No disrespect, Mama, but you weren't here for Serena or me. Church was your life after Daddy died and I was left to try to raise Serena while you popped in from time to time when needed. Maybe my relationship would have lasted and just maybe Sherry wouldn't have felt like she had to go to those clubs to get attention if . . ." Jonathan didn't want to go there, but it was time to come clean about his feelings.

"Just be a man about it. Don't try to blame me for your skeletons just because they are now coming to the light," Crystal snapped.

"Mama, I'm not perfect. I just believed that it would be better for everyone if I left. We didn't have normal childhoods because we were a preacher's kids. You know how you folks are and I didn't want to embarrass you."

Jonathan went in as his emotions took over. He hoped to gain back his freedom and peace of mind. He'd hidden in the closet long enough.

"Okay, mister, you are going to hang yourself with your own leash. Keep right on talking like you are, with all of that attitude, and I'm going to have to pull some rank up in here to remind you who the head of this house is." Crystal stood up and got up in Jonathan's face to make her presence known. "Did you ever go hungry? Huh? One time, were the lights cut off? Did you get what you asked for when you asked for it? When you were sick, who was here to nurse you and your sister back to health? It was me! I was out trying to solidify your future and you complain to me over some rebellious chick who dropped you? If she really loved you . . ." Crystal was out of breath.

Jonathan moved out of range of his mother before she was able to make physical contact again. "You're right about all of that, but one thing was missing and that was you. You were here physically, but the church had taken everything and you gave it freely. Serena and I went without. All you had by the time you came home to us was what was left of you. Crumbs, Mama. Emotionally, you were missing in action. After Sherry dumped me, I wasn't good for anything or anyone. You witnessed firsthand what the breakup did to me, but what you didn't know is that night, my life was torn apart.

"I went to a party after sending Serena over to one of her girlfriends' houses." Jonathan cried as he tried to collect himself. "That night, Mama, you were in revival service and I didn't know how to release the pain I was feeling. I went across town and stopped by my friend Thomas's house where he was having a party. There was alcohol there along with other recreational drugs. I took my first of many drinks that night." He couldn't bear to look into her eyes, so he paced around the kitchen and continued sharing his truth.

"That night, I had my first encounter with a dude. I know it was the pain from the breakup and the alcohol talking when I accepted an invitation from the guy to go into one of the empty rooms. I knew better and should have declined, but I wanted to drown out my feelings of despair. One drink led to another and another and as the hour grew late, I was inebriated. I wasn't a drinker so it didn't take much, but I shouldn't have ever had the first drink. I didn't care about myself, felt as if no one valued me. The guy showed me a little attention and I clung to it. He knew I was vulnerable because I told him what happened and he took advantage of the situation." Tears streamed down Jonathan's face.

Crystal didn't know what to say. She was literally at a loss for words. Her heart was breaking in what felt like a million pieces and she didn't have the strength to do anything about it at the time. A few minutes had gone by and the silence was deafening. Finding her voice, Crystal spoke through her tears. "I'm sorry that you felt as if your only recourse was to dabble in homosexuality. I don't know which is worse: that or the drinking." She threw her hands up in the air dramatically. "Oh, what am I talking about?" she asked herself out loud. "There is no sin bigger than the other. It's all sin just the same.

"Is that the reason you left Amina with us so that you could run off and live out the sexual lifestyle that you opened the door to? I mean if this is the case then I praise God that you did leave her here to be raised in the admonishment of the Lord." Crystal felt angry now that her tears had dried up. "Must I take the blame for everything that went wrong in your life? I have enough guilt to take me to my grave. I'm sorry if I failed you, son, but you have to take responsibility for the bad choices you've made and do something about it. You can't continue to use your past trials as an excuse to disobey God's Word." Crystal ministered Jonathan, hoping it made a difference.

"Mama, you will never understand. You just can't. When I left home, I swore that I wouldn't come back here because of my shame of what I had done. I didn't want it to get back to you that your son had turned into a fag. I got busy filling out as many job applications as I could in the New York area. I felt as if my sins would tarnish you and everything that you worked so hard for. I was confused and angry and I blamed the world for a long time for my troubles," Jonathan admitted.

"You've been brought up to know the difference between right and wrong. You know how God feels about homosexuality. Need I remind you of what happened in Sodom and Gomorrah?" Crystal's voice broke, followed by an avalanche of tears.

Jonathan didn't know what to do. He walked over to his mother, who was standing, and hugged her. "Mama, I'm sorry. The truth of the matter is that I've been living as a homosexual ever since I left home and drinking is my vice to numb the pain that I've put myself through and to dilute the situation itself. My excitement for the relocation was twofold. I was ecstatic that I had gotten the job I applied for. Now I'm one of the top accountants working in the firm." Jonathan needed a drink.

Recollecting herself, Crystal exhaled deeply before speaking. "Jonathan, would you like to come to church with me this morning? I'm sure that the Lord will have a word waiting just for you when you get there." Crystal wrung her hands and didn't realize that she was holding her breath as she waited for a reply.

Jonathan knew the question was coming; however, he wasn't prepared mentally or otherwise to go to church. Wiping his stubbly face, he answered without looking at her: "No, I won't be going to church this morning. I have thousands of things on my mind and God isn't one of them." Jonathan's appetite had returned and he rubbed his grumbling stomach.

"I don't know why you are speaking that way. What do you mean that God isn't one of them?" Crystal shook her head in disbelief.

"What I mean is this: God surely wasn't thinking about me when he allowed me to have my heart shattered or when I lay down with that dude. So like I said, I have things on my mind and you know what else? I had a late night last night and I probably wouldn't be able to stay awake past praise and worship." He knew that would ignite a fire in his mother so he followed it up with an empty promise that he would take her to church for the midweek services. It was his hope that she would leave him alone about the situation, which really wasn't a situation. He was dealing with much more than she would ever understand.

The phone began ringing again and Crystal decided to let Jonathan slide for the moment and answered the phone. "Good morning, Pastor Sampson speaking." She attempted to mask the sadness in her voice. She wasn't sure who it was on the phone since she refused to get rid of her rotary phone from back in the day. She had a cordless as well, but her preference was the traditional mustard yellow phone she had been using for years. There was no caller ID, so she waited for a response.

"Pastor Sampson, it's me, Sister Jalisa. I was just calling to see if you need anything extra this morning so that I can have everything that you need," she said.

"Good morning, Sister Jalisa; you doing all right this morning? I'm running around now trying to get myself together. You know I have to have my cup of coffee so I can make it through the day. I can be pretty on edge if I haven't had my caffeine, but you already know that huh? Well, let's see, do I have two extra pair of pantyhose? You know how I usually go through two pair a service. Oh and please make sure I have the strawberry Crystal Light and a breakfast bar."

"Pastor, I will make sure that I have everything to help make your day go smoothly. Would you like me to come and pick you up or should I just meet you at the church?" Jalisa asked.

"Meet me at the church. I just need to drive and listen to some worship music this morning. I want to make sure that I am in the right frame of mind and pleasing to God," Crystal said and wrapped the phone cord around her pointer finger as she turned around to see if Jonathan was still sitting at the table. To her dismay, she saw only an empty chair. "Sister Jalisa, I will see you soon; and drive carefully, sweetie. Love you."

"I will and will see you soon. I love you, Pastor." The call was disconnected.

Crystal hung up and turned around in a circle counter-clockwise to unravel herself from the long phone cord. She didn't know what was going on in her own house and although her son was grown, she knew that she would have to remind him of who the Indian chief was and who was the Indian. She ran through the house one more time, making sure that she hadn't forgotten anything. Time was running out and she needed to eat a little something but after the conversation with Jonathan, her appetite had disappeared. Crystal grabbed her bag and left her ark of safety with a heavy heart. Before getting into her car, she looked upward and said, "God be with me."

Chapter 17

Church was a cloud. Crystal drove to her daughter's home, oblivious to how she arrived there safely. "Lord, thank you for getting me here without a scratch." She didn't want to come across as clingy, but she felt lonely. Her heart ached as she missed her daughter's and granddaughter's spirits in the midst of it all. More than anything, it hurt her to feel as if her children were excluding her from the most trying time in their lives. Her feet felt bound to the floor of the car as if twenty-pound weights had a hold on her. Pulling down the mirror, Crystal was taken aback by the reflection that stared back at her. Red eyes, runny mascara, and tear-streaked makeup changed Crystal's mind about visiting Serena. She flipped the mirror back up and started the car.

The door opened and Nathaniel exited the house with James by his side. Crystal wished that she could disappear, but it was too late. She had been spotted. "Darn it. Why didn't I just go on home instead of driving over here?" Pasting a fake smile on her face, Crystal put the car back into park and took her time getting out.

"Pastor Sampson, it's good to see you." Nathaniel walked up to her and gave her a gentle hug and genuine smile.

"Hello, Brother Nathaniel. Missed you in church today." She returned his hug and wiped her eye behind his back. Standing and straightening her suit with her hand, she turned to acknowledge James. "Young man, I didn't see you at worship service either." Crystal assumed that James had no church home. Without giving thought, she added, "I do hope that attending church will become a part of your Sunday routine since you are now dating my granddaughter." She eyed him warily.

"Pastor Sampson, I have a church home and I was in service this morning." James was put off by Crystal's rude assumption.

"Oh? Well, I stand corrected. Forgive me, I need to go check on my daughter." Crystal tapped her heels on the concrete driveway. She dismissed them both as she turned and began to walk up toward the house.

"Nathaniel, how is Serena today? I wanted to surprise her." She hadn't expected a reply since she was already at the door and had placed her hand on the knob, entered the house, and pushed the door closed behind her.

"Man, she's straight to the point, isn't she?" Nathaniel patted James on the back, laughing.

"Yeah, she got me over here sweating. I mean the way she spoke to me had me second-guessing where I had been this morning. Those Sampson women, whew, bro, we got our work cut out for us." James shook his head.

"Well we've already won half the battle," Nathaniel said confidently. "We have the hearts of the ladies. Don't take what Pastor Sampson said personally. Give her some time; she will come around and if we do right, then she'll love us and one day we will all be a big, happy family."

"I hope that you're right. One thing is for sure and that's the fact that we are outnumbered and need to stay in the ladies' good graces at all cost." James raised his hand for a high five.

"We men have to stick together, my brother. You have my back and I will have yours." Nathaniel raised his hand to complete the covenant between them by giving James a fist pump.

"I guess we should go ahead and get on out of here. I have to get ready for my next road trip. I will back, in a few days." James moved in the direction of where his car was parked.

"Where you on your way to?" Nathaniel asked.

"Philly. There's a big ol' school shebang going down up there and this up-and-coming group of musicians pay really good. Cha-ching!" James turned around and smacked his pants pockets.

"I heard that and you're right. If it don't make money, it don't make sense. Godspeed, my man. I'll keep you posted on the goings-on around here." Nathaniel respected James's grind, but thought there would be a place for him with his youth center in the near future.

"All right, take it easy. I'll see you soon." James hopped into his Camry and drove off.

Nathaniel went back into the house, just in time to hear the ladies in the kitchen laughing. With all that had transpired in the last couple of months their jovial behavior made his heart long for his own mother and father. The memories of family made him happy that he had Serena and her family in his life. He decided to join them and partake in the fun that was going on around him.

"Sounds like you all are having a great visit." Nathaniel sat at the head of the rectangular oak table and poured himself a glass of lemonade.

"Gran-Gran was telling us something funny that happened during service last week," Amina filled Nathaniel in. "But nobody can tell the story like Gran. Go on, Gran, tell him so I can laugh all over again," Amina said.

"It's a miracle I can even remember what happened last week, but Brother Tremaine asked me if he could sing a song his daddy used to sing. I didn't give him the green light right away. He wasn't aware that I would be honoring his request to sing during the morning service.

I called him up to do his solo right after the choir finished praise and worship. His face turned pale as if he'd seen a ghost.

"He came on up and looked at me before beginning to sing. At first his voice was real squeaky like a mouse, but I knew it was just nerves." Crystal didn't share that she'd already heard Tremaine sing once before. "Laughter could be heard in the congregation and Brother Tremaine stopped as quickly as he had started. I began to clap, you know, to encourage him to go on. Eventually, others caught on to what I was trying to do and they began to clap as well." Crystal took a long swig of her lemonade before finishing the story.

"Well, when Brother Tremaine opened his mouth again, he belted out two verses of 'I Won't Complain.' The bass in his voice had me on my feet with the quickness. His voice was strong and steady. The whole church joined in with him as he sang, giving him the courage he needed. By the time he sang the last note, most of the church was on their feet. They gave him a standing ovation."

"Gran, wow! God knows what He's doing when He brings people together, doesn't He? I can only imagine how Brother Tremaine felt having all of those eyes on him and not to mention that you blindsided him." Amina and Nathaniel laughed as Serena smiled.

"Mommy, from what Amina tells me, you've gotten a little chummy with Brother Tremaine. Is that true? Don't try to deny it. I see the stars in your eyes," Serena said softly.

Nathaniel sat quietly until the women started talking about crushes. He gave Serena a soft kiss on the cheek in preparation to leave. "Well, ladies, I think this is where I exit. I don't want you all to have to change the subject on my account. I have some work to do over at the youth center. Ladies, enjoy the rest of your social call." He stood and cupped his hand, sticking his thumb up and pinky down and put it up to his ear. Nathaniel mouthed, "I'll call you later." He winked at Serena and bid them farewell.

Amina couldn't wait to grill her grandmother some more. This was a first for her, but Amina believed that she wanted to be loved by someone special. "Gran, come on and spill. I've seen you with Brother Tremaine and you laugh like I've not had the pleasure of witnessing since before. He seems to want to get to know you better. Are you ready for love, Gran?" Amina prodded.

Crystal wiped her sweaty palms down her pants suit under the table. She got nervous just thinking about the almond brown brother who made her sit up and take notice. If someone would have told her that she would fall in love again, she would have rebuked that sister or brother and started to pray earnestly that their moment of temporary insanity wouldn't last long. Crystal sat with her daughter and granddaughter, unable to deny that she felt something for Brother Tremaine. "I like him. I really like him a lot." Crystal placed her hands on top of the table and reached for her glass of lemonade, noticing the glass was empty.

Serena picked up the pitcher and poured more of the sugary, pulpy lemonade into her mother's glass. Amina had squeezed fresh lemons and added sugar and ice earlier. She was happy that her mother was there, but she couldn't help but to wonder where Jonathan was. He'd broken his promise to be with her until the storm passed. He promised that he wasn't going anywhere yet and he'd been MIA for too long. Placing the lemonade back down on the table, Serena grabbed one of the muffins that sat on the table. She said a quick prayer and picked the blueberry muffin, testing it out.

It was no secret that her taste buds had been out of whack since she began therapy; however, she needed to take her medication. "Mommy, where is Jonathan? I thought he was staying with you." Serena said, putting a small piece of muffin into her mouth and chewing slowly.

"Your brother has been holed up in the house practically since he got here. It's usually hit or miss when we bump into each other. I'm up and gone and he's still in his room with the door shut. When I get home, he's usually out. I saw him briefly this morning and asked him to accompany me to church, but he declined. He also said that he would swing through soon." Crystal didn't want to discuss what was really going on with her son in front of Amina.

"I called him since he hadn't called me and asked him when he was coming over to see us," Amina spoke up. "Gran, do you know how much longer he will be here in town? I have been by at least twice and there's never an answer. I just figure he's going through something and that eventually he'll reach out to me. There's so much I want to talk to him about." Amina glanced at Serena and smiled shyly.

"Baby, I'm not sure how long he will be here. We didn't discuss that this morning. I'm just so happy to have someone at the house with me that I hadn't even thought about how quickly time has flown by. I am shocked that he's been here this long." Crystal hoped that the subject would switch to something else soon.

Amina's cell phone chirped, alerting her of a text message. Even though she was wondering what was going on with her dad, her thoughts were consumed with James. When she looked down, she saw it was Jalisa. "Excuse me, ladies. I need to take this." Amina hurried to her bedroom to call her sister.

"Hello?" Jalisa answered on the first ring.

"Hi. Didn't your mother teach you that you don't answer the phone on the first ring?" They both laughed, and then silence.

"So, I'm going to get straight to the point. You told me that I could call you if I needed to talk. Are you free right now?" Jalisa examined her face in the bathroom mirror.

"Are we going to discuss a possible relationship? Or something else; either way, I have time." Amina flopped onto her bed, which remained unmade from earlier that morning. Not liking the bumpiness of the bunched covers, she put Jalisa on speakerphone and hopped back up to close her door for privacy. She sat on the edge of her bed and waited for Jalisa to open up.

"I went on a date last night." Jalisa paused for effect.

"OMG! You've got to tell me all about it. Is this someone I know, or what? Where did you go and how did the date turn out? Is he cute? Whoa, let me back it up; is the brother saved?" Amina threw the questions at Jalisa so fast that she couldn't keep up.

"Pump your brakes, lady. Well, I know him. Not well, but he seemed to be really interested in getting to know me. He's a music major at North Carolina Central University and he is the ministry leader at Church on the Rock, in Durham. He lives here in Bahama. The first thing I asked him was he saved or just going to church. We all know that everyone who goes to church ain't saved. There's only one thing . . ." Jalisa explained.

"Girl, what's the problem? He's saved and he has a plan for his future. Makes me wonder about what James will be doing as far as work in the long term." Amina mentally left the conversation.

"I guess you're right. My issue is that he stays on campus and there are tons of girls. I don't want to get tied up with him and then he's two-timing me with some other chick. What do you suggest? Should I proceed or just shut him down now?" Jalisa waited, and it was so quiet she started to think that the call had gotten disconnected somehow. "Amina? Girl, are you still on the line?" Jalisa heard minimal noise on the other end, which let her know that the call definitely was not disconnected. "Amina! What are you doing?" Jalisa huffed, feeling as though she had wasted the last three minutes of her life on nothing.

"Oh, I'm so sorry, sis. I had a moment. What were you saying?" The cloud over Amina's head vanished as she was brought back to the conversation.

"Never mind. I hate repeating myself and obviously you are distracted." Jalisa rubbed the side of her face, wiping a tear away.

"Sister, I apologize. It's just that it seems like we are both in fresh relationships and my mind went to the what ifs concerning James. I'm not too busy or distracted to listen to you. Can we try this again?" Amina felt bad and didn't want to hang up on a bad note.

"Apology accepted, and as I was saying . . ." Jalisa told Amina again where her insecurities stemmed from. They sat on the phone for the next hour giggling like schoolgirls as they encouraged one another to fight for their men.

Chapter 18

The dreaded moment had arrived, but Crystal just didn't know how to begin the much-needed conversation with Serena. She knew that it was now or never, so she prepared herself for the inevitable. "Serena, baby, how would you like to go into the den so we can relax a little. I can bring the glasses and freshen up the lemonade if you'd like." Crystal had to concentrate on keeping her voice from wavering.

"Okay, that would be nice." Serena got up to go into the den, wondering what was going on with her mother. She knew it was more than she let on, but prayerfully, whatever it was, Serena hoped that her mother would be freed up by whatever burdens she was bound by. With all that was going on in her life, she vowed to let go of any of the trivial things that she had tucked away in her heart.

Crystal followed up the rear with fruit, muffins, and lemonade. "Oh, Mommy, can you get me a bottle of water?" Serena asked slightly above a whisper.

"Sure, sweetie." Crystal gladly returned to the kitchen to retrieve a bottle of water for her daughter. She smiled upon returning and handing her the cool drink.

"Mommy, why are you smiling so hard?" Serena asked, smiling in return.

"Baby, it's been such a long time since you have needed me for anything. Sometimes I have to laugh to keep from crying." Tears formed in Crystal's eyes as she talked. They overflowed her eyelids and fell onto her face.

"Mommy, what's wrong?" Serena reached over to her mother and hugged her. She wasn't quite sure what was going on at that moment but the last thing she ever wanted was to see her mother cry. It touched her deeply.

"I was just thinking about how blessed I am. God has truly been good to me all of these years. He blessed me with Jonathan and you and I'm grateful. I know I've said as much before but it was at the most stressful time for you. I don't want you to think that I was only speaking from pure emotion or the feeling that you wouldn't come through the surgery. So, I'm blessing God that I have the opportunity to tell you again." Crystal almost lost her nerve due to Serena's steady gaze.

"Mommy, is something deeper going on here? I mean are you physically healthy and is Jonathan okay?" Panic built inside Serena's stomach and she didn't want to think the worst.

"I just want to let you know that your brother and I had a little heart-to-heart this morning and for someone who has always been so introverted about everything, he let me know the content of his heart. I feel like I've failed you both as a mother and for that I'm sincerely sorry. You both are grown now and there's no way for us to go back in time for a do-over, but I've prayed that God would redeem time for this family so that everything broken would be made new in Him," Crystal said.

"Aw, Mommy, you are not a failure. Granted, you and I don't have the type of relationship or friendship that I've desired all of these years. I have to take responsibility for the foolish things I did in the past. I was always placing blame on you, but only because I wanted you to notice me. I needed you, Mommy. We had lost Dad and it seemed like we had lost you as well, although you were still alive," Serena said softly. "I was no angel and for all that you endured because of me, I'm sorry. Mommy, I love you and sometimes we suppress negative things that have happened in our lives and it births unforgiveness and strife. That's all we have shared throughout the years. Playing nice and really not wanting to deal with one another any longer than a few minutes or hours at a time." Serena's emotions were taking over and this was one of the few times that she allowed herself to be vulnerable in front of her mother.

"Aren't we a mess? We preach God's Word and encourage His people in different arenas, you all over the world, yet we have been bleeding on the inside due to our own brokenness. Isn't it funny how we can minister to everyone else and see the light at the end of their tunnels, yet not be able to reveal our own hurts and failures to one another?" Crystal laughed through her tears.

"Yes, but praise God that He isn't through with us yet. In the book of James, He tells us that we are to confess our sins to each other and pray for each other so that we may be healed. I know God had blessed me with a double portion of the anointing through the power of the Holy Spirit, but I couldn't see my own faults. I blamed you for so long for our strained relationship and I was wrong. I'm still believing God for restoration of my health and my vocal cord so that I can continue to glorify Him." Serena grabbed her throat and rubbed her neck.

"Are you in pain?" Crystal almost knocked her glass of lemonade over.

Serena shook her head and pointed to the kitchen. "I'll be back, gotta take my medication." She went back to the kitchen and crushed one five-hundred-milligram Vicodin and poured it into another cup of lemonade.

"Sweetie, do you need me to do that for you?" Crystal walked up behind Serena, taking in her fragile-looking frame. She was wearing the same jogging suit she'd worn the day of her surgery and it hung loosely off of her. An emotional tidal wave hit Crystal. "Serena?" She gasped, clutching her chest, and turned away.

Serena swung around so fast that she almost knocked her glass onto the floor. "Mommy, are you okay?" Serena ran to her side and rubbed her back while her mother swayed from side to side.

"Why, God? Why my baby? Wasn't my husband enough? I've apologized for my faults and repented. Haven't I been punished enough? Perfect I'm not, but I've been faithful." Crystal hollered upward and doubled over, grabbing her abdomen. Her posture could have easily been mistaken as an illness, but Serena knew that her mother was travailing and releasing the pain that the enemy used to keep her bound.

Amina got there as quickly as she could upon hearing the screams from inside her bedroom. "Gran, Auntie, what happened in here? Is she going to be okay? Do we need to call nine-one-one?" Amina asked.

Serena nodded her head yes, but didn't speak. She hugged her mother, hoping that it would bring comfort. It blessed her as she had never been afforded the opportunity to be there for her mother that way. Taking hold of her mother's hand, in the midst of Crystal's cries, Serena met her mother on the floor and began to pray for her mother that every chain be broken so that the freedom to live, love, and forgive would be deposited within the trio. Feeling drained, Serena motioned for Amina to connect and lead them to the throne of grace.

Amina's eyes widened and she shook her head no frantically. She hated to defy her aunt's wishes, but she hadn't ever seen her grandmother acting that way. Amina looked back at Serena, knowing that she shouldn't be down on the floor straining with her grandmother.

Amina was depleted spiritually and she didn't want to be needed right then. Not really sure if she had anything more to offer, she kneeled down and laid one hand on her grandmother and one on her aunt. She gained the strength from the pit of her belly and she prayed one of her most powerful prayers.

Chapter 19

Jonathan looked at the caller ID on the cordless phone and saw that the number was restricted. He had hoped that it wasn't Amina calling to ask him when he was coming through again. "Yeah," Jonathan bellowed into the phone over the running water.

"Mm, is that a shower I hear in the background?" Sedric laughed in his high-pitched voice.

"Why are you calling from a restricted number? Why are you just calling me back after the trouble you caused me and money you cost me? Did you think it was funny? Playing games like that can get you hurt. You wouldn't take my phone calls and now it's been three months since you pulled that stunt. And how did you get my mother's number?" Jonathan fumed.

"Oh, I can tell you miss me. When are you coming back to New York, lover?" Sedric asked, turned on by Jonathan's anger toward him. His toes curled, knowing that the man he loved was still affected by him.

"I can't believe you would do that to me. At the expense of me getting to my sister?" Jonathan hissed.

"Oh, darling. I guess I should apologize, but I won't. By the way, how is your darling sister? The sister you hardly talked about throughout the years we've been together. You were so upset the days after you received the news about her. You treated me bad, Jonathan. Hurt my feelings, kicked me out of your bed, heart, home, and your life," Sedric continued his rant.

"How did you get this number?" Jonathan tried to remain unaffected by what Sedric was saying.

Sedric ignored Jonathan's question and unleashed his fury. "You used me, Jonathan. Even after you kicked me out, you called me back for your benefit only. I helped you, but I also wanted to punish you the best way I knew how. I obviously don't have your heart, but I know how to mess with your wallet." Sedric gloated at first for messing up Jonathan's tickets, but as he talked about it, he felt a tinge of remorse.

"Life is too short to sit around hashing and rehashing what once was." Jonathan tried to redeem himself. "I'm sorry if I hurt you, but you knew that I wasn't ever comfortable with being with a man. We've had many conversations about this and something about you drew me to you."A knock on the door interrupted Jonathan's train of thought. "Hold on," he whispered. Without waiting for Sedric to reply, he placed the phone on the clothes hamper and threw his towel over it to conceal it. "Yes, Mama," he answered.

"Are you okay in there?" Crystal asked on her way out to church service.

"Yes, why do you ask?" A wave of fear ran through him and he grasped the corners of the sink to hold himself steady.

"It sounds like you were having a conversation with someone. Who were you talking to?" Crystal pressed her ear to the bathroom door knowingly.

"No one, Mama. I was just talking to myself, that's it," he lied. He hated feeling like he needed to do so. If he'd been in the comforts of his own home, he wouldn't have to answer to anyone.

"Son, I know what I heard. Never mind that; have you changed your mind about accompanying me to church?" Crystal was in an uphill battle when it came to her son and she was ready to fight until he was free of the demonic holds that homosexuality and alcoholism had him entangled in.

"Ah, nah, Mama. I haven't changed my mind." He rubbed his head, hoping that the conversation would end so that he could get back to Sedric. The call itself had stirred up some unresolved desire inside of him.

"Jonathan, you promised me that you would go. It's been three weeks since and each time I ask you to come, you decline. Evangelist Curry and some of the other long-time members ask about you all the time," Crystal pleaded.

"Just tell everyone I said hello and that I will be to church soon." Jonathan sighed.

"Soon? What is soon, Jonathan? How long are you planning to be here and not connect with your family? You have yet to reach out to Amina, your daughter. How can you behave so callously? It's like you don't give a hoot about anyone, but yourself." Crystal was ready to unleash the lion and if it came to that, Jonathan wasn't going to like it.

"Mama, not now, okay? I'm trying to take a shower. I don't want you worrying about me. Keep your focus; you're on your way to minister to God's people," he shouted through the door.

"Don't try to shut me up by dismissing me. I'm still your mother even though you up and left us here to raise your daughter while you decided to go and live a double life. I can't even believe that you of all people, who knows God, would even open the door to that foul and perverted spirit. You need to prepare to make tracks on out of this house. I refuse to continue to tolerate your pigheaded attitude. I'm sick of tiptoeing around you like you run the show around here." Crystal paused to catch her breath.

"I'm going to clean my house, beginning right this minute. How does it look for me, a pastor over many of God's flock, to preach to others about homosexuality and my own son is gay? I guess I'm just going to have to face the fact that you're gay and you're a drunk. You're gonna have to take it outta here and you'd better go and see your sister and daughter because if you don't, I will expose your behind. Makes me sick just looking at you." Crystal stomped off down the stairs, grabbing her satchel and keys. She made sure that she slammed the door extra hard.

Jonathan waited to hear the garage door open and jumped to peep out of the blinds to see his mother descend the driveway. He meditated on their conversation and he knew that Crystal was a devout Christian. She wasn't playing with him and he knew it. Fear and shame attempted to hold him hostage once again, but he vowed that no longer would he be enslaved to people's opinions of him.

Fuming, Jonathan didn't even respond to his mother. She wanted him out then he would get out. *You make me sick . . . tolerate you . . . you're gay* repeated itself in his mind like a record that had been scratched and stuck. He turned and snatched his towel off of the hamper and saw the phone hit the floor. He wondered if Sedric had heard the exchange between him and his mother.

Angrily, he threw the phone into the toilet when he heard Sedric calling out to him. His voice disgusted him and he wished that he could go back in time and undo all of the foolish things he had done in his life. Tears fought their way past his eyelids and he felt like all hope was lost.

He wailed as he finally was able to come to terms with his alcohol dependency and his alternate lifestyle and call them what they were. "I'm gayyyy! I'm damaged and I'm a drunk who was a respectable man who's been turned out." Jonathan lamented and screamed as loudly and long as he could until he had nothing left to release.

Drained yet still angry, Jonathan was overtaken in shame and fury. *I will tell them about you, gay, homosexual.* All he wanted was for the voice of his mother to be silenced in his mind. He tried to talk to God, but gave that thought up with a smirk.

"God is the reason I'm here, the reason I turned out to be a failure. He took my father from me. He didn't care that he was a pastor. Yeah, he appointed my father because he loved God, and what did God do? Let him die. I'm a dude on the down low who covers up his ultimate sins by drowning his sins with alcohol. I'm out of here. She wants to expose me? I will go and do it myself. Everyone has been on me to go see my family, so I'm going and I hope they are ready for me and the news I have for them," Jonathan declared as he threw on some clothes.

Jonathan walked over to his closet where shoeboxes housed cans of alcohol and beer. He'd hidden them there for times like these. He needed anything that could numb his senses. Jonathan shuffled through the boxes and saw that his stash was running low. He knew that he would have to go out to get more before his mother got home from church.

He snatched the bottle by the neck and twisted the cap off. His eyes caught a picture of him holding baby Amina not long after she was released from the hospital. He picked it up with his free hand while he grasped a Samuel Adams beer in his left hand. Gazing at the picture, he took a swig of the beer and then another and another. He didn't know when to stop, so he didn't. Five beers later, Jonathan was still holding on to the picture. Thoughts of falling into temptation that night with a complete stranger interrupted thoughts of loving, living, and raising his daughter.

The next sounds that could be heard came from the picture frame crashing into the wall. Shards of glass were everywhere and Jonathan didn't have time to get out of the way before catching some in the face. Blood ran down his face from the impact. Due to his drunken state, he didn't feel the pain. The emptiness in his heart surpassed anything he could have felt physically. Stumbling down the stairs, Jonathan snatched the car keys from the key holder on the kitchen wall. Five minutes later, he was sitting in the car that he'd recently had cleaned and peeled out of the driveway in the direction of the nearest corner store.

The grace of God kept Jonathan as he made it to the store. He ran into the convenience store and left the car running. Making several trips to the counter with armfuls of beer and liquor, Jonathan pulled out his billfold to pay the cashier.

"Sir, are you okay?" the cashier asked. Her smile was replaced by a look of horror and then her mouth involuntarily turned downward into a frown.

"I'm fine. How much?" Jonathan asked with slurred words.

"Sir, are you sure that I can't get you some assistance? Your face is bleeding," she offered.

"I said I'm fine. Now how much for the booze?" Jonathan asked.

"Fifty-seven eighty-eight," the cashier replied.

"Here, check these out," Jonathan instructed the cashier and handed her a stack of credit cards.

She took one and placed the remaining in the stack back on the countertop. Fifteen minutes later, Jonathan sat in his car and let it sit idle. He had opened one drink and chugged it down like he was drinking water and not a fresh, cold beer. His plan was to chase away the thoughts of negativity, failure, and the low-down lifestyle he had been dabbling in for the last eighteen years.

Jonathan pulled out of the convenience store parking lot feeling a little more at ease. Those feelings dissipated when the voices started taunting him and calling him out of his name. Jonathan took one hand off of the steering wheel and swatted at his head in efforts to make the noises stop. "I've got to get to the church. Mama, I need you. The demons are running loose and I need you." He was in and out of consciousness by that point and he pressed his foot down on the gas pedal, trying to outrun the devil.

He never saw the officer sitting off to the side of the road, lying in wait for someone like him to break the speeding law. Jonathan was oblivious to what was going on around him because he was preoccupied with the voices. They laughed at him and told him he would be nothing but a drunk for the rest of his life. He pleaded with the voices to leave him alone and even called on the name of the Lord to help make them flee.

The police car had been flashing its lights since the time that Jonathan sped by the officer unaware. When the police officer realized that the person he was pursuing didn't heed to the red and blue, he radioed for backup and turned on his mini bullhorn attached to his side mirror. He turned on the sirens and gained speed to catch up to Jonathan, who was clearly driving at a dangerously fast speed.

Bile rose up in Jonathan's chest as he realized that he was going to jail. He looked down at the speedometer to see that he was driving seventy miles per hour. He wasn't sure what the speed limit was, but figured he had surpassed it if the cops were trying to get him. His eyes spotted the open cans of beer. Instead of pulling over to the side of the road and taking his chances, Jonathan pressed his foot harder onto the pedal.

A car chase ensued. It was on, but it didn't last long. Jonathan tried to outrun the police officer en route to Abiding Savior. He hadn't thought about the fact that there were now five cruisers on his trail and they had given to full chase. At that point, Jonathan didn't think that there would be anything he could say to explain why he was speeding and had a barrage of open and unopened alcoholic beverages in the car.

Jonathan couldn't stop. His life flashed before his eyes and he cursed the voices, cursed his daughter's mother, and cursed the men who floated in and out of his life. Tears streamed down his face and his vision became blurry. Reaching over to turn the music as loud as it would go, he didn't see the eighteen-wheeler as he veered over the center lane and crashed. Everything went black.

Chapter 20

James rang the doorbell. He had come to see his lady and check on Serena's progress. He'd just gotten back from his third road trip in the span of a month and he had missed Amina. Her eyes lit up when she answered the door and saw James on the other side of it.

"James, oh my gosh. What? When did you get back?" Serena ran and jumped into his arms. She held on to him, not wanting to let go.

"Hey, beautiful." He laughed. "Whoa, you going to make a brother drop these flowers I got for your auntie." James hid one hand behind his back that held a single red rose for Amina.

"Oh, I apologize. I am just so surprised to see you. Especially since you told me that you wouldn't be back in town for a couple more days. I'm so happy that you're back." Amina kissed his lips quickly.

"I missed you too, beautiful." James's eyes grew wide in shock that Amina had kissed him first.

"Let me help you with those." Amina dropped her gaze, not believing her own boldness in the moment. She had prayed that she didn't get too caught up too quickly. She reached out to take the flowers.

"These are for your aunt. I hope that she's doing well." James handed the vase to Amina, waiting to see if she would invite him in.

Amina admired and sniffed the flowers. "Did you just say that these are for my aunt?" Her eyebrows furrowed before turning and leaving James standing there.

She was well into the kitchen when she heard him ask: "What's the matter? Are you going to invite me in, or what?" James felt the shift in her attitude by her body language. He smirked and shook his head.

"Suit yourself," Amina hollered through the house over her shoulder with her back turned.

James walked in and shut the door. He followed Amina into the kitchen, where she stood rearranging the flowers. Quietly, he leaned up against the counter and watched her in awe. She was beautiful. He had learned a little about what made her happy and what angered her. James was excited about their relationship and he hoped that standing before him was his wife-to-be. Finally, Serena turned around to see him staring at her. Anger flashed in her eyes before he pulled his arm from behind his back, revealing a beautiful red rose in full bloom.

"For you, *ma cherie amour.*" His white teeth sparkled as he held the rose out to her.

Amina ran into his arms and lay her head on his chest. "I was a little jealous. I thought that you hadn't thought about me enough to bring me something. My mind was all over the place. I'm sorry for leaving you standing at the door." Amina stared James in his eyes and she felt fireworks. She wasn't sure if he'd forgiven her because his reaction was delayed.

"You're my lady. Did you really think that I would bring another woman flowers and neglect to show you how much I'm into you?" James wrapped his arms around Amina's waist. "I missed you so much that I broke all kinds of speed limits trying to get back here. I wanted to surprise you by coming over." James kissed Amina lightly on the lips.

"I like the sound of that. To be honest, I didn't realize I had a jealous bone in my body. I guess I'm learning new things about myself as well. I apologize for my behavior. Now that I know that I have an issue with insecurity, I will begin to pray about it immediately. I don't want to run you off. I really am a mature adult," Amina pleaded her case.

James chuckled to lighten the mood. "Come on, let's go sit down." James led Amina to the living room. He felt her tugging on his hand, not really sure why. He continued to go in the direction of the living room with resistance from Amina. Getting a little impatient with her resistance, he gave her a questioning look.

"Auntie would have a fit if she came home to find us in the living room. She usually entertains in there and is a germaphobe. Every time someone leaves, she has me wipe down everything with Clorox wipes and mop the floors thoroughly." Amina pulled him into the public sitting room behind her and gestured for him to go in before her.

James sat down and pulled Amina down onto his lap. "What's that you're wearing? Mm, you smell good, girl." James relaxed.

"Oh, you like this fragrance?" Amina giggled. "It's called Indian Sandalwood and it's my favorite. I'm glad that you like the way it smells on me. How was your trip?" she asked.

"It was good. Happy to have made it back in one piece. How are things going around here? Has there been any noticeable change in her health?" James was genuinely concerned, as he respected Serena.

"Well, she's actually at the cancer clinic right now at UNC. This whole ordeal has weighed her down. Her esteem is a little low right now, especially with the tabloids coming up with all kinds of scenarios about her illness. She doesn't go out much, but when she does, those who recognize her are always snapping pictures on their phones and tablets. Have you seen the gossip magazines? It's too much." Amina filled James in on what was going on with Serena.

He massaged her shoulders, hoping that she would be able to relax. James wasn't really good at being there emotionally for anyone. Being an only child, he only had to worry about himself. His grandmother raised him after his mother was placed into a mental institution after his father was hit by a drunken driver one night. "I'm really sorry that she's going through all of this. Truth is I have seen some of the tabloids that had her plastered across the first page of the magazines, looking sickly and smaller than I remember her to be. One thing I know is that she is a woman of great faith. And for all of the women and men alike that she has been a blessing to, I believe that God will cause her to win this battle with cancer. I continually pray for her." James's voice seemed to fade as his mind drifted to all of the times he'd called on Serena for prayer or spiritual guidance.

Amina looked surprised. "James, I didn't realize you were a praying man." She smiled and poked him in his chest playfully.

"Yes, I am. I take my salvation very seriously and I have Prophetess Serena to thank for that. She singlehandedly changed my mind about church and Christianity and as soon as my work schedule slows down, I will probably come and join you all at Abiding Savior. I've lost my zeal over at Grace Baptist Church." James was ready to make some major changes in his life, but he wasn't quite sure of how he would do it all right then.

"Thank you for your prayers. Please keep them coming. She needs them. When she comes home from therapy she's usually tired and only wants to sleep until the nausea kicks in. If she's lucky, she'll wake up in time and get to the bathroom when she gets sick. It's hard to prepare meals for her because she complains that everything tastes like metal." Amina paused as she thought about what her aunt was having to go through and tears came to her eyes. "It's hard watching her day in and day out, but she's a fighter, that's for sure." Sadness settled on Amina's shoulders.

Changing the subject from something that made her sad, Amina jumped up from the couch and headed toward the kitchen. "Would you like something to drink or eat? We have all kinds of soups, fruit, and drinks if you're hungry or thirsty."Amina prepped two glasses with ice and pulled the iced tea from the refrigerator.

James followed Amina into the kitchen." You know, we haven't been out together yet. I would love to take you for a bite to eat and maybe go to the park for a while. I don't want you to worry so much. God has this thing under control," James said confidently.

"What are you smiling so hard about, Mr. Man?" Amina asked, handing James an iced tea.

"Just thinking about you, me, us. It's enough to make a happy man smile. So what do you say? Would you like to spend some time with me at the park after getting a bite to eat? I still would like to get to know more about you and I'm sure you have questions about the man I am." James smiled again, never taking his eyes off Amina as he sipped his tea.

Feeling bold, Amina stepped to James and took the glass out of his hands. Her hand shook from nervous energy but she pressed on. She leaned in and kissed James fully. She didn't want a peck; she wanted to feel more of a connection with him. Amina was all in with him and at the same time she was afraid of disappointing God. James put his arms around her waist and gave himself to her. Throwing all caution to the wind, they both blocked out warnings of the spirit to slow it down.

James was the first to break away from the kiss and from Amina. The smell of her skin was intoxicating and the feel of her lips ignited the desire inside of him. *Click!* He heard the lock click on his heart and was ready to grow with her. Collecting himself as best he could, he didn't rush to speak. He rubbed his hands down the leg of his pants, trying to calm himself down and redirecting his thoughts. "Wow! Now that was a mouthful." James laughed nervously. He led Amina back toward the den and they sat down.

"Was I being overbearing?" Amina blushed with embarrassment. She hoped that she didn't turn him off by bum-rushing him.

"Oh no, you're fine." James flashed his pearly whites at Amina. "I don't want to give you the impression that all I want is your body or that we can only really connect on a physical level." James stared at Amina long and hard, hoping that she believed what he was saying. "Amina, I admire your boldness. Confession: I have watched how you carry yourself and I never took it personal when you would order me around.

"I've been looking for someone I could grow with for a long time. Someone who doesn't feel the need to flaunt their Christianity in everyone's face, but allows their light to shine by their actions and the way they carry themselves." James sighed before speaking again. "I've done some things in the past that I am not so proud of, but I am truly thankful that Prophetess Serena trusts me enough to transport you both to and from your destinations. It is an honor to be able to watch you blossom into the woman of God I need in my life." James knew he was blessed.

"James, I can appreciate what you're saying. One question: how long had you been checking for me?" Amina smiled.

"Honestly, I'd been checking you out for almost a year. I've always known you are younger than I am, so I never let on that I was watching you." He closed his eyes and reminisced.

"Oh wow, so you knew that you would be sitting here one day?" Amina shook her head as if she knew the answer.

"Hold up, that's not what I said. I must say that I'm thoroughly pleased that you give me the time of day. While I hoped for an opportunity to get with you, I wouldn't say I assumed that would be the case. I didn't think you'd want to be bothered with the help." James twiddled his fingers.

"I guess you thought wrong, Mr. Jones. I would say that God knows our beginning from our end. I didn't even know that this would be happening, but I am so blessed to be able to be your lady," Amina said. "Oh, and I know your favorite color must be blue because you're always wearing it," she added.

James felt at peace with Amina and prayed in his heart that one day he would feel comfortable enough to share his life with her. He wanted to hold on to the moment and hoped that she wouldn't ask too many questions. "I'm twenty-three years old and my birthday is in December. It's on the twenty-fourth, to be exact. You're very perceptive and I like that about you. You're a woman who pays attention to detail. I guess I can assume that you won't forget my birthday or my favorite color. Christmas can't come soon enough for a brother." They both laughed.

"Well, I had been talking about you to my auntie and I wanted to speak with my dad concerning our relationship. I've been feeling some kind of way about him staying away. I haven't seen him since we were all at the hospital together. He's been gone most of my life and my prayer is that God would help us to build, but without a foundation . . ." Feelings of anger and sadness collided. Amina was on an emotional rollercoaster.

"Whoa, you've been talking to Prophetess Serena about me? Ah, man, what did she have to say? She didn't prophesy about me, like anything bad, did she?" James was visibly shaken up by the thought of Prophetess Serena telling Amina that it wouldn't be a good idea to get involved with him because of his past.

Amina laughed at the serious look on James's face. He made her smile through her tears. She hoped that he didn't think she was this emotional all the time. She knew that he respected her aunt to the utmost and her opinion of him as far as being a male suitor meant the world to him. Amina let him ponder her aunt's response about him just a little longer.

It wasn't until she witnessed him wringing his hands together that she decided to end his torment. "Auntie didn't have anything negative to say about you and she didn't have a prophecy concerning you either. She did caution me to depend on God so that He can direct my paths concerning every aspect of my life," Amina said.

It was James's turn to let out a huge sigh of relief. "So, if we have Prophetess Serena's stamp of approval, then I only have to go through the approval process of Pastor Sampson and your dad?" James was visibly nervous.

"It doesn't matter if they approve. It's you and me until you show me something different. I make my own decisions, so don't worry about Gran-Gran and my dad," Amina said with determination.

"I hear you, but what about your grandmother? She didn't seem too thrilled with me the last time I saw her. She hinted that she knew about us and didn't hesitate to let me know that I need to be in church if I planned to date you," James said with a serious expression on his face.

"What? Why are you just saying something about that? It's totally unacceptable. Please forgive her." Amina was embarrassed by her grandmother's behavior but not surprised. "My grandmother can be so crass. She doesn't do well with tactfulness; whatever she feels, she's just going to say it."

"It's cool. You should be happy that Pastor Sampson loves you and wants who is best for you. She knows what God has anointed you to be and she's right to get at me early on. At least I know what I need to do to remain on her good side." James smiled.

"We have to take things slow. I want you to know up front that I am saving myself for marriage. If you can't handle that, then I will understand and we can continue to have a cordial friendship."

"You're taking me too fast. If it makes you feel any better, I want you to know that I am also keeping myself until the day I am married. My intentions toward you are pure, so the only things you have to worry about are my tiny imperfections." James used his thumb and pointer finger to signify what he meant. "I know we are both young, but I don't plan to date forever. I am ready to be a good husband to some lucky lady and, who knows, that could be you."

"Okay, Mr. Jones, you know that the just live by faith. I know that God favors me, and luck has nothing to do with it." Amina playfully nudged James on the arm and they both laughed. They talked and laughed like two high school kids until Serena and Nathaniel came through the door from her chemotherapy appointment. It worked out well since James's main reason for coming was to see how she was doing. The laughter stopped when Nathaniel, who was attending to Serena, held her arm and led her through the living room straight to her bedroom.

Amina and James both jumped up to see if there was anything that needed to be done. Nathaniel explained that Serena had an allergic reaction to the heparin flush the nurses used in order to make sure there would be a good blood flow after accessing her vein. He further explained that the nurse used Benadryl to reverse the allergic reaction and Serena was pretty much out of it when she was released from their care.

"So how was the appointment itself?" Amina asked as her voice followed Nathaniel and Serena to the back of the house.

Nathaniel reappeared and said, "I guess for the most part all was okay. Your aunt is a trooper, even when she complained about being hungry after having had a hearty breakfast. She was famished and wanted more food after the first bag of chemotherapy hit her system. She sent me on two food runs, but I didn't mind. There wasn't anything she could ask me for that I wouldn't have done for her. She was also unhappy that there were only two bathrooms in the bay area, where all of the patients were getting various treatments during the same time. She said the liquids had her running to the bathroom and once she had forgotten to unplug her medicine pole. She said that she was only able to travel so far before the pole snapped back and by the time she could walk the pole back to the wall to unplug it, there was a line formed at both of the bathrooms."

"I'm sure that had to make for a long day. That would be exhausting in itself. Add the allergic reaction and, man . . ." James felt bad for one of his favorite people and he vowed to pray even harder on her behalf. He missed going out on the road with such a phenomenal woman, but he was just glad that he had a legitimate reason to come over anyway. He was becoming family since Amina and he were dating.

"She's going to be just fine. I am going to go check on her and make sure she's settled in and I'll be back out to rap to you all some more." Nathaniel left them alone.

Amina turned around and bumped right into James, who was on her heels. They laughed and James backed up so that Amina could get by to go to the kitchen. He picked up their tea glasses and followed her. She ran some dishwater in the sink and mouthed, "Thank you, Lord." She placed the glasses into the sudsy water and turned around to see James staring at her. "What's wrong, James?" Amina asked.

"Nothing's wrong, nothing at all. I was just enjoying the view." He smiled and reached for her hand. Amina instantly forgot that her hands were wet as she received James's hand in hers. She walked into his waiting arms and laid her head on his chest. Amina held on to James, not wanting to break the embrace because it felt so right. The two were caught up in their separate thoughts when they heard a sound behind them.

"Erhmm." Nathaniel cleared his throat and coughed into his hands as an alert that he had entered the room, certain that what he saw was more than just a friendly hug. Amina and James dropped their hands to their sides abruptly and moved away from one another as if the other had the plague.

No one said anything and if one had a knife, the tension could be sliced. Nathaniel was the first to speak up. "Uh, I hope I didn't interrupt anything."

"No, no, you didn't. We were just um . . ." James jumped.

Finding her voice, Amina jumped in to help out. "I was feeling a little emotional after talking to James about my father and all we are dealing with and he provided the comfort I needed." She smiled at both of the men, who both wore silly looks on their faces.

"Okay, well I'm outta here. Your aunt is resting peacefully and probably will until the effects of the chemotherapy wear off. If you need me, you know what to do. Now, I'm leaving, but you two behave." Nathaniel laughed and shook his head as the door closed behind him.

James smiled at Amina, hating to have to tell her that he came home early only to have to leave again. "Sweetie, I wanted to let you know that I am driving Pastor Mack to Charleston, South Carolina for the Men's Empowerment Conference first thing in the morning. I won't be back until Thursday and I need to get going so that I can make sure the Town Car is clean and gassed up."

The phone rang before Amina could respond to James, but her spirit sank at the news. It took her a moment to move toward the kitchen for the cordless phone to answer it. She remembered that Serena was resting in her room and dashed toward the phone, but it was too late. The voice mail had answered the call, so she decided to check it later and spend those last few moments with James. She was sure that he needed time to get himself together before heading out of town again. "Lord, please. I hope that our relationship won't only consist of stolen moments and high cell phone bills due to talking all of our minutes up and going beyond each month." The phone began to ring again and Amina felt like something was wrong because no one called anyone back-to-back if everything was okay.

"Hello?" Amina said into the phone as she cradled it between her chin and shoulder. She held up one finger to let James know that it would only be a minute. Her face transformed into a scowl and her breath caught in her throat before the shrill scream gurgled from her throat. "Noooooooooooooo."

James sprang into action and ran over to Amina to take the phone from her. He finished up the conversation with the person on the other end of the phone. Clicking the off button, James led Amina to the chaise longue and literally placed her down on it. She was crying hysterically and was talking gibberish that he could not understand. She was already going through so much. "Sweetie, we need to get to the hospital as soon as possible."

"I can't go! I don't want to see him like that. I have already lost my mother and I wouldn't be able to live if something happens to my dad." Amina rocked back and forth on the chair, not really thinking that she had heard what the caller said correctly. "I need to call my grandmother." Shaking and crying, Amina dialed Crystal's cell phone number and waited impatiently for her to answer.

"Hello? Hello?" Crystal pulled the phone from her face and looked at the caller ID to see that it was Amina calling. She wondered why Amina was crying. She placed the phone back up to her ear. "Amina? Baby, what's wrong?" she asked.

Tremaine heard the panic in Crystal's voice and placed his fork back on his plate. Worry lines creased his forehead, but he remained quiet.

"Gran-Gran, I need you to meet me at Duke's Regional Hospital in Durham." Amina could barely keep it together long enough to give her grandmother the correct information about her father.

"What's wrong? Who's in the hospital and why are you crying? Are you okay? Is it Serena?" Crystal wasn't satisfied with the lack of information she had. Whatever it was, Amina had her nerves in a bunch. Covering the mouthpiece of her cell phone, she asked Tremaine to get the check. The pending emergency caused her to lose her appetite.

"Gran, it's Daddy. He's been in a car accident. He's been hit by an eighteen-wheeler and was in critical condition and had to be removed from the car with the

Jaws of Life." Amina cried and rocked on her knees on the floor where she'd fallen to. The thought of him dying made her cry out in agony.

"Amina, I need you to calm down, honey. Nothing will be accomplished with us sitting here getting hysterical. First thing's first: have you told Serena what's going on? If not, she needs to know that her brother has been in a serious accident. Can you both get there? If so, we will prepare to meet you there at the hospital," Crystal said calmly, yet she wanted to cry out.

"Okay." Amina had calmed some, but she'd awakened Serena with the hysteria moments before. "We will see you soon and yes, that shouldn't be a problem since James is here. I'm sure he won't mind driving us. Love you, Gran, and please get there safely." Amina hung up the phone.

Serena dragged herself from her room with sleep written all over her face. She looked tired. "Jonathan? Did I hear something about a car accident?" Paralyzed with fright, she stood there swaying from side to side.

Amina ran to Serena's side because she feared that Serena would pass out. "James, please help me get Auntie to the chair." By then, Amina's tears had subsided and she knew that once again she needed to be strong for her aunt. Once Serena was settled on the chaise longue in the living room, Amina treaded lightly before confirming what her aunt had heard.

"Please answer me. Why were you in here hollering and screaming? What's happened to your father?" Serena didn't want to be coddled; she wanted the truth.

"Daddy's been in a serious accident. The Jaws of Life had to remove him from Gran's car, which is totaled. Life Flight was called to transport him to Duke in Durham and he's supposedly in critical condition." Amina didn't fight to hold back her tears any longer. She thought she could be the strength that Serena needed, but repeating what happened released a new set of tears.

When it sank in for Serena that her brother's life was hanging in the balance, she screamed, "What's next?"

Amina rushed around trying to get things together so they could get to the hospital. She had to pack another bag for Serena filled with snacks, anti-nausea medications, an extra blanket, and bottles of water. When they emerged from their bedrooms, James stood up and headed toward the door in preparation to take them to the hospital.

"James, are you sure that you can take us? I know you are supposed to be getting on the road soon and you need your rest." Amina didn't want him to be the next victim of a car accident.

He took mental notes on what he loved about her and the list was growing quickly. He was pleased that the current situation didn't make her insensitive concerning him. "Yes, sweetie, I'm good. I just want to make sure that my two favorite ladies make it safely, so I'll be waiting outside." He smiled. Once outside, James shook his head and also asked God why. "I've always heard the saying that God wouldn't put any more on you than you could bear, but when is it too much?" James asked out loud as he walked around the car to make sure it was clean for the ladies.

"Auntie, do you need me to help you get ready?" Amina yelled from the kitchen.

Serena felt as if everything was moving in slow motion. The effects of the liquid treatments had altered her gait and she walked around her room in a cloud. She wasn't sure how long it took her to get it together, but her body was shutting down and she had to fight the desire to lie down. Instead, Serena bent down to her knees to pray.

Amina wasn't sure what was keeping Serena, so she followed up and went to her bedroom to see what the delay was. What she saw made her jump. She stood at the door entrance trying to assess the scene. Her pulse raced with the anxiety she was feeling. Then she heard it: Serena's murmurs and moans. The ramblings sounded like Serena was petitioning God. Her voice got louder and Amina could hear clearly that Serena was indeed praying for her family. She joined Serena down on the floor and petitioned God with her aunt for her father and for their family.

Chapter 21

"Gran-Gran, how is my daddy?" Amina ran ahead and James assisted Serena as they brought up the rear. Crystal was standing at the nurse's station speaking to one of the nurses. When she turned around to face her granddaughter there were fresh tears in her eyes. She opened her arms and Amina fell into them. Serena had finally reached them and her mother opened her arms to her daughter and enveloped her in a hearty hug.

"Baby, I just got here myself. The nurses don't really know too much, but said the doctor should be coming out as soon as she can." Crystal looked at Serena's frail-looking frame and had to fight back more tears.

"Hello, James, thank you for getting my family here safely. You are always such a dependable young man. I appreciate all that you do for them." Crystal acknowledged James with her heart full of gratitude. She reached over and shook his hand.

"Pastor Sampson, it's my pleasure. God always has a ram in the bush. When there's a need, He supplies." James smiled at the look of surprise on Crystal's face that turned into a smile.

Amina was happy to hear that her man knew more about God's Word than she initially gave him credit for. Serena gave him a knowing look. She'd been pouring into James spiritually for a while now and she knew that his desire to learn more of God was sincere. It showed just how serious he was about his relationship with God at that moment. The chair she'd been sitting in was hard and uncomfortable, even though she'd only been sitting a minute or two.

Crystal was stunned beyond her own belief. She didn't want to let on, but she really was beginning to like the two men her girls had chosen. She wasn't totally sold on Amina dating but she would have to get used to it considering the fact that she, too, was opening her heart to the new man in her life. She became detached from what was going on and began to think about her own situation. *I'm getting too old to go slowly. I haven't realized how lonely I've been all of these years that I've closed myself to the idea of allowing God to send me someone new. Truth is I want someone to hold me and make me feel like a woman again. I want to be loved.*

"Gran? Scotty, can you bring back my Gran?" Amina waved her arms in front of Crystal's face, struggling to get her attention. Serena and James chuckled, but Amina had questions that only her grandmother had answers to. She needed Crystal to come back from la-la land where she had disappeared to.

Crystal was totally still as if hypnotized. Her eyes weren't moving, but she wore a frown that creased her forehead and caused her lips to pucker in dismay. She seemed to come back just like that. "Yes, dear. I'm sorry. I was just thinking." Crystal pulled herself together and forced herself to smile.

"Can you fill us in on what was going on with Dad? When I got the call, the officer said something about the fact that Daddy had been drinking and the front of the car was full of alcohol cans. I didn't even know that Daddy drank. What's going on? When did all of this start happening? Gran, please tell us what you know," Amina pleaded.

"Mommy, there are obviously some things that are happening right here in our midst but are being kept from Amina and me. Did this have to happen before we could find out that my brother is not as good as he claimed he was all those times we talked on the phone? If you know something and aren't telling us then nothing can get better. Secrets can kill, Mommy. Jonathan could die, right, Mommy?" Serena said.

Crystal's nerves teetered on frazzled as all of the different situations she had going on fought to control her mindset. She thought back to the argument she'd had with Jonathan before leaving for church and prayed that wasn't the reason he went out and tried to hurt himself.

"There she goes again. Either she's ignoring us or something deeper is going on here." Agitated, Serena shuffled in her seat again, seeking some type of comfort.

"Don't talk about me as if I'm not in the room. Jonathan and I weren't seeing eye to eye on some things and I demanded that he leave my home. I never thought it would come to this, but there are things that should not be explained in this setting that I couldn't allow. One thing I will say is that your brother has been living a destructive lifestyle and if he makes it out of this alive, he will be the one to fill you both in. It's not my place." Crystal regretted backing her son against a wall concerning his chosen lifestyle and the fact that he was covering it up with the alcohol.

Crystal never looked up to see the reaction from her words and how they affected her family. Their strength had been compromised by the multiple fiery darts the enemy continued to fire upon them; however, it wasn't time for added strife. "We are a family and we need to pull together and show the devil that our faith is on fire. This is not the time to hash our family business in this very public place." Sweat poured down Crystal's back as she felt uneasy sitting in the hot seat. Regaining her composure, the fire in her eyes pierced their souls.

No one spoke, each left to their own thoughts of regret. "Amina, can I speak with you over here for a moment?" James was already up and leading the way to an empty area by the vending machines.

"Yes, James." Amina's voice was pinched. "I can't believe that she shut us down like that as if we can't know what my father's issues are. It's not like he was coming around to have any heart-to-hearts with us and she's acting like it would be robbery to give us the insight we need." Her feelings were visibly hurt.

"Shhh. God is still working, bae." James reached out to hug Amina. She welcomed his hug and felt secure in his arms. Tears slowly trickled down her high cheekbones and found their way to her mouth. Licking away the salty wetness on her face, she could feel the tenseness in her back and shoulders recede. James held her tight until she got over the brunt of her emotional tirade.

They walked back over toward where Serena and Crystal were sitting and it wasn't missed on them that a heated discussion was taking place. Silently, Amina and James sat and held hands while they watched, curious about the outcome of this disagreement.

"Focus, Mommy. This, all of this, is not even about you. My only concern is how Jonathan is doing. I can't believe that you are sitting here worrying more about what church folks are going to say and the embarrassment your son has cost you. What about your son? Will he live? Or will he die? There is such an attack on us right now and instead of praying to God to remain faithful and strong, all you're concerned about is the church. Why does that not surprise me?" Serena looked at her mother disgustingly.

"I am still your mother, Serena. You will not address me in that sort of manner again. I am very concerned about my son. When Amina called me to let me know what happened, I wasn't sure what to think. Your brother has pretty much secluded himself from the rest of the world.

"I had been trying to talk with him and find out why he hadn't come to see you since the hospital. I wanted to know why he wasn't bonding with his daughter and what was keeping him locked in his room all the time. Now I know that he's an alcoholic. My car was full of empty beer cans and his blood alcohol level was three times the legal limit, according to the nurse. It frightens me that I don't know what drove him to this." Tears were on deck for the women. It hit them in waves.

"No, Gran, please don't think the worst. I can't lie; I was upset that Daddy kept standing me up, but maybe he has some serious issues that we know absolutely nothing about. I now know that you know what's going on with him and it's frustrating being shut out." Amina rocked back and forth from side to side.

Crystal needed to pray but she couldn't. She wished that she had asked Tremaine to stay with her, but she didn't want to involve him in too much family stuff yet. He had made things pretty easy for her by not pressing the issue when she told him that she would speak with him soon.

There was a whole lot of dirty laundry that needed to be washed before Crystal allowed Tremaine to become aware of what they were dealing with. She was afraid to hit him with too much too fast and she was determined not to run him away. She blew her nose into her handkerchief. When the tears started falling, she didn't try to stop them. Crystal stilled her thoughts and she heard the Spirit say, "Many are the afflictions of the righteous, but God delivers them from them all."

Serena felt her head wrap and it felt loose. Amina was watching Serena and got up to rewrap her head for her. Serena stood and allowed Amina to work with the scarf since she didn't know how to fix it herself. Amina carefully unwrapped her aunt's head. The colorful scarf reminded Amina of the coat of young Joseph. It was adorned with many colors and was very pretty, so pretty that his brothers were jealous that their father favored him over them. Amina took her time and fixed the scarf, wrapping it perfectly. Once she was done, she twirled Serena around slowly, making sure that the wrap was tight and wouldn't later cause embarrassment for her.

"Thanks, sweetie. That's why I love you so much. You are always there when I need you. I'm doing okay. You know the meds have got me losing this weight. Look at me! I know I am looking like a crack fiend," Serena shrieked.

"Oh, Lord. Auntie, aren't you speaking a bit drastically? You haven't lost that much weight, but you do need to force yourself to eat more," Amina said.

"Well, you know it isn't easy being me. I am sure that people are talking about me all over the free country and no doubt wondering if I am going to make it through this mess or die. Every time I check my Twitter account, I see that new vultures have attached themselves to my page. It's a shame that I don't even know many of those women. And they don't even have the fear of God in them to know that He sees everything they say and knows what they don't say," Serena fussed.

"I don't have the energy to respond to most of the foolishness because you know that I am not confrontational. I guess folks don't care that I'm dealing with enough without them swearing that I am sick because I am living in sin." Serena was too angry to cry, but she wasn't finished speaking her mind. "Look at Mommy, sitting out there crying and carrying on. She didn't say anything about wishing that Jonathan makes it through this; her concerns lie with what church folk are saying about the police report."

Amina pulled Serena off to the side before saying, "Auntie, I'm sorry. You know how Gran is. Sometimes she speaks out of turn and what she says would make passersby question her convictions, but she loves us each in her own way. I know that she is all wrapped up in her image, but I believe that God will show her what she needs to be focused on because life is so short. Please don't hold it against her."

"Well, we'd better get back over there before she starts wondering if we are plotting," Serena said.

"Yes, you're right." They both walked over to see that the chairs they were sitting in were being occupied by other people. They planted themselves into whatever chairs they could find and waited.

"Did anyone call Brother Nathaniel to let him know what's going on?" James had to ask rather loudly due to all of the craziness going on in the waiting room. Kids were running around like they had no home training. The adults they were with had no interest in preserving anyone else's sanity besides their own by letting them govern themselves. He looked back and forth from Serena to Amina and they both shook their heads no. "I think it would be a good idea, Prophetess, if you would call him. I'm sure that he would want to be here for the family," James suggested.

"I don't think we need a cheerleading squad up here." Crystal broke into the conversation like a thug. "You know once you tell someone and they find out where we are, it will be like putting honey out for the bees. Nosy folks and the reporters will make their way up here soon enough. I hate to think about it. They will come in swarms like flies fighting over a dead carcass." Crystal was sure that the news had already spread through the church like a wildfire, but she still wanted the privacy the family deserved until they could make heads or tails of the attempted assassination that had no doubt been plotted by Satan himself.

"There you go again." Serena laughed, not because it was funny to her, but it was predictable of Crystal. Her focus was on the wrong thing and Serena prayed that her mother would come to her senses before she ended up losing her family.

"Excuse me. Did you say something, Serena?" Mother Crystal cut her eyes in Serena's direction, daring her to say something fly.

"It doesn't matter, Mommy. Surely we don't want the world to see that we are human and have issues just like the next sinner saved by grace." Shaking her head, Serena pulled herself up and walked off with her cell phone in hand. She placed a call to her man. Shivers ran up and down her spine in anticipation of hearing his voice.

"Hey, you." Nathaniel's smooth voice caused her frustration to dissipate like melted ice.

"Hey, yourself." Serena's voice sounded stronger than she felt, but she didn't want to alarm Nathaniel with hysterics before she gave him the news. "Just thought I'd give you a call to let you know that the family is at the hospital in Durham. Jonathan was involved in a serious car accident and his life could be lost. I don't want to keep taking you from your work, but I want you here with me if it's at all possible. If you're in the middle of something with the kids, then just let me know and we'll be fine. I'll just see you later on. I just needed to hear your voice." Serena was totally out of breath but was still trying to talk.

"Hold on. Wait a minute. One thing at a time. We can talk about what's going on when I get there. Lady, you must not remember me telling you that I wouldn't leave you. I'm going to show you that I'm in this with you. Whatever that means. If you're involved then I'm involved. Now tell me, which hospital in Durham are you all at?" Nathaniel needed to find someone to take over, but most of the staff had already left for the day. He would work it out.

After ending the call, Serena had returned just in time to see Dr. Campbell lead them all to a conference room. He told them he would return to give them the update on Jonathan. It hurt to know that he was in a coma and that it was only up to God whether he would come out of it. Questions hung in the air about his recovery if he did come out of the coma. The blessing was that the truck driver escaped with minor cuts and bruises. He was checked out and then released.

There was a box of tissues on the table and bottles of water were there as well. Being left in that conference room for an hour reminded them of what had brought them together that day. They were all preoccupied in the waiting room with all of the busyness going on around them, but in the room where no one was talking, emotions were riding high as the fresh wounds of Jonathan's condition continued to replay in their minds.

Tears of sadness and questions of why this happened to their family plagued each of their minds. Crystal wondered, for what had to be the hundredth time, where she went wrong in raising her kids and why they were determined to bring shame to her. Serena was always in trouble as a child and now her sweet boy was an alcoholic.

Across the room, Serena and James tried to console Amina. They were in for the battle of their lives. She had every right to feel the way she did, knowing that her father was in a coma. James made many trips to the cafeteria, bringing back food for everyone because he didn't feel as if he was able to really do anything for Amina or the prophetess, but be there. James was en route to the cafeteria again and saw Nathaniel running up to him.

"Hey, man, I've been looking all over for you guys. How's it going? Can you fill me in?" Nathaniel rubbed his bald head and waited impatiently for the answers to his questions.

"Hey, bro." James gave Nathaniel their brotherly handshake before he continued. "Yeah, he reportedly led the police on a high speed chase and he lost control of the car and veered into the center lane. An eighteen-wheeler tore the car up and made such an impact that the Jaws of Life had to come and extricate Jonathan from the car.

"The police also reported that the car was full of open beer cans and a case unopened. Jonathan's alcohol level was almost triple the legal alcohol limit. They didn't even think twice about charging him with driving while under the influence and one count of reckless endangerment. He recently got out of surgery and is now in a coma. Everyone is taking it hard, especially Amina, which is understandable." James was out of breath by the time he finished filling Nathaniel in.

"Wow, man. I think I had better stroll with you for a minute while I digest the news you just gave me." Nathaniel rubbed his head in disbelief. He'd purposely driven to the hospital with the radio off in case the media had gotten ahold of the accident.

"Yeah, bro, I'm heading to the cafeteria. The ladies haven't really been eating much, but the coffee and snacks seem to keep them going. Prophetess has enjoyed the jelly-filled doughnuts, so I will get them for her to keep her going." James laughed.

"James, I am telling you that I am just glad she has found something that she can keep on her stomach. I can't wait to see her. She's going through so much right now and I can only pray that this situation with Jonathan doesn't push her over the edge," Nathaniel said.

"I heard that. Prayer and our trust in God is the only way that we can get through this."

"You said a mouthful right there, my brother. Since I got you alone, do you mind letting a brother in on the scene I walked into earlier?" Nathaniel had a smirk on his face, but was intrigued to hear about young love. He felt like he could direct James when it came to his relationship. Nathaniel had seen a lot of things and been to a lot of places. He thought about some of his conquests and shook his head as if to shake the bad memories off.

The two men walked along in silence. James was happy that he had someone to talk to since he was an only child. He wanted to be sure about Amina before even bringing her up to his grandmother. It was James's intention to get all of the data he could before giving her his heart. That's what he thought anyhow. James pointed the way to the cafeteria and motioned that it was up ahead. Nathaniel followed and as they entered the cafeteria, which was usually bustling with traffic, it was nice and empty. Before gathering the goodies for the ladies, James asked Nathaniel if they could sit down for a minute and Nathaniel obliged, excited to hear what the lad wanted to share.

"Well, let me see. Where do I begin?" James twiddled his fingers and kept his gaze lowered on the empty table. Nathaniel kept quiet and gave James the time he needed to proceed. "It's like this: Amina and I are officially dating. We had a long talk and she let me know that she saw me as a different person other than just the driver. She is new to all of this relationship stuff and wants to go slowly. I'm in agreement of us moving slowly, man. She's not like those other girls I've dated in the past," James acknowledged. Nathaniel didn't say anything, but allowed James to get everything off of his chest before speaking.

"I've never told another man this, but I understand what she means by wanting to wait and save herself for the man she would spend the rest of her life with because I am a virgin as well. I respect her feelings and totally agree with her. I've always wondered what Amina was like outside of doing ministry and being around church folks all the time. I'm surprised that she would even fall for a brother like me. Bottom line is I really like Amina and I'm falling fast, bro."

"Man, you're still a virgin?" Nathaniel rubbed the stubble on his nearly bald head. "I owe you a high five. If more of our young men and women would save themselves for marriage, there would be fewer teenage and unwanted pregnancies."

"Yes. I mean being the type of brother I was, I had a reputation to protect. So I've done some things, you know what I'm saying? Just gave the brothers enough to talk about, but I've never consummated with any female. Especially knowing the dudes I have to chauffer here and there. I don't want to have to wonder who my girl has been with. So many times those one-night stands left lasting impressions, if you know what I mean." James winked at Nathaniel. "Man, you sound just like my old friends. They thought I was gay just because I wasn't out macking on girls and trying to bed everyone who had a big butt and a smile. I'll just say this: that's why they are no longer my friends. I am saved and I love serving in the capacity of being a highly sought after driver, whether it be male or female. My character and integrity speak for me," James said proudly.

Nathaniel rubbed his head again and pulled on his chin hairs. He smiled at James, certain that he would be a good fit for Amina and his kids at the youth center. She needed someone who was already rooted and grounded in the Lord. Also, it didn't hurt that James was just what he was looking for to head up the center in his absence. He wanted to take some time off to be around more while Serena completed her chemotherapy treatments.

"For being the type of guy I wish I had the guts to be earlier in life." Nathaniel reached out his hand to give James a real man handshake that employers gave to employees upon offering them the position and them accepting. James took the handshake as to mean that Nathaniel had faith in God that their relationship was for the good of them both.

Nathaniel led a prayer for James and Amina. Then he petitioned God to cover them and lead them as the men in the relationship. His prayer was that God would equip them with the qualities needed in order to be successful with their communication, their love languages, keeping open minds, and being slow to anger when conflict arose. Once the prayer was done, they hustled to get what they had come for and got back to the ladies.

Serena was seated facing the traffic coming off of the elevators so when the door opened and she saw Nathaniel, her face lit up. She'd moved faster in that moment than she had all day. He had food bags in his arms and had to hold his left arm up in order to keep her from crushing the goodies. "Heyyyy! I'm so glad to see you." Serena hugged him as he tried to walk and he laughed.

"James, can you help a brother out? My woman is about to take me down and I like it." They laughed. Nathaniel passed the bags to James. He caught Serena up in his arms, kissed her quickly, and set her back down gently.

Crystal tried to ignore the public display of affection. She shook her head in disbelief that Serena would act like a crazed woman in love in the general public. Crystal busied herself by pulling out her cell phone. She scrolled through her call list checking to see if she'd missed any calls. She cringed when she saw over sixty missed calls. Voice mails were left by half of those and there were over one hundred texts that she would have to read at some point. The only ones that interested her at the moment were the ones Tremaine had sent. She replied to his texts, feeling giddy like a schoolgirl.

Suddenly hungry, Crystal put her phone away, satisfied that she'd communicated with Tremaine. She decided the rest of the madness could wait. "What did you all get? My stomach is growling and now that everything is kind of calming down, my appetite is returning."

"Hey, Pastor Sampson, I'm sorry to hear about Jonathan. I got here as quickly as I could." Gesturing toward the food, Nate said, "Well the café was selling salads and cold cut sandwiches so we got a few of those. Do you like ham?" Nathaniel started pulling the food items from the bag, wanting to make sure that Crystal got the first pick.

"Nathaniel, what kind of salad did you buy?" Amina asked. "A girl's gotta watch what she eats. I don't want to gain too many pounds." She winked at the group and laughed.

"I have a couple here. One's a chef's salad and the other is grilled chicken. Which do you want?" Nathaniel asked.

"I'll take the chef's salad, as long as it has meat on it, too," Amina said.

"It does; what type of dressing do you prefer? They only had red French and Italian," Nathaniel advised.

"Hmm, I'll take the red French if that's okay with you." Amina reached up to grab the dressing.

Finally, everyone was served and eating. Nathaniel and Serena wiped their mouths with napkins after they had shared the chicken salad. "Mm, that was good, babe. Sure beats the fruit and crackers I have stored in my bag. I can't believe that I thought I would want that and not real food. I was hungrier than I thought. Seeing you has restored my appetite and is helping me to remain hopeful about my brother."

"Rest, baby." Nathaniel pulled Serena's head to his shoulder and they rested their eyes until an update was given.

Crystal sat rod straight up in a leather recliner until she couldn't any longer. She was worn out and eventually, she gave in to the heaviness of her eyes and she slept. James and Amina followed suit and tried to rest until Jonathan woke up. They wouldn't leave until he did.

Chapter 22

Crystal, Serena, and Amina were called to the hospital two weeks later. They headed down the hall to the intensive care unit with the message that Jonathan had been stable enough to be moved to a regular room. "Oh God, this is the moment we've been praying for." Crystal thanked God for keeping her son. Nathaniel stayed back at Serena's house, hoping the best for Jonathan.

"Mommy, I'm tired. Why didn't they wait to call us to come down here once he was settled into his new room? Once you get an update, I think we should go back home and get some rest." Serena yawned and her eyes filled with water.

"Yeah, I'm glad that Nathaniel didn't come because he would have been waiting on us all day for nothing." Amina was disappointed in the slow transition in her father's condition and she made no secret about it.

"Don't you dare act like God isn't still in the midst of working this thing out now. One thing about God is that He isn't troubled by our timetables. God has His own timing, or have you forgotten?" Crystal chided Amina with her voice in annoyance.

"Well, I'm ready to go as well. We can come back when Daddy is awake. I can't handle seeing him lying there. I'm sick of it and I'm going home. I'll get James to come pick me up." Amina left the ICU determined that she wouldn't be back until her father was moved into a regular room.

Time had passed from afternoon into evening, and then the day slipped into the night. Serena finally had Nathaniel come pick her up and Crystal was left alone. In between her nearly stalking the ICU nurses she took walks until she couldn't hold out anymore. "Tremaine? I was wondering if you could come and get me from the hospital and take me home?" Crystal held her breath waiting on his reply. She was trying to get used to having someone in her life besides Jalisa, who was there for most of her needs. She liked calling Tremaine better; she just hoped he didn't mind.

"I was waiting for you to call me. I've missed you, Crystal, but I respect your wishes of handling your family on your own for now. Can you give me twenty minutes? I've gassed my car up and can be on my way to you. I'll call you when I get to you." Tremaine felt like he'd just won a million dollars. Maybe Crystal was serious about letting him be her man after all. It had taken her some time to come around and with all that she had going on with her son and daughter, he wasn't so sure that he would get to first base with Crystal.

Crystal called Amina next. "Hey, sweetie. I pray that you are feeling a bit better."

"Hey, Gran. I'm feeling a little better. I've prayed and asked God to forgive me for my ungrateful behavior. At least Daddy is still alive. I've been acting like a total brat. I wanted to let you know how sorry I am for disrespecting you earlier," Amina apologized.

"Baby, I understand. I've been angry as well. Waking up each day since your auntie got sick and now with your dad's accident has convinced me that God is trying to tell us something during this season of testing. I've been hard to deal with at times and I owe all of you an apology. I'm calling to let you know that the doctors are still weaning your dad from the medications that they had been using to keep him heavily sedated, in order for his body to begin the healing process," Crystal said.

"Thank you, Jesus!" Amina shouted directly into Crystal's ear.

Crystal pulled the cell phone away from her ear and waited until Amina was done before placing the phone back to her ear. "I'm glad that could make you happy, but I don't want you to get ahead of yourself. We won't know everything as far as if there is any memory loss or anything until days after he wakes up." Crystal worried that there may be some damage.

"Yes, Gran. Your news has given me even more hope because I've been praying really hard for him." Amina's spirits had been lifted. "I will let Auntie know in the morning before she leaves for her treatment, since she's already asleep. Do you have a ride home? I could have James come to make sure you get home safely," Amina offered.

"That won't be necessary. I have a ride home; so don't worry about me because I'm in good hands." Crystal snickered.

"Gran, I've been meaning to ask you. When I called you the day of Daddy's wreck, you said that 'we' were on the way. Who was 'we'? I never saw you with anyone. Who's the mystery person? Do we know her or him?" Amina badgered her grandmother, showing no mercy.

Crystal wasn't ready to share too much about Tremaine yet, so she stalled. "Too many questions for an old lady at this time of night. I just wanted to give you a positive update and, my darling, I will speak with you tomorrow if the good Lord wills. I love you."

"Oh, don't worry, old lady, I'm slowly figuring things out. It won't take long when I take you to God. He will give me the answers I am seeking and I love you too. Good night, Gran."

"Good night. Sweet dreams." Just as Crystal clicked the off button, it wasn't long before her knight in shining armor called.

"Hello?" Crystal sang into the phone.

"Your chariot has arrived. I'm out front," Tremaine sang back into the receiver.

"I'm on my way out." Crystal ended the call, said a little prayer, and headed out of the hospital.

Chapter 23

Nathaniel watched as Serena tossed and turned. He hadn't been able to get much sleep because he was worried about her. Serena was in the middle of a nightmare and the longer she flipped from side to side the more worried Nathaniel became. He sat on the edge of the recliner chair and in his heart he wanted to take her fears away. Relief washed over him as Serena woke up. The sliver of light emanating from the bathroom cast a shadow on Serena's bed. He watched her silhouette rise, twist, and turn in the night.

Seeing Nathaniel sitting there staring at her made Serena smile. "Hey, you. I had the worst nightmare. You care to hear about it?" Serena's eyes adjusted to the darkness and even in the dark, she knew that her man was fine.

"Tell me about it." His voice was husky and the sleep deprivation could be heard.

"My dream was vivid with images flashing of me lying on a hospital bed. I watched what was happening from where I was suspended in the air. I saw my members crying as the doctor informed them that they had done all they could for me. That all the treatments they tried wasn't strong enough to keep the cancer from spreading. It was too far gone." Serena paused.

"It was the weirdest thing I'd ever experienced. All I could do was watch as my spirit hovered over her sick and frail body. I mean I could hear everything that was being said and the cries and moans from my family members made me cry." By the time she was finished telling him about her dream, she noticed that Nathaniel had moved from the chair to the floor in front of her bed.

"The scene was a real one and could very well be my reality if God decides not to intervene on my behalf. I know now that I won't ever be comfortable in another hospital room." Serena stopped talking as her tears distorted what little vision she had.

Serena talked and Nathaniel listened until Serena became sleepy again and when she fell asleep, he stayed by the foot of her bed until the next morning.

"I'm too blessed to be stressed. God's going to do it for our family. I know He will," Serena declared as she stepped out of the house. They were on their way back to the hospital now that Jonathan had awakened.

"Good morning, dear." Crystal was driving them to Duke and she was in a much better mood than she had been in the beginning of the trials her family faced.

"Good morning, Mommy." Serena leaned over to give her mother a kiss on the cheek before putting her seat belt on. "Amina should be on her way out any minute now."

"All right. It's going to be a great day in the name of the Lord. He really has been in the midst of our valley experiences. Don't you agree?" Crystal asked while checking her makeup in the mirror.

"Mommy, indeed God has been working on our behalf. Jonathan is out of the coma and I'm feeling pretty decent, even though I've been poked and prodded. The nurses had a hard time trying to find a vein to use to administer the chemotherapy. I'm all dried up. See." Serena pulled her sleeve back on the jacket she wore and showed her mother her battle scars.

"I'm sorry you're having to go through this. You don't deserve any of it." Crystal's upbeat attitude deflated a tad bit. She kept on talking despite the nervous energy in her belly. "We are going to beat this disease. I don't care what the doctor's statistics are. We will believe the report of the Lord. Can I get an amen?" Crystal tooted her horn, wondering what was taking Amina so long to come out.

"Amen, Mommy. I trust God, and you know what else?" Serena looked at her mom and lifted her hands in the air. In unison they said, "We've got faith on fire," and started praising God in the car.

Amina finally came out of the house with her cell phone glued to the side of her face.

"Mmph, she must be talking to James," Serena teased.

Amina hopped into the car and planted a big kiss on Crystal's cheek and flopped back onto the leather car seat. She resumed her conversation.

"Are we ready to see Jonathan now?" Crystal asked.

"Yes, let's go and see what today shall bring," Serena said.

Crystal made it to the hospital in record time. The traffic was light and the ride was peaceful. Pulling into the front of the hospital, Crystal waited patiently for one of the valet attendants to come to her window. The hospital was always busy, so it took a few minutes. Finally, it was their turn. Seeing the valet parking fee on the booth outside, Crystal asked, "Do you have change for a fifty?" She waved the fifty-dollar bill out of the window.

"Good morning, ladies." He peered into the car and then straightened back up. "Yes, ma'am." His smile was genuine. "I can take care of that for you so that you ladies can get on your way."

The attendant took the crisp fifty-dollar bill from Crystal's hands and trotted over to the booth that looked like the command center.

"Young man, you came back pretty quickly." Crystal held her hand out of the window for her change and without counting it, she handed him back a twenty-dollar bill. "Take care of my baby while I'm gone."

"Oh wow! Yes, ma'am. Indeed, today is going to be a great day." He smiled even harder this time before reaching over to open her car door and then Amina's and Serena's as well.

The ladies exited the car and stood on the sidewalk. They joined hands for a quick prayer and entered the hospital with smiles on their faces.

"We're here to see Jonathan Sampson," Crystal announced when they had made it to the seventh floor.

"Who is we? We have special orders for the patient." The security guard barely acknowledged them. He was working on a crossword puzzle.

"It's Crystal Sampson, Amina Sampson, and Serena Sampson," Crystal spoke up on behalf of the trio.

"There's a two-visitor limit at a time. Please decide who will come in first and then when two of you are finished the other can go in."

"Thanks." Crystal turned her attention to her family. "I think it would be best if Amina and I go in first and then I will come out so that you can go in." She directed her attention to Serena.

"Okay, sounds good. I'll be waiting over here." Serena pointed to the waiting room area.

Amina and Crystal washed their hands and walked over to where Jonathan was being seen by the doctor. They watched him work. The doctor was pleased with Jonathan's condition. He gave Jonathan commands that consisted of squeezing his hand or blinking his eyes if he could hear what the doctor was saying. It proved that his brain was functioning more than what they believed it to be when first brought in. It also proved that prayer changes things.

"Doctor, how is he?" Amina stood on the opposite side of her father's bed holding his hand.

"He's doing much better than we expected. I'm pretty ecstatic about the minimal damage done to his head. If you'd seen the car, you would know that someone has a guardian angel. The scans done on his head showed a concussion at most. He has some other injuries that may get worse before they get better and will need to be addressed, but other than that, in time he will be all right."

"Thanks so much, Doctor, for everything. I'm so happy to see my son alive. God bless you."

"We're just doing our jobs, ma'am, and we love what we do." The doctor smiled and walked away to confer with the rest of his team. They believed that no matter what happened now, Amina's father would recover one hundred percent; although he would require rehab due to the shattered bones in both of his legs.

Crystal gave God thanks for His faithfulness concerning her family. Crystal stood by her son's side and petitioned God for direction in how to be there best for her son as he progressed and eventually would have to face the court system. Jonathan was sleeping, so she kissed his forehead and headed out behind Amina so that Serena could come in for a bit.

Exhausted, Serena was happy to see her brother breathing. "Jonathan? Big bro. I'm here, baby. It's Serena." Jonathan twitched. She rubbed his head and soothed him. "Don't fret. I'm not going anywhere. I will be here for you until all of this is just a bad memory. Everyone is here who loves you. Rest, and we will see you tomorrow." Serena kissed her brother on the cheek and she walked back to the waiting room to meet up with her mother and niece.

"Are we all ready to go home?" Nathaniel stood and greeted Serena with a hug when she got back to the waiting room. He'd hoped that they were satisfied with the most recent developments.

"Hey, you." Serena's face lit up with a glow. Pecking his lips gently, she said, "Let's go. I'm at peace knowing that Jonathan is on the mend." Serena was more than ready to go home. She had been suffering from insomnia and wanted desperately to get into her bed for the next day or so.

"Me too," Amina agreed.

"Me three," Crystal concurred. They left the hospital together, ready to face whatever came their way.

The group headed out to the hallway and onto the elevator. Serena was the last to step on as she began to feel nauseated. Her head swooned and she lost her balance. Thankfully, Nathaniel was there. He grabbed Serena around the waist and held her steady.

Everyone asked at the same time, "Are you okay?" Alarm then relief masked their faces as they watched how swift and alert Nathaniel was when it came to Serena.

"I'm okay, yes. I believe so. Just the thought of riding the elevator made me feel sick to the stomach. But I'm going to be okay. Let's just get this ride over with." Serena mustered up a little smile and held on to Nathaniel with one hand and the elevator rail for dear life with the other. She closed her eyes, readying herself for the dropping of the elevator car to each floor as they descended to the first floor.

Nathaniel had Serena and Amina wait in the hospital lobby while he went to get his car. Crystal decided to wait with them until he returned. People from everywhere were coming into the hospital or leaving and saw Serena and recognized her right off, and some spoke. People wished her well and said that they were praying for her and her family, while others walked up to her and put money in her hands.

Amina was on guard for anyone who might have stopped by and meant harm toward her aunt. She covered Serena while keeping some folks at a distance until Serena let her know that it was okay if they came closer. Amina questioned each one to make sure they didn't have colds or other illnesses that were contagious and detrimental to Serena's already compromised immune system. There were even a few people who were standing around who didn't give positive vibes and Amina could discern that they weren't truly interested in her well-being, but were hanging around to see what they could find out.

The ladies sighed with relief when Nathaniel returned to get them. The valet had returned with Crystal's car minutes before. His absence was felt and Serena felt cherished and special that people who she didn't know gave her money and wanted her autograph. A couple of ladies wanted pictures with Serena in spite of Serena's protests due to her attire. They didn't care how she looked; they just wanted a photo with the lady who had helped them along their spiritual walks by way of the conferences that she held.

Nathaniel wasn't sure what he was walking into. The crowd put his senses on heightened alert and caused him to jog over to where his girlfriend was seated. When he was able to make a hole and get through to her, he saw that she was smiling, and although her face was plastered with the jovial smile, the dark circles were a result of not just the chemotherapy but due to the fact that she was extremely tired and needed some rest. Nathaniel could appreciate the throngs of fans who gathered around, but it was his responsibility to get the love of his life home so that he could take care of her.

"Excuse me, ladies. I'm sorry to interrupt, but I need to get Prophetess Serena home so that she can get her rest." Nathaniel broke up the crowd. "I'm sure that she appreciates all of the love you all have shown her and for that, I want to thank you. I ask that you will continue to pray for God to do what man cannot do as it relates to healing her and her recovery. I'm sure that Prophetess Serena will never forget your act of love that you have shown to her and family. Now if you will allow me to take the woman of God home, I would greatly appreciate your consideration."

Nathaniel moved around Amina and held his hand out to his queen. She was drained and happy for the rescue so she could get out of the hospital. Serena thanked well wishers and placed her hands in Nathaniel's and they walked away. Shouts of encouragement followed Serena, causing her to become overwhelmed with emotion. It was just what she needed to know that God was indeed working things out for her good. Once outside the door, Nathaniel scooped Serena up into his strong arms and whisked her to the car. Amina opened the passenger door and he placed her ever so gently on the seat and then reached over her and pulled on the seat belt to strap her in. Serena's head hit the headrest and she was asleep before Nathaniel could pull away from the curb of the hospital.

Chapter 24

Serena was nervous as she struggled to prepare mentally for her first set of scans to see if the treatments were working in her favor. It was necessary, as she was halfway through the treatment regimen she was on. Her nerves were frayed; although she prayed and had everyone praying for her. She even requested that Crystal speak from the pulpit about her health and the need for continual prayers. Serena was aware that this was only part of the process and with all she had been through this far, humble was her new middle name.

The receptionist was calling out the names of patients who had already checked in at UNC for various tests. Serena had been led to the area where tests would be performed. She would be getting the computerized axial tomography: a CAT scan for short. Her doctors from the cancer center explained to her what the test was for and how it would be administered. Nathaniel sat down beside her. His efforts of trying to calm Serena's fears by telling jokes didn't go over too well. It became obvious that Serena wasn't in the mood to laugh or talk.

Finally, the door swung open and a male nurse came out. "Serena Sampson?" the lab technician yelled out into the lobby of people, waiting for someone to answer his call. Serena got up from her seat and looked at Nathaniel, motioning him to follow her. Nathaniel gathered her things and stood next to Serena. A calm feeling came over her and she knew then that everything would turn out for her good.

"Ma'am, verify your birth date for me?" the male nurse asked over his shoulder as he led the way to the back.

"It's February the second. I was born in the year 1971."

"Awesome. My name is Todd, the lab technician, and I will be getting you set up for your testing today. If you need anything once we get started, please don't hesitate to let me know." The male nurse directed them to a small waiting room and told them he would return for Serena shortly.

Serena twisted her hands together as the sweat built up in her palms and in between her fingers. She wiped them down the front of her sweatpants and flopped back into the leather chair. Nathaniel rubbed her back and kissed her gently on the cheek.

"Relax, Serena. God is with you. I wish you would try to lighten up just a little. Hasn't God shown you His faithfulness?"

"Nathaniel, don't start with me. I trust God, really I do. It's just that this is all new to me and I am entitled to my feelings. I can only imagine how awful that chalky stuff is they give you to drink." Serena shuddered at the thought.

"Okay, okay, baby. Look at him." Nathaniel gestured with his eyes to the gentleman who sat across from them slurping on a straw that held some flavored drink. "He's taking it down like a champ. If he can do it, then surely a strong woman like you can as well. It's mind over matter. If you focus on the taste and the procedure itself then you will make it harder on yourself to get it done. I'm here, baby, to cheer you on." Nathaniel's voice was soothing to Serena's psyche. His words of encouragement massaged her temples and brought forth a peace and that umph that she needed to get through the next two hours.

"I love you, Nathaniel, and I want to thank you for being right by my side when I need you the most. Even though you were cracking those corny jokes, I am thrilled that you are here with me. I am so amazed at the way things have progressed between you and me."

"I'm happy to be here. It's not a burden but a joy for me to be able to support you every step of the way through this. I'm not going anywhere, so you are stuck with my corny jokes. I do it because I love you and cherish the gift that you are to me. I've been taught that you can tell the way a person feels about the gift he's been giving by the way you treat it. Lady, you are my every dream come true." Nate leaned over and kissed Serena softly on the lips.

The moment was interrupted when Todd, the lab technician, returned and asked Serena to follow him down the hall. Nathaniel gave her the thumbs-up sign and smiled at her. Serena winced like she was already suffering and trudged behind the nurse until they reached their destination.

Todd spoke. "This is where you will change into a gown. I need for you to remove all of your clothes, top and bottoms. You can keep on your underwear but if you're wearing a bra, you will need to remove it. One of the gowns needs to be put on and opened in the back and the other gown will open at the front. You can leave all of your personals in the locker below and once you are ready, remove the key and sit here. I will come back around to get you." He pointed to the dressing room behind them.

Once she had emerged from a room, Todd came back for her like he said he would. He ushered Serena into one of the small rooms that held only a school desk and some other medical supplies. She clutched at her throat and started to perspire.

Todd watched her closely. "Are you okay, Miss Sampson?"

"No, I'm not. I can't breathe." Serena's breath became ragged and she began to hyperventilate.

"Miss Sampson, I need for you to listen to me. Take a deep breath in." Serena obeyed. "Now exhale. Deep breath in, hold it and release again. This exercise will open your blood vessels and allow oxygen to flow to the heart easier and it calms you down. Sit here." Todd coaxed Serena into the chair and had her repeat the breathing technique until she had calmed down.

"How we feeling? Better I hope." Todd showed that he was genuinely concerned about Serena's well-being.

"Better, yes. I think that it's okay for us to proceed now." Serena felt calmer.

"Good, you will be fine. I'm sure that this part won't take long at all. I have to start an intravenous drip in order to administer the contrast. That will come at the end part of the scans. Your responsibility is to continue taking slow, deep breaths," Todd instructed.

Serena prayed and thought about the sweet nothings Nathaniel had said to her before being called to the back. The peace she experienced earlier was coming back and she relaxed. Todd only had to stick her one time and it didn't even hurt. Serena was surprised that the size-twenty-two plastic tubing was in place. Todd was an excellent sticker and he had good eyes too. Serena's veins had taken a beating as the effects of the chemotherapy dried her veins out. The big, juicy veins that used to show up at the smallest bit of strain were now replaced by traces of veins that rolled or ran away from needle sticks.

"Miss Sampson, you have been great," Todd said.

"I needed to remind myself that this is only a test and that everything would be all right, but I must go through this process in order to get the results I was promised," Serena said.

"Yes, it's only a test and it will be over before you know it. You have conquered the hard part and if you could get through this then drinking the contrast won't be too difficult for you. We have different flavors. Your choices are chocolate, strawberry, and vanilla. Which flavor would you like today?" Todd smiled at Serena and because of his expertise and compassionate heart, she couldn't help but to return the smile while she kept her arm straight. He noticed that she looked afraid to bend her arm. "Miss Sampson, you can bend your arm; there is no needle in your arm, but there is plastic tubing there. See?" Todd showed Serena the tube and then he pulled the hard plastic piece back just enough to show her what was in her arm.

Serena took a deep breath and relaxed. She didn't want Todd to pull the whole thing out for her to have to go through being stuck again. He may not have been as fortunate the second time around as the first. When she realized that Todd really knew his stuff, she smiled, remembering it was only a test. She pondered which flavor of the drink she would prefer and decided upon the chocolate. "I will have the chocolate."

"Okay, sit tight and I will be right back with it. Once I give you the first cup, you will have thirty minutes to drink all of it, and thirty minutes after your first, I will bring your second cup and then the third after another thirty minutes have passed. I need for you to know that if for whatever reason you don't finish all cups, you will have to retake the test. The contrast is needed to illuminate the areas in your neck and chest that the doctor uses to see if your treatments are stopping the growth and spread of new cancer cells. Before I go, can you tell me when is the last time you have had something to eat?"

"My last meal was around eight p.m. last evening," Serena said.

"Good. Hang tight," Todd said.

Serena was ready to get this over with. Todd came around the corner a couple of minutes later and asked her to follow him. He was holding on to an identical white sixteen-ounce Styrofoam cup with a straw in it as the man Serena saw earlier drinking.

"Miss Sampson, you are going to need to drink as much water as you can to flush this contrast from your system for the next twenty-four hours. Once you are halfway through the picture imaging, you will be injected with iodine dye. This, too, will need to be expelled from your system. If you need anything or have any questions, just let the nurse at the window know and she will page me."

Serena was anxious to get back to Nathaniel. Even though Todd was nice enough, she wished he would hurry and finish saying what he needed to say so that she could get back to her man. She was going to need him to further encourage her to get this chocolate drink down. She knew that just because it looked good didn't mean it would taste good. She didn't want to seem rude, so she looked as if she were listening. He gave her the drink and gestured for her to go back into the waiting room, which she did with gladness.

"Hey, baby. How did things go? He didn't hurt you, did he?" Nathaniel asked, smiling at Serena.

"Hey, you. No. Things went better than I expected. I only had to get one stick." Serena held her arm out for Nate to see Todd's handiwork. "See, this thing bends just like the ones at the clinic. I tell you, we sure have come a long way. Now, if I can just drink three cups of these within the next hour and a half, we will be one step closer to get out of here."

"Piece of cake, baby," Nathaniel encouraged.

"Oh Lord." Serena screwed her face up as she took a sip. "There isn't any amount of chocolate flavoring that could mask the horrible medicine taste." She held her breath and sucked on the straw for as long as she could before exhaling and taking in another breath and drinking some more.

Thirty minutes later, Todd brought over her second cup of cold chocolate drink. He walked in just in time to see Serena hand her cup to Nathaniel for him to throw away. It took her the whole thirty minutes to get it all down. He handed her another cup and walked away down the hall in the same direction he had come. Serena started to feel nauseated. She looked into the full cup and gagged.

"Honey, are you going to be all right? It looks like you're about to be sick to your stomach. You look pale," Nathaniel said, feeling helpless.

"I feel like I'm going to lose everything I've already drunk. I can't go with the third cup. My stomach is gurgling. Can you hear it?" Tears stung Serena's eyes and she felt hot all over. "It's the most horrible thing I've ever had to ingest." Anxiety crept up on her and she started to doubt that she could go any further.

"Serena, remember, if you can't keep it down now, you will have to start all over from the beginning. Baby, you're too far in the game to quit now," Nathaniel encouraged Serena.

She asked that the Lord help her get the rest of the drink down without losing it. Nathaniel got up to locate the nearest restroom. He told Serena that he would be right back, but she didn't hear anything that he had said, nor did she realize he had left the waiting room. She could hear the cheers of the audience of the game show coming through the waiting room television speaker. The cheers made Serena think about the scripture in the book of Romans. It talked about how the saints of God who had gone before them were cheering them on. "A great cloud of witnesses" was how it was stated.

Serena's stomach settled down. She thanked the Lord for coming to see about her and for allowing her to have the waiting room to herself. Serena returned to the chair she had been sitting in and nursed the drink. She gulped sometimes and sipped at other times. Nathaniel had returned with some wet paper towels and some dry. He was worried about his girlfriend and wanted to make things better for her, not sit by and do nothing at all. "Take these. Are you going to be okay, babe?"

"Thanks, love. I know I had you worried a few minutes ago. I didn't plan on coming here and going through the emotional rollercoaster that I have been riding on since we've been here. I really thought I was good, but being here and going through this is more than what I bargained for. I don't think I need those now, but just in case, hold on to them." Serena grimaced.

"I'll be honest. I was afraid that you were losing control. I didn't know what to do, so I left you here and went to the restroom and prayed. I am telling you one thing I am learning is that trials and misunderstandings in our own minds lead us straight to the Lord." Nathaniel reached over to hold Serena and he kissed her cheek.

Serena hadn't finished the second cup before Todd whisked around the corner with the third and final cup of the drink. "Miss Sampson, how are you doing? Is the taste really that bad? You really should drink them a little faster. It's not a great tasting drink, but it is a bit more bearable really cold." He stood there for a moment and watched her suck down the last bit of the now lukewarm contrast. Serena struggled to get the first two cups down and she would take the full thirty minutes on the last if she felt the need to. She liked Todd, but he was beginning to sound like a nagging woman.

Todd held the cup out for Serena to take it, but she just looked at it and continued slurping the last of the drink, which was now thick and gooey. Seeing as though Serena took her time in taking the cup, he pushed the cup into the direction of Nathaniel in hopes that he would relieve him of the duty of holding the cup. He had other patients to tend to. Todd spoke to Nathaniel this time.

"I will be back to check on Miss Sampson shortly. When I return, we will be ready to begin her testing." Todd did an about-face and walked off.

Two people were escorted back to where Serena and Nathaniel sat. They seemed to be as nervous as Serena was when she first came in. Serena was no longer afraid of what was to be. She sucked down the fluids from the cup and in order to keep them down, she thought of her favorite: chocolate milk. She sat as still as possible while Nathaniel rubbed her back. She closed her eyes and counted from one to ten, inhaling and exhaling as slowly as she could. Todd was back to get Serena. Those last thirty minutes zipped by and finally, it was time for the scans. She blew a kiss to Nathaniel and dropped the last cup into the trash.

"Do you need to go to the bathroom before the tests?" Todd asked like he did all of the patients who had to drink three cups of the contrast. The fluids usually swelled up in their bellies and filtered to their bladder.

"Yes, I'd better go. How long does the test take?" Serena asked.

Todd ushered her into the restroom and told her he would answer her questions once she was done. He waited patiently until she was finished and then ushered her down the hall and into a room where a big machine stood. It was hollow on the inside and there was a starch white sheet covering a thin board-like apparatus that had minimal cushioning on it. On the other side of the room was a big, clear window that showed the room where the lab technician would control the machine and take the pictures needed.

Serena looked around until she saw a young lady who had the clearest mocha-colored skin approaching. She wore a white lab coat that fell beneath her knees, black pants, and moccasins. Her hair was styled with pixie braids that matched her eye and skin color. She was very pretty.

"Miss Sampson, my name is Treva and I will be conducting your testing today."

Serena smiled at the lady. "Hi. Okay. I'm ready to get this over with."

"Follow me this way and we will get started," Treva instructed.

"Miss Sampson, I need for you to lie down with your head here." Treva directed Serena where to lay. The lab technician instructed Serena to lie down on the cot-like bed with no handles or anything to grab on to for security.

"Ma'am, are you sure you want me to lie down on that sliver of a board? It doesn't look like it will be able to stand all of this." Serena pointed to her frame and laughed halfheartedly.

The lab tech laughed along with Serena before answering. "It's going to be fine. It's a lot sturdier than it looks, I know." Treva worked efficiently and quickly to get Serena set up for testing.

Serena lay down and looked around the sterile room. She clasped her hands together on her legs to keep them from dangling off the side of the thin table. Serena lay there waiting to go into the big machine with all of the buttons on both sides. It was hollow yet extremely large. It made her think of a shark eating a whole person. "I'm nervous about this test," Serena admitted to the lab tech.

"I understand. I mean I can't relate directly, but indirectly, I see thousands of patients a year with some form of cancer. I don't want you to be worried." Treva paused, staring into Serena's face. "You sure look look familiar. When I saw your name on the medical record, I racked my brain trying to figure out where I heard your name before. TV?"

Serena knew that she didn't look the way she did before she got sick and started taking chemotherapy. "Who do you think I am?" Serena humored the woman.

"Okay, okay. Please don't get upset with me if I'm wrong, but are you the Prophetess Serena?" Treva stood in front of Serena with a serious look on her face.

"How did you guess?" Serena asked, surprised.

Treva started jumping around like a kid in the candy store. She clapped her hands and pulled her cell phone out of her burgundy scrubs. "I knew it. I knew it. My mother watches you on the Christian networks. You are famous and I know that she won't believe you're really here." Stepping outside of her professional role, Treva did a little victory dance in small circles.

Serena laughed with the lab tech and then noticed the cell phone. The smile fell from her face. "Um, what do you plan to do with the phone?" Serena knew that if a picture popped up any place reminding her of this day, she would sue the hospital and shut it down.

"I'm sorry if I'm being insensitive, but once everything is done, could I please make a call to my mother and you just tell her hello? I've never done this before and I really shouldn't be doing it now. I'd get fired if anyone found out; however, my mother loves you and now that I think about it, she has traveled to each of the cities you were in to attend your conferences. I'll understand if you tell me no," Treva said.

Serena was quiet. She didn't know what to think, but she was compelled to oblige the woman's wish. Treva started working again. "How's this?" she asked Serena after placing a pillow under her head.

"I'm comfortable I guess," Serena confirmed.

"Great, I'm not going to try to keep you here too long. If you'll hold your knees up, I will place this pillow under them so your legs won't cramp. Now, I will give you a few commands while you are taking the test. The first half of the test will consist of picture taking of your head, neck, and abdomen without contrast. The second part of the test will be with contrast. I will administer the contrast slowly and run back to finish up. Do you have any questions for me?"

"No, I'm just ready to get this over with." Serena tried to smile, but it looked more like a grimace.

"Awesome. I have picked out some jazz music for you. I hope you will be happy with my selection. The music will help to distract you from the loud noises the machine makes during the test. Now if you will hold your head up just a tad, I will place these headphones on your head. The noise from the scanner is extremely loud and these will help to deflect a lot of the clicking sounds. You ready?" Treva asked Serena.

"I believe I am," Serena answered.

"Okay, here we go." Treva pressed a button that slid Serena all the way through the scan machine until Serena could feel the air on her head from the other side. She left the room and got situated in the control room and pressed play on the compact disc player before starting the exam. "You okay in there?" she checked in with Serena. That went on for about ten minutes and then everything stopped, including the music that was keeping Serena encouraged.

"Okay, we are halfway finished." Treva advised Serena as she walked around the machine to prepare for the contrast injection. "You still doing okay?"

Serena heard Treva speaking near her head and she turned her head to respond. "Yes, and thanks for the music. I'm ready. Let's get it." Serena turned her head back around and waited for the machine to start roaring again.

Finally, it was over. "You did awesome," Treva said as she pushed the button that brought Serena and her face-to-face again. "Let me get you out of here. I just have a few instructions for you today. Before I do that, do you have any other tests scheduled for today?" Treva asked.

Serena couldn't get out that time machine quick enough. "No, I don't have anything else to do here today. I'm getting out of here so I can put some food on my stomach. Those shakes almost took me over the edge and my bladder is full. Is it normal to feel nauseated after drinking all of that stuff?" Serena asked Treva with a disgusted look on her face.

"You should be able to eat. The shakes will usually run through your system. You should drink sixty-four ounces of water or more to completely flush your body of the contrast. Hopefully, you'll be feeling back to normal in a few hours or so. Now, let me take your IV out and then you can get dressed." Treva removed the plastic tubing and swiftly threw it in the trash can. She applied pressure to Serena's forearm and held it for sixty seconds. "Let's see if you've clotted." Treva pulled the gauze from the small hole in Serena's arm. Happy that it had stopped bleeding, she stuck a Band-Aid on it and cleaned around the area. "Now you can get ready to get dressed and go home."

"Thanks for making this experience bearable. Now, if you will give your mother a call, I'd like to say hi to your mom." Serena smiled. Even at her lowest, she was still willing to bless someone else's day.

After Serena had spoken to Treva's mother, Treva showed her the way back to the dressing room.

"When you're done getting dressed, you can leave the key in the locker and then you will be free to go. Don't forget to drink plenty of water," Treva reminded.

"I won't. I mean I will drink lots of fluids. Does it only have to be water or can I drink whatever I want?" Serena asked to make sure she had a clear understanding. She didn't want to set herself back, but knew that she wanted to drink a couple of glasses of sweet tea before the end of the day. It always made her feel better.

"You can drink whatever you'd like. Make sure that you are drinking water as well and everything should be fine. Take care and thanks again. Oh and Miss Sampson?"

"Yes?"

"I just wanted to let you know that I will be praying for your recovery."

"Thank you. Your mother told me the same thing. God bless you both. If I have the pleasure of seeing you again, I plan to have a great report." Serena gave Treva a hug and they parted ways. Serena changed clothes as quickly as possible and put the hospital gowns in the wooden container labeled DIRTY GOWNS. Walking out of the dressing area, Serena left her concerns behind.

Chapter 25

"Doctor, how is my father doing this morning?" Amina inquired of the doctor before going in to see him. She had been faithful in coming to see him every few days since the accident. It had been three weeks and he was finally on the mend.

"Mr. Sampson is a living miracle. He's progressing by leaps and bounds every day. Someone has been praying for that young man because he continues to amaze us. I am more than confident that he will make a full recovery, but may need to use a cane for a while. Other than that, the swelling in his brain is gone, his ribs are healing nicely, and while we thought at first that his neck was fractured, it wasn't. I'm telling you that it's hard to believe that the man we see in there today is the same man who was brought in through emergency Life Flight almost a month ago. He wants to get out and walk, but his leg injuries will take time to heal. We are just going to keep him here a few more days and if things keep going this good, he will be out of here by the end of the week. We are recommending some outpatient physical therapy to strengthen his legs depending on how he does. We will take one day at a time."

"Thanks so much, Doctor. I am going to go in and see him now if that's okay." Amina smiled at the news that her father would be going home soon.

"One more thing and I will let you go. Your father is still facing serious charges from the Bahama Police Department. I recommend that he go to Alcoholics Anonymous and get counseling for whatever it is troubling him. He could have very well lost his life that day and caused another life to be lost. Have a nice day." Dr. Messina bid Amina farewell.

Amina knew that her father would have to deal with the legal ramifications due to his drunken state, but she didn't want to think about anything but his getting better. She called Crystal and Serena, asking them to come down to the hospital. Amina pasted on her happy face and went in to see her father. Upon entering the room she noticed that the blinds were closed. The television was off. When Amina glanced over at her father he was staring straight ahead. She was almost certain that he had heard her coming in, but he chose not to acknowledge her presence for some reason or another. Amina sat down in the chair on the opposite side of the door and remained silent for as long as she could.

"Daddy, how are you today?" Amina waited but received no answer. She was fed up with her father's inconsiderate behavior. It was time that they had the much-needed discussion she had been waiting to have until he got better. His stubborn spirit was irritating her and she needed to get to the bottom of what was going on with him.

"Daddy, I've been here day after day and I have respected the fact that you are on the road to recovery, but you had been evading me ever since you got home. I can see that you don't want to talk to me but I have a lot to say to you, and since you aren't going anywhere, you can just listen."

Amina stood up and turned her chair toward Jonathan's bed and seemed to gather her thoughts before speaking again. "I'm not understanding why you've been acting the way you have and why this has happened, but I feel the need to remind you that the day you were in that horrible accident, you were extremely drunk. Daddy, I didn't even know that you were a drinker. I guess there is a lot that I don't know about you. You were eluding the police and crashed into an eighteen-wheeler truck. When did you start drinking and why were you drinking and driving?" Amina waited, but the silence caused the air to get thick and tension had settled in the atmosphere.

"Daddy, why won't you speak to me?" Still nothing. He was lying so still that you wouldn't even know that he was coherent if the tears hadn't been freefalling from his eyes. Amina decided that she shouldn't press further because she didn't want her father to go into total shut down if he hadn't already. She accepted his silence for now. The more she sat there looking at the pitiful man she called her father, the angrier she became and before she could shut her mouth she regurgitated a flurry of words. "What has happened to you? I never thought that you were so disturbed. The man I thought I knew wouldn't be caught dead drinking beer. Not the way I know Gran-Gran raised you. What did you do? Go to New York so that you wouldn't have to take responsibility of the fact that you left me here without a single parent? I mean, wasn't it bad enough that I lost my mother right after I was born and then you chose to leave me too?"

Amina was acting out in her emotional state and knew she needed to calm down. She still waited for him to respond.

Jonathan turned his head away from Amina. His vision was blurry from the tears that he couldn't stop nor wanted to stop from rolling down his cheeks. The magnitude of his sins weighed down on him like a force that had paralyzed him as he realized his failures. His life flashed before his eyes time and time again, yet he had nothing to say. He couldn't even look at his daughter in the face because he'd been an epic failure in her life. He focused his attention on the eraser board glued to the wall that had his nurse's information, his room number, and a note that read GET BETTER written in big blue letters.

Finally, he whispered, "Your father is a broken man. I'm so broken that I can't even accept God's grace for sparing my life. I know I should thank Him for sparing my life, but I wish I would have died in that car accident." He continued to avoid her gaze because he didn't want her to see him as he saw himself. "It was my intention to tell you about the alcoholism while I was here, but each opportunity brought fear and torment. I would pick up a beer instead of the phone." Jonathan started the process of his healing.

Jonathan didn't know how to answer his daughter without sharing with her the whole story of how he got there. He knew that today wouldn't be like any other day in his life.

"Daddy, I wish that you would have said something. You have distanced yourself from the family for many years and we have never really had the chance to bond as father and daughter. I am nineteen years old and I have never been in a relationship with a guy until now. I don't know how to keep my man from running off the way my mother did. I needed you to show me how to choose the right mate. I have heard many times that you should pick a mate based on the attributes of your father, but I was robbed of the opportunity to know what you were like."

Amina thought she would feel better just being able to talk to her father, but the more she talked she believed that he wasn't really hearing her heart.

Jonathan didn't want to see his baby crying over his negligence, but he didn't know how to comfort her. He felt bad because she didn't know how it was to have a mother and father. He'd robbed her of having one parent in her life who could make a difference. "Amina,

I thought I was doing the right thing by leaving you with Gran and Serena. I was young and foolish. A man who was brokenhearted over losing the only woman I wanted to love. I know what I'm saying probably doesn't make much sense; however, it was the best that I could do at that time. I didn't know how to hold things together after losing your mother." He was tired of hiding his life and keeping up the facade that he had it all together. It was time.

"Please don't cry, baby girl. I'm so sorry for all the messed up things your mother and I put you through," Jonathan said.

Amina's head popped up to look at her father. He had finally turned his head to look at her. His eyes were bloodshot and he looked exhausted. His legs were propped up on pillows and one hand was handcuffed to the bedrail. "Daddy, I accept your apology," she said. "I'm grateful that God has sustained your life, Daddy." Amina wiped her tears away. "No matter what, I will be here to help you get through the next few months or however long it takes for you to make things right. I want to know you and I want you to know the woman I've become."

"Baby girl, I just don't think anyone would understand why I did what I did, how I've lived the way I've lived and believe the way I've believed. I just can't go into it right now, but in time I will. One thing at a time, please," Jonathan pleaded.

"Daddy, I'm not here to judge you, but to support you. I love you and I've never stopped. If you don't reveal your hurt then it can't be healed. The enemy would love to make you feel ashamed of the things you have done. God isn't a God of condemnation, but of redemption. Can you trust the God in me not to look at you strangely when you talk to me? I understand that we all have issues and none of us are perfect. You have completely shut Gran, Auntie, and me out of your life in the past. Now that you've come face-to-face with it, we want to be included in helping you come to terms with those struggles." Amina's voice soothed Jonathan's wounds like a healing balm.

Jonathan listened with his heart as his daughter poured out hers. He didn't think anyone would understand what he had been going through and he wanted to be free. Her words caressed his emotions and he remembered that his family loved the Lord. Tired of hiding behind the mask of yesterdays gone by, Jonathan had one request: "Sweetie, call the family and ask them if they can get over here as quickly as possible. I have something that I need to say," Jonathan acquiesced.

"I called them before I came in to see you." Amina grabbed her father's hand in hers. She squeezed it for reassurance, to let him know that she was there and wasn't going anywhere. At that same time she was praying in her spirit that God would prepare her for whatever her father admitted to. Her prayers were that no one in the room would look at her father any differently and would accept the facts that would be laid on out for them once they got there.

"Daddy, you remember James? He came to see Auntie when she was in the hospital. He's a driver for Auntie and many other celebrities. We're in a relationship. It's all new to me, but I wanted to get your thoughts on it. He's twenty-two years old and he's a Christian. He's a really great guy and I want you to be able to talk to him and get to know him better before you go back to New York." She hoped that her father wouldn't act overprotective considering he had hardly been there at all.

"Whoa, you're only nineteen, you know that right? Isn't twenty-two a little old for you? He's a grown man and you, you are still a kid." Jonathan wasn't sure how he felt about his daughter growing up and loving some other man beside him. He couldn't put his finger on why he reacted the way he did; it's not like he was really around to bond with his daughter. Once he left for New York, he hadn't looked back.

Amina didn't hear anything but her father insinuating that she was not mature enough to be in a relationship. Amina chose her words carefully. "A kid? Is that all you see me as? Daddy, take a good look at me. I've surpassed the stages of diapers, formula, and pacifiers. That's who you remember me to be because you chose to leave me in the hands of other people. You've missed out on monumental phases of my life. Graduations, school dances, awards ceremonies, my prom, and many other things. So trust me, my kid days are far gone, never to return. I need you to try to guide me through my first real relationship outside of my family; but then you may not be the person to do that since you ran my mother off." Now that Amina's rant was over, she felt bad. She was usually more in control of her feelings and not a person who liked confrontation.

Jonathan was shocked at the anger that his child held inside of her. He couldn't fault her even though her words stung. Unsure of what to say to his daughter, Jonathan kept quiet. He wondered if he could ever make up to her how he had disregarded the majority of her life. She wouldn't remember all of the days he kept her and made sure she was safe. Before the terrible breakup, Jonathan fed Amina, bathed her, and prayed every night that God would show him what was best for his baby girl. He did it out of love, he thought.

Amina reached over to her father's breakfast tray and poured some of his fresh ice water into one of the Styrofoam cups. She settled back down into her chair and thought about what her father would say to the family once they got there. She was having a hard time trying to understand why her father was acting so mysterious as if he had something going on in his life worse than anyone else. Amina's main concern was how her grandmother would deal with whatever the news was.

The door swung open and Crystal, trailed by Serena, came through the door with a worried look on her face, but they visibly exhaled when they saw that the room wasn't full of doctors waiting to bear some bad news. "Hi, son, Amina." Crystal gave her son a kiss while Serena gave Amina a kiss and then they switched places. They both walked over to greet Amina and Jonathan with hugs and kisses on their cheeks.

"Hi, Gran, Auntie. How are you feeling today?" Amina gestured for her grandmother to sit in the chair that she had recently vacated.

"Feeling fine, baby, and how are the two of you?" Crystal asked, watching both of their tense faces.

"Um, okay I guess," Amina answered for herself. She didn't want to bring up the conversation she had with her father because she knew that her grandmother wouldn't approve. "Auntie, I'll get you a chair."

The room was still quiet when Amina returned. She pushed the door, dragging two chairs behind her. With no help from anyone, she got wedged in the door with one chair in and one chair that she struggled to pull through. Breaking out in a sweat, Amina dropped one chair on the floor outside in the hallway. "Can I get some help here?" Amina asked, peeved.

"I'm sorry, baby, let me help you with that. I don't know where my mind was." Serena seemed to shake herself off and opened the door and slid one of the chairs into the room.

The silence continued. Crystal's mind was on the argument that she and her son had the morning of the accident. Serena's mind was on her next phase of treatment and she'd resumed worrying about the results of the scans. Amina was still feeling some kind of way about the blowup she'd just had with her father.

Jonathan felt that his daughter was right. If he didn't reveal his hurt there was no coming back from that, no healing. He didn't want to die from feelings of unworthiness and he wanted to tell his family the truth about him before his mother did. He looked over at her and saw the remorse in her eyes. She tried smiling at him, but tears fell instead. Jonathan didn't try holding back his own tears as he looked at his family. They were all he had left and he would need them by his side.

Breaking the silence, Jonathan used the control on the bed to raise the bed. Hearing the noise, Crystal jumped up. "Let me help you with that, son." She extended an olive branch as she desperately wanted to make things right.

"I've got it, Mama." Jonathan looked at her reassuringly and she sat back down. "I wanted you all here to talk to you. There are some things that you need to know about me and I don't want them coming from anyone but me." Jonathan looked at the most important women in his life.

"I'm sure glad that you are ready to talk, Jonathan. I hope that your recovery goes well, but I must say you pick a fine time to want to break bread with the family. You've been in this city going on five months and I haven't seen you since I was the one lying in a hospital bed. Now that you're lying in one, you want to talk? I have to admit that even though I'm sorry that you're going through what you're going through, in case you've forgotten, I'm going through some things too. I'm very upset with you, big brother," Serena admitted sadly.

"First of all, I want to apologize. Mama, sis, baby girl, I'm Godly sorry for not being there for you all the ways I should have. Mama already knows what my demons are.

This all happened because when I exposed myself to her, I felt like the world had been lifted from my shoulders; however, it was the furthest thing from the truth." Jonathan began coughing and the ladies hopped up.

"Daddy, are you okay? Can I get you some water?" Amina went to her father's side, waiting for him to tell her what he needed.

"Nah, I'm okay, baby girl. Thanks. Mama, sis, I'm going to be okay. My throat is just a little dry. Please sit. I'm already nervous as it is." Jonathan's voice became stronger. He waited until everyone was seated before he continued baring his soul. "As I was saying, I'm sorry for not being the son Mama thought she raised or the father that Amina needed in her life."

"Jonathan, what do you mean you're not the son Mommy thinks that she raised? Who exactly does she think she raised? What's going on with you? We know you weren't here for Amina physically, but you've always been a part of her life. It was decided that she would stay here with Mommy and me so that we could raise her. Where is all of this coming from?" Serena asked, bewildered.

"Sis, please let me finish!" Jonathan bellowed.

"Serena, let your brother talk now," Crystal urged.

Amina sat quietly. She anxiously waited to hear where this conversation was headed.

Serena sat back in her chair and looked straight out the window. She was determined to keep her mouth closed until given permission to speak. There was an uncomfortable stillness in the room as no one said anything. Jonathan wondered if he should go on or just forget about it. He'd already apologized to his family. His mother knew about him and he hoped that she was praying for him. Outside of his physical ailments, his soul was ailing as well.

"Never mind. I just wanted to apologize for all of the hurt and disappointment I've caused you. Mama, I'm sorry for blemishing the ministry that you've worked your whole life to build and brand. I wasn't thinking. I was upset when I got behind the wheel of that car. It's evident that I have a drinking problem."

"Son, bad things happen to good people. Just because life happened to you doesn't make you a horrible person. The blessing is that this situation could have been a lot worse, but God was in the midst. No one was hurt besides you. You are in a safe place; don't be afraid to share your heart. As far as Abiding Savior's concerned, just know that God's got us. He is our protector and our shield. We won't miss a beat, you'll see." Crystal hoped that her family would be restored and the only way that could happen was if they all opened up to one another. She hoped that Jonathan would tell his truths so that real healing could begin.

"Remember, Daddy, I promised to be here for you no matter what," Amina repeated.

Jonathan exhaled and used his free hand to hold on to the bedrail for support before taking off the mask and uncovering who he'd been the last nineteen years. "The night Sherry broke up with me, I was devastated." Jonathan paused. "Each time I tell this story, I get emotional. I remember going to Ms. Paxton's house and asking to speak to Sherry, but she wasn't home. I didn't get the chance to try to win her back. Her mother had said that she'd packed her clothes and said she wasn't coming back. I'd lost the woman I'd planned to spend the rest of my life with." He cried like a newborn baby. Sadness overwhelmed him as the scab was removed and the wound was fresh because he would tell his family of the sordid lifestyle he'd gravitated to.

Crystal moved closer to Jonathan's bedside and peeled his fingers from the bedrail and held his hand. She'd already heard the story, so she knew what to expect and her shock had worn off. It had taken her days to digest the information her only son had shared with her. She'd talked to God many times and prayed for understanding, but the only response she received was that it's his life and he would find his way back.

Jonathan appreciated his mother being by his side. It gave him the courage he needed. "Once I found out that Sherry had left home, I just snapped. I didn't know what to do or where to go. I ended up in one of my boys' neighborhoods. A party was going on and I heard the music from down the block. I ended up at the party. I had a few drinks and I ended up in bed with a guy I'd never met before. There it is." Jonathan couldn't face anyone, but he squeezed his mother's hand tightly like he was afraid a bomb would go off. He braced himself for the backlash, the judgment, but none came.

"My life has pretty much been a lie. I mean as far as working, I am an account executive with J.P. Morgan. However, everything else in my life is all wrong. The night I ended up in the bed with that guy was the start of my desire to be with men. Alcohol became my way of dealing with the guilt and shame of what I'd been doing. I didn't mean for it to become a lifestyle, but it was my life. I danced with everyone, someone, then myself. I didn't have a care in the world. Someone tapped me on the shoulder from behind. I turned around and we began dancing together. One dance turned into another and another until we moved to one of the bedrooms and there it happened." Jonathan exhaled.

Serena appreciated Jonathan's honesty, but that alone didn't make her not want to slap the taste from his mouth. Instead of saying what she was really thinking, she thought before speaking. "Jonathan, we all make mistakes, brother. You know how many mess-ups I had while in my rebellious state. I didn't have a care in the world because I didn't think that Mommy cared for us or what we wanted. Mommy always down talked Sherry, never having anything good to say about her. She demonized Sherry, point blank," Serena said.

"Excuse me. I am in the room and I can hear very well," Crystal fumed.

"Sis, I can't use Mama as a scapegoat for why I did what I did. No, she wasn't the easiest woman to deal with when it came to Sherry. Mama informed me that there were things going on that I didn't know about, which would explain why she didn't like Sherry. It was my fault that I did what I did. When it was going on it, exactly what I wanted. I wasn't too concerned about where the attention came from and that's why I did it," Jonathan confessed.

Amina sat upright in her chair. "Sooo, are you saying you're gay?" Amina looked at her father for an answer. When he didn't defend what he said she got up and left the room. No one tried to stop her.

Chapter 26

Crystal remained in her study before service and paced the floor. She hadn't been able to sleep or eat much since Jonathan's release from the hospital three weeks ago. Jonathan's legal problems were just beginning and he'd been going to rehab a couple times a week. It broke her heart to have to take him downtown to turn himself in to the police department, where he was fingerprinted and placed into a jail cell. Upon Jonathan's release from the hospital, he was cuffed and his rights were read. The nurses wheeled him down to the waiting police car in a wheelchair. She followed the police cruiser, crying the whole way.

After Jonathan spent three days in jail, he was finally released on reduced bond. He pleaded guilty to the charges of drunk driving and reckless endangerment and his court date was set. Crystal's heart was hurting because she had to find a way to tell Jonathan that his boss had called while he was in the hospital as the news spread of his accident and the charges against him caused him to be terminated immediately. Years of memories came flooding back into Crystal's mind, although she tried to focus on her prayer. Selfishness was the only thing she could hear echoing in her ears. She prayed even harder to quiet the voice in her head. Conviction blanketed her as she fell to her knees and cried out to God to fix it.

A knock on the door interrupted Crystal's pleas to God. Slowly, Crystal rose from the floor and went to answer the door. She didn't care that she looked disheveled and forlorn. Her suit was wrinkled and her face stained with tears. Jalisa was at the door and rushed in, shutting it behind her.

"Pastor, there are some more news reporters here. They are requesting to speak with you about Jonathan's upcoming trial," Jalisa advised her.

"How did they know that Jonathan is my son?" Crystal snapped.

"Well, the rumor is that there was an anonymous tip from one of our church members," Jalisa revealed.

"Humph, I wonder how much they were paid to talk to the reporters. You already know that I will not be speaking to any reporters about my family's personal business. They can read the outcome in the news or just show up on the courthouse steps. They act like he committed murder or some other horrible crime." Crystal paced the floor.

"Yes, ma'am. I'm sorry that things are seemingly getting out of hand. I thought we kept things under wraps pretty well, but there's always one who will sell out," Jalisa said.

"I mean yes, he was drunk driving and yes, he ran from the police. Stuff like that happens daily around here, but my son is the one who is in the news and has been on television. Worse things are going on in the city but they want to be able to mock the God I serve just because the preacher's kid isn't perfect! Tell them that if they are outside after church is over I will call the police and file trespassing charges. Please find Elder Shaw and send her back here. I am going to need for her to bring the Word this morning."

"Yes, ma'am. I'll go now." Jalisa left the office as quickly as she'd come.

Crystal went to her bathroom and washed her face and fixed her clothes. She checked the mirror to make sure that she looked presentable before Elder Shaw arrived. Moments later, Elder Shaw knocked at the door and was summoned inside. "Elder, thank you for coming as quickly as you did. I need for you to preach in my place this morning. Jonathan has been home a few weeks and I haven't taken any time off to be there for him. I've been clinging to the ministry here, but I need to be home. He's still on the mend. I trust that you have a prepared Word today," Crystal said.

"Pastor Sampson, I'm prepared to stand in your place. I will let the church know that you had to leave and to keep your family in prayer," Elder Shaw said.

"Just keep us in your prayers and please let the church know that we appreciate their many prayers, phone calls, and get well cards. Also let them know that I will make a formal statement soon. I need for you to send some men of valor to escort me out to my car. I don't want to have to deal with the news reporters right now. We are dealing with enough. I expect for you to hold down the fort until I get back. I love you, Elder Shaw, and will see you soon. If anything goes wrong, please call me right away."

"Thanks so much, Pastor Sampson. Don't worry about anything. I will do as you have asked. I'm going out to get you some guys for cover. We love you, Pastor."

Crystal went to her mahogany desk and sat down. She swiveled around to look out the window at all of the people outside wishing they could get to her. They were vultures seeking their prey, but they had the wrong one. She got her things and waited to hear the knock on the door before exiting her office. Toney came with two of the other men in tow. Toney and Larry walked on either side of their spiritual leader as Trent followed up the rear. They escorted Crystal to her car and to her surprise, no one bothered her, although they snapped pictures from a distance. She bid her spiritual sons adieu, locked her doors, and drove home.

Chapter 27

Amina drove up to her grandmother's house and called her father. "Daddy, I'm outside. Can you come and unlock the door?" Ten minutes later, Jonathan came to the door with his walker. He smiled at his daughter as he stood back from the door and opened it wide enough for her to enter.

"Hey, baby girl. How are you?" Jonathan smiled at his daughter.

"Hey, Daddy. I'm good. How are you feeling?" Amina gave her father a hug and walked into the house. She dropped her pocketbook on the kitchen counter and sat at the oak table in the dining room and waited for her father to join her.

"I've had better days, sweetie. Your grandmother is at church right now. She's probably preaching a hole in somebody's head about folks sinning and being in sin." He laughed and shook his head.

"Daddy, Gran-Gran lives at the church, but you know that already, don't you? Have you guys spoken since she brought you home from the hospital? I would have come over sooner, but I wanted you to get your rest and get stronger. How has rehab been? I know that you have had a lot going on since being released and I just wanted to give you some space to figure things out."

"Well, your grandmother hasn't really had much to say to me. She was there when I was released from the hospital and followed me to the county jail. Three days later, I went before the judge and she was there, waiting to post my bail and bring me home. Rehab is a beast, baby girl, but I need it," Jonathan said eyeing the walker.

"Gran called Auntie to let her know that you were able to come home and what the stipulations were. It's been crazy since all of this happened." Amina shook her head. "Daddy, I want to apologize for walking out on you at the hospital that day. I guess I was just surprised by your confession of being gay. It took me by surprise, but after I had time to think about it, I realized that hurt people do things they wouldn't ordinarily do because of pain they've endured. I don't want you to think that I agree with your lifestyle. But regardless of what you've done, one thing that will never change is that you're my daddy and I love you."

"After all of the trouble I've caused, there's no way I'd be caught with a bottle up to my lips unless it was a bottle of water. Your grandmother made sure there were no traces of alcohol anywhere to be found. It messed with me when she drove into the garage and her other car was no longer there. I felt really bad all over again for wrecking her car. To have you here today is another blessing. I didn't do the best by you, but I know that I have another chance. I also realize that, in a way, I did the same thing to you that I have accused my mother of. I'm sorry."

"No one is expecting you to never mess up; that's impossible. Wallowing in self-pity won't change what has happened," Amina encouraged her father.

"I have so many things to figure out, but first thing's first. I need to get through this. I am definitely coming back home. Mama told me that I was let go from my job due to my recent extracurricular activities. I guess everything happens for a reason and I hope that I can bounce back once I've fulfilled all of my legal obligations here. I'm sure that my boss isn't too happy that I've been gone for as long as I have. I just hope that you all will forgive me in time, accept me for me, and keep on loving me," Jonathan said, turning his ears toward a sound in the garage.

Crystal had turned her car off and sat quietly for a few minutes. She had to get her thoughts together before going into the house. After getting hot and sticky from the outside heat, Crystal peeled herself off of the leather interior of her seat and ambled into the house.

Amina met her grandmother at the door and squealed, "Hey, Gran-Gran. What are you doing home so early? Surely, church hasn't let out yet. Is everything okay?" She kissed her grandmother on the cheek and grabbed her pocketbook and led her into the house.

"Hey, baby, yes, everything is okay. Can't a woman come home and make sure her son is all right?" She grunted and walked over to the table where Jonathan sat. Looking down at her son, she saw the little boy who never gave her a hard time after his father passed. He was young and innocent then, but life had done a doozy on him and it was up to her to help restore him back to God. "Hey, son." Crystal dropped everything on the kitchen counter and grabbed a glass for something to drink.

"Mama, thanks for coming home early to check on me. It's not like you to let church services out early. You feeling okay?" Jonathan looked at his mother, concerned about her health.

"For your information, I didn't let church out early. I had Elder Shaw preach in my absence because I needed to come home and talk to you." Crystal pulled out a chair and plopped down in it.

"Do I need to excuse myself?" Amina asked out of respect but really hoped that she wouldn't be dismissed from the kitchen.

"Naw, baby, you come on in here and sit down too. What I need to say, I can say in front of you. Jonathan, I know I am a hard woman, but that's all I know how to be. I have had to take care of your sister and you after your father died alone. I tried to honor your father's memory by making sure that the church took off, which required a lot of hard work and dedication. You see, it's hard for a black woman to lead a congregation where men are speckled throughout, doubting that I could fulfill the position. Many have missed the scriptures where God talked about using women for ministry. See, son, I was dealing with a double standard. I can admit now that I lost focus on everything but the church. I neglected my first ministry, which was my family." Crystal regretted her past.

Amina reached across the table and grabbed her grand-mother's hand. She could hear the pain in Crystal's voice. It was encouraging to her to see them talking to one another and not at each other. This was what she had been praying for: that God would restore their family and bring them closer together. She was ecstatic that her father would be moving back home. In her heart she knew that God was going to turn his situation around and they all would be one happy family. Testimony time was on the horizon; she could just feel it.

"Come on, you guys, group hug!" Amina stood up and moved over to where her father was sitting and waited for him to stand up and Crystal was right there, ready to make amends. They all hugged and kissed each other's cheeks. Amina wished that Serena was there, but it was okay because they were all family and God was in the healing business.

Chapter 28

"Jonathan, are you ready to go?" Crystal called from the kitchen.

"I'm almost ready, Mama." Jonathan wasn't feeling well, but he was prepared to go see the judge. His court date was happening at nine a.m. He was grateful that Nathaniel had hooked him up with one of his lawyer buddies, Robert Shearin. He was supposed to be a topnotch professional who won most of his cases. Jonathan had never been in trouble in his life and he was very scared of what the outcome would be. He hoped that would account for something. He looked in the mirror and saw a different man.

Jonathan didn't have any alcohol in his system. He hadn't had a drink in over four months. His mind kept telling him that he needed a drink when he was feeling stressed, but he wanted to be free of snares and entanglements with sinful things. He brushed his teeth slowly, methodically, thinking about how blessed he was to be able to still do the things he was able to do before the accident. Moments of clarity were growing longer and longer for him.

Jonathan felt a tug in his gut and felt a longing for something more. He knew now that it was Jesus that could fill the void. Jonathan had tried the alcohol, being with a man versus being with a woman, and deceiving himself into thinking that he would be fulfilled and find the love that had abandoned him years ago. Those things that he'd indulged in didn't make him feel good about himself; that's why he'd hidden them for so long. Now he wanted something more and he knew where he would get it.

Jonathan washed his face and tied his tie, feeling better than he had since being home from the hospital. He could see the hand of God in his relationships and he trusted God to work this out for him. After speaking with Robert, Jonathan was confident that since he didn't have a criminal record, he would be able to get off with probation and restitution. There wasn't anyone hurt in the accident, but he was told to be prepared to be ordered to attend Alcoholics Anonymous faithfully. Robert warned that the press would be after a hot story since they were looking for an interview from him. Jonathan was advised not to worry.

"What took you so long, son? I thought you were going to stay up there and not even come down at all. Are you nervous?"

"Sorry for my delay. I was just thinking about some things and I can actually say that I'm good and ready to get this over with. If you are ready to go, I am also. Robert said he would meet us down at the courthouse." Jonathan pushed his walker over to his side of the car, where Crystal held the door open for him.

She locked up the house before heading back to the passenger side of her car to fold up the walker and place it in the back seat. Sweat beads popped out on Jonathan's forehead as his mother backed out of the garage and driveway.

Crystal sensed how apprehensive he seemed and she reached over to hold his hand until his anxiety passed. "Son, I love you and I am so proud of you," Crystal said.

Chapter 29

A month had passed since Serena had completed all of her medical treatments and this was her first Sunday back to church. She felt a little awkward sitting down in the congregation as she was used to sitting up in the pulpit doing ministry. Serena didn't allow that to dampen her spirits as she turned to her right, and as if reading her thoughts, Nathaniel draped his long, chiseled arm across her shoulders. Water in her eyes, Serena was thankful all over again and she smiled at her man.

The music played and the atmosphere had been set for worship. Serena watched and thanked God for another day, for another opportunity to be able to walk into the house of the Lord. She remembered the last time she was there. She was being carried out on a stretcher. An overwhelming spirit of gratitude saturated Serena's psyche and tears flowed freely from her perfectly made-up face. As her shoulders shook with force from the emotion leaving her body, Nathaniel held her tightly and she laid her head on his shoulder and continued to reverence God.

The events of the last six and a half months played in her mind over and over again. Amina sat on Serena's left side and she removed tissues from her travel bag and stuffed them into Serena's hand. She had been such a great help during that season in Serena's life and she had even been able to reconnect with her father during this. She smiled gratefully as he sat on her left side, having made up his mind to relocate to North Carolina and be closer to his family.

Crystal took the microphone from Elder Shaw and the applause for her was astounding. She waited until everyone calmed down and then spoke to her church family.

"Praise the Lord, saints." She held the microphone out toward the congregation as she awaited their response.

"Praise the Lord," came the jovial reply.

Crystal was grateful for the faithful members who weren't there to judge or mock her or her family. She smiled and cleared her throat. "I just want to thank God today for all of the wonderful blessings that He has given to my family today. I'm blessed because I'm still standing here with a church of committed and sold out saints of God. Give yourselves a hand clap of praise." The church went wild and if one was on the outside, they would have thought that the church was overflowing with people due to the loud noise coming from the building. God must have been smiling.

"Thank you for sticking by Abiding Savior and me when the enemy came to sift us as wheat. I have had to really learn how to lean on Jesus and listen to those who speak the truth for my good. Saints, we have all sinned and fallen short of the glory of God, but I'm so glad that God looks past our sin and sees our need, which is His mercy and unfailing love. My family has been through a lot and we're still going through it, but we know that trials and testing are the way of life for the Christian. I'm asking that you continue to keep your pastor in prayer and keep this in mind: this too shall pass. I give God praise for my daughter, my son, and my granddaughter today. They have helped me to see that God can still do a new thing in any of us who want to be changed," Crystal said.

The church erupted in applause and hollers. Crystal held up her hand to quiet the congregants. When she was satisfied that she had their undivided attention, she spoke. "Beloved, when I say praise the Lord, your response should be Hallelujah. Now let's try this thang one more time. Praise the Lord, church." Crystal thrust the microphone out toward the crowd again and waited.

"Hallelujah." The church erupted in praise once again and then the musicians began to play.

Crystal led the congregants in worship. She had so much joy that particular morning because of the many blessings that God had manifested during her family's season of testing.

The presiding minister replaced the pastor at the pulpit and carried on the spirit of worship in the place. Once Crystal was back in the pulpit and had taken the microphone, she began to speak. The church was silent and only the soft harmony of the keyboard could be heard.

Sweat poured from her face and neck. Crystal gave God praise for her family, who was sitting on the front row. She motioned for the microphone to be passed to her. "Saints, I am just so full of love for God this morning. I'm blessed, family. I want to give God praise for my daughter, Prophetess Serena; welcome back, baby. My son, Jonathan, God has great things in store for you. Amina, my only grandchild, Gran-Gran loves you with all of me. Brother Nathaniel, thank you for loving my Serena and being here for our family. I'd also like to extend a warm welcome to Brother James Jones. Thank you for blessing Abiding Savior with your presence. Give God some praise and let the music play."

The congregation went up in spirit again. It seemed as though they genuinely cared about Serena and she blushed at the fanfare. She didn't jump up or do any of her usual celebratory actions due to the fact that she was still weak and didn't want to overdo it, and not only that, she had been babying her throat and not using her voice the way she had before the illness.

When the church came to order, Nathaniel felt honored to escort his queen up to the pulpit. He led her up the steps on the side of the pulpit closest to where they were seated and Amina followed closely behind her. Serena took her time and great care in stepping into the pulpit. Nathaniel returned to his seat down in the front and beamed at her beauty and grace. She looked radiant in her silver and purple suit with matching hat and shoes. Her makeup looked flawless and she had a glow about her. The church members and visitors alike stood in honor of the return of their teacher, preacher, and friend. The clapping, the music, and the praise team were all on one accord and it was refreshing for Serena to stand there in awe of all that was taking place.

The dancers came out with streamers and flags while waving them up and down the aisle, prancing around in their royal purple dancewear. Amina stood to the side of the podium keeping a close eye on Serena. She stared at her aunt in awe of the love being poured out for her because Serena deserved to be honored today. Serena had come so far and had to battle so much, but by and by, what they couldn't see during the storm was that the rainbow was to be manifested and some changes were taking place for the better. Amina diverted her attention to her father. She began to weep when she saw his head drop onto his chest and his arms stretched upward.

Seeing that the congregation had quieted some while others were shouting out "I love yous" to Serena, she needed to get started, but was thankful for the timely delay. She had learned so much and she knew that she would share her testimony today. Patiently, she waited for about three more minutes before speaking.

"It's so good to be back among the saints." The applause was astounding.

"We love you, Prophetess," one of the sisters stood up and shouted.

"I love you too. I love you all," Serena said to the whole church. "I just want to take this time to thank each of you for the prayers and visits when I was in the hospital." The congregants were ecstatic and began applauding the living miracle stamding before them now, speaking and defeating the report of the doctors. Serena's voice still felt weak as this was the first time she was stretching it and she was now stepping out on faith that her voice would carry her through the sermon.

She scanned the crowd with her eyes, she saw that everyone was staring back at her intently. She twisted her neck around to look at her mother, and when she did, her mother smiled and nodded her approval, encouraging her to continue. "Sisters and brothers, I am a blessed woman. A woman who stands before you healed from throat cancer." The crowd applauded and started screaming in praise to God. Serena didn't wait this time for the crowd to calm down; she gripped the microphone in her hand and reared her head back and hollered hallelujah to God. Her voice sounded off like fireworks full of authority and energy.

"I take nothing for granted but I am thankful to be back where I belong. See, God has healed me from cancer that has the ability to break down even the strongest man or woman. I was given a sixty percent chance of beating this thing." Serena heard amens from the pulpit to the front door. It gave her a chance to recollect herself because this was all still fresh to her. She didn't think that she could go on, but then she felt the support of her mother who stood behind her telling her it was okay and to take her time.

Serena felt like she could go on now that her composure was in check. She cleared her throat lightly after sipping water from a glass handed to her by Amina. "You see, there are times in our lives when we lose focus of what's really important. I've been in church all my life because for those of you who know my mother, Pastor Sampson, church was her life. I was saved at an early age and I grew to love the Lord in spite of my one foot in and one foot out of the grace of God. I had to grow up and realize after my first heartbreak that God could heal my hurts and disappointments with what life offered. So I threw myself into working in this ministry and answered my call to God to walk in the office of a prophet.

"The problem was that I was still empty on the inside and regardless of the fact that I knew God, there were some things I was upset about. I continued walking in the things of the Lord, being obedient to the authority placed over me." Serena nodded to her mother and smiled.

Crystal sat and listened to her daughter, knowing how hard it must be for her to stand up and expose herself to all of those people. She also realized it was much needed, not just for Serena but for someone in the congregation and for her own family. With tears in her eyes, she returned her daughter's smile and put her hand to her mouth and blew a kiss to Serena.

"Saints of God, I got caught up and became lacka-daisical in the things of God. I'd received invitations to travel the world to bring forth the Word of God so that women in all kinds of dire situations could be delivered. I believed that God would do exactly what they were asking for according to His will and healing power concerning them." Amens and "unh hms" came from all corners of the massive sanctuary. Women were dabbing their eyes and whimpers could also be heard faintly in the midst of Serena's testimony.

"The thing is this, God has a sense of humor and will use the things you've said to others to encourage and edify by placing you in a situation that will test your faith. Aw, y'all ain't hearing me." Serena beat her hand on the podium for added effect. "I said that God will take you from the palace and place you in a pit just to see what you gon' do. I had a decision to make and that was to give up and die or exercise my faith in the power of an omnipotent God and live. I know it sounds like an easy decision to make, but some days I was up and some I was down."

Applause erupted from the church members who stood up and began to applaud and give God praise for their own situations. In the pulpit, the reaction was no different. The ministers and elders jumped to their feet and cheered Serena on, saying, "You'd better preachhhhhh, Preacher." Crystal waved her handkerchief as if to stir the anointing in the air while jumping up and down.

"And let me tell you, children of God, that when God has a divine assignment on your life, He will allow you to go through some dark places in order to bring you back to Him. See, God commands His people to worship Him in spirit and in truth. What we do for God should not be done out of duty or obligation, but of sheer love for who He is." The congregation began to get hyped by the word going forth and that encouraged Serena to continue to speak revelation to them.

"God had to strip me because my mindset was business as usual. There were engagements I wanted to turn down because there was an unspoken question in my heart. Why was I doing everything for God but He wasn't giving me my heart's desire. I knew that God was expecting me to go out and preach and prophesy to the women at those conferences and revivals, so that's what I did. God honored the anointing on my life more than I did. He went with me and prepared the way for me at each place I visited. Women were freed, delivered, and healed all by the power of God, but I wasn't free. When one looked at me, they saw success and a highly anointed woman who loved the Lord. One thing I've learned is that you can't get caught up in stuff." Amens rang out from the congregation.

"I began to notice that each time I went out, my voice would fail me and I would be more tired than the time before. Little did I know that God was crashing my party of pity. Never did He leave me, never did He forsake me, but when He was done with me, I had let go of all of the things that could have separated me from the love of my God. Cancer was my curse and my blessing; it almost took me out. My trials became my blessing. In the wee hours of the mornings, when my body was racked in pain due to chemotherapy and the surgeries, I would helplessly lie in my bed and cry. His Word says that if you draw near to Him, He will draw near to you." Many were crying and ladies were rocking side to side with young children on their laps.

"God began to break up the hardness in my heart. He has a way to make it seem like you are going to lose the very thing that He ordained inside of you. When we begin to take for granted what God has done for us and through us, He will make you hunger and thirst for it until you are back in the place He placed you in the beginning. See, your gift will make room for you and while you are in spiritual war, He will show you what could be and what's going to be." Serena paused, hoping that the people received what she said.

"Saints of God, you have to fight for your miracle. God told me, He said, 'Serena, when I deliver you out of the lion's den, then you will give me the praise. I'm giving you your heart's desire because you are finally giving me mine: your love. I've always loved you, but you didn't always love,'" Serena ministered.

"He went on to say to me that no longer will I serve Him out of duty or obligation, but I will serve Him because my heart is pure for Him. God said that when you come out of this, you will no longer just do ministry, Serena, you will be ministry." The congregation went wild with praises and shouting. The music started up again, the praise dancers began praising, and the worshippers started worshipping. Many were slain in the spirit, yet still others were trying to eat the word she was serving up.

In the midst of the spirit of praise Serena turned and placed the microphone in the hands of her mother. She was oblivious to the throngs of people running down to the altar throwing money near her feet. Serena bowed down and honored her God. In her body she was tired, but she still laid hands on herself and claimed supernatural restoration, trusting that God would restore her fully as she spoke life. Amina was right by Serena's side and she helped her aunt up from the pulpit floor and back down to her seat. When she got to the front row Nathaniel stood up and grabbed her hand.

Serena wasn't aware that Amina had brought one of the cordless microphones down until she handed the microphone to Nathaniel and smiled. He'd signaled for her to do so. Amina moved off to the left and her father stood up and hugged her. They sat back down and held hands, waiting on what was coming next.

Crystal stood at the podium in the pulpit and quieted the church. She motioned to some of the ushers and trustee board members to bring the collection buckets and gather the money up from the floor and around the pulpit. She then turned her attention back to the waiting congregation, who had certainly been on an emotional rollercoaster that morning.

"Praise the Lord, everyone. I believe that Brother Nathaniel has something that he would like to say, so please turn your attention to the front. For those of you who can't see, just focus your attention to one of the big screens near you. Brother Nathaniel?" Crystal cued him in to take over.

Nathaniel took the microphone and said, "Prophetess Serena Sampson, you are the most beautiful, intellectual, and anointed woman I know. When I first saw you, I was intimidated by the authority that exudes you." He bent down on one knee and continued to speak. "I have grown to know you and love you. I love almost everything about you and while I acknowledge that there are many facets of you, I am excited about being able to be the one who gets to learn about them all.

"Thank you for allowing me to be a part of your life. I want to be there with you during your mountaintop experiences as well as what you have just walked through. It would bless me even more if you would do me the honor of spending the rest of your life with me because I'm more than sure that I can handle the favor of God on your life." Nathaniel looked deeply into Serena's eyes, which were brimming with tears.

He got down on one knee. "Serena, my queen, will you do the honor of making me the happiest man in the world by accepting my proposal to take my hand in marriage?" Nathaniel wanted to make it official in front of those who would be in attendance that he was marrying the love of his life.

The atmosphere was pregnant with anticipation. The members looked as if they were on the edge of their seats as they waited for Serena's response. Crystal exited the pulpit with the assistance of one of the men of valor and stood by her son and granddaughter. She hoped that Serena accepted Nathaniel's proposal because she could feel it in her soul that he was sincere and really loved her.

Crystal may have had her doubts before, but Nathaniel had been like a rock for them during the course of Serena's illness. When he had invited her out to dinner at the Fish House located in Durham, North Carolina, she knew it was serious. The conversation was light and the calamari was some of the best she had ever eaten. She knew something was up when he started stammering and messing over his food. Crystal acted like she didn't really know what was going, but had figured that he wanted her blessing on the proposal and pending marriage. Finally, after he asked for the check, he then asked Crystal if she would bless and perform the marriage ceremony if Serena accepted.

Serena just stood there. She didn't say a word, but she cried like a newborn baby. Nathaniel had beads of sweat popping out on his freshly cut head, causing a burning sensation to distract him momentarily. He rocked on his knee, hoping that his lady would hurry up and answer the question. Serena calmed down moments later, which seemed like an eternity, with only the sounds of the clock ticking on the wall echoing throughout the sanctuary. She held her left hand down in front of his face and wiggled her fingers. Everyone could see every move either firsthand or up on the big screens that captured the momentous occasion. Nathaniel took her gesture as a yes to his proposal. He took her ring off of her finger and removed the official rock from the box and slid it onto her perfectly manicured ring finger, which sealed their engagement.

When Serena looked at her finger blinged with the four-carat solitaire diamond-cut nugget that rested upon her hand, she turned to the cameras and held up the beautiful ornament as it graced her hand. The congregation roared in cheers and salutes. The musicians began to play the wedding song and everyone was shouting. No one realized that it was nearing two o'clock in the afternoon. It was like the party was just getting started. Serena whispered something in Nathaniel's ear and he kissed her tenderly on the lips with the biggest smile on his face. They each turned to hug their family members and soon-to-be family.

Serena was overjoyed by the events of the day. "How about we get out of here and go celebrate. Mother, will you be accompanying us?" Serena asked softly.

"Baby, I wouldn't miss this fellowship for the world. You all go on ahead and text my phone to let me know where you are meeting. Once I do the benediction and make sure everything is in order, I'm handing over everything else to the deacons so that they can lock up the church when they are done." Crystal hugged her family members once more and told them that she loved them before turning back toward the pulpit with her spirit humbled and full of joy.

Crystal was determined not to allow another opportunity to bond with her family pass her by. She had been out of order for a long time. God had redeemed time for her and family. He had brought her son home and even though he had a long way to go, God had saved him from destruction.

Jalisa circled the parking lot of the Cheesecake Factory out at Southpoint Mall. Not finding anywhere to park due to the moviegoers and shoppers, Jalisa opted for valet parking as to not waste anymore time. Crystal was anxious and getting impatient due to the delay of getting inside, sure she had missed the whole dinner.

Once inside Crystal exhaled and patted her weave down on the sides and straightened her dress. Jalisa asked for the party of seven, adding that they were expecting them to the greeter at the front of the restaurant. There was a young man dressed in black and white who greeted them. He informed them that he was waiting on them to arrive and he promptly led the way to their waiting party. They arrived just in time and hadn't missed much according to Nathaniel. He stood up and pulled out a chair for both of the women he now called family. A few minutes later,

Brother Tremaine showed up. Crystal's eyes lit up when she saw him and she stood to receive a hug and kiss on the cheek.

"Everyone, I hope you don't mind. I invited Brother Tremaine to have dinner with us and help us celebrate all of the good that God is causing us to have," Crystal said.

"Hi, Brother Tremaine," everyone said in unison. He waved.

Amina smiled a knowing smile. "Gran, is there something that we need to know?" She cut her eye at Brother Tremaine, who was preparing to join them at the table.

All eyes were on Crystal as they waited for her to say something. "Well, family, I guess it's a good time for me to let you all know that Tremaine and I are dating." Crystal smiled shyly at Tremaine and he held her hand.

"Well, praise the Lord," Serena said and laughter rang out in the back of the restaurant as they ordered the delicious flavored lemonades in wine glasses. When the waiter came back with the sugar-crusted rims of tall glasses filled with ice and the sweet and sour mixture of liquid, they each took their glass and held it up.

"Let's toast to God's mercy and grace." Serena, Nathaniel, Jonathan, James, Amina, Jalisa, Crystal, and Tremaine all held their glasses up and said, "Go get the devil and tell him I'm back!"

Everyone clinked their glasses together and laughed.

UC HIS GLORY BOOK CLUB!

www.uchisglorybookclub.net

UC His Glory Book Club is the spirit-inspired brain-child of Joylynn Jossel, Author and Acquisitions Editor of Urban Christian, and Kendra Norman-Bellamy, Author for Urban Christian. This is an online book club that hosts authors of Urban Christian. We welcome as members all men and women who have a passion for reading Christian-based fiction.

UC His Glory Book Club pledges our commitment to provide support, positive feedback, encouragement, and a forum whereby members can openly discuss and review the literary works of Urban Christian authors.

There is no membership fee associated with UC His Glory Book Club; however, we do ask that you support the authors through purchasing, encouraging, providing book reviews, and of course, your prayers. We also ask that you respect our beliefs and follow the guidelines of the book club. We hope to receive your valuable input, opinions, and reviews that build up, rather than tear down our authors.

What We Believe:

—We believe that Jesus is the Christ, Son of the Living God.

—We believe the Bible is the true, living Word of God.

—We believe all Urban Christian authors should use their God-given writing abilities to honor God and share the message of the written word God has given to each of them uniquely.

—We believe in supporting Urban Christian authors in their literary endeavors by reading, purchasing and sharing their titles with our online community.

—We believe that everything we do in our literary arena should be done in a manner that will lead to God being glorified and honored.

We look forward to the online fellowship with you.

Please visit us often at:
www.uchisglorybookclub.net.

Many Blessing to You!

Shelia E. Lipsey,
President, UC His Glory Book Club